T0285526

THE SOHO MURDER

By Mike Hollow

THE SOHO MURDER

Mike Hollow

Allison & Busby Limited
11 Wardour Mews
London W1F 8AN
allisonandbusby.com

First published in Great Britain by Allison & Busby in 2024.

First Edition

ISBN 978-0-7490-3039-1

Typeset in 11.5/16.5 pt Sabon LT Pro by
Allison & Busby Ltd.

By choosing this product, you help take care of the world's forests.
Learn more: www.fsc.org.

Printed and bound by
CPI Group (UK) Ltd, Croydon, CR0 4YY

For Neil,
a straight bat, honest and true

CHAPTER ONE

Eric Thompson trudged along Romilly Street with his hands in his pockets and fury in his heart. In the distance, at the junction with Dean Street, he could see the ravaged remains of the parish church of St Anne, a Soho landmark for more than two hundred and fifty years but now reduced to an ugly shell by Hitler's bombs. The eastern façade was still standing, as was the tower beyond it, but the roof was burnt out and most of the side walls had been reduced to rubble. The magnificent stained-glass window that had once graced the church at its eastern end was now no more than a gaping hole through which the charred remains of the roof timbers were silhouetted against the December sky. If the mad Nazi tyrant had stepped out of the newsagent's with the *Daily Mirror* tucked under his arm at that very moment, Thompson would gladly have shot him on the spot.

If pressed, he would have to admit that the number of times he'd been inside the church could be counted on the fingers of one hand, but that didn't alter the fact that he appreciated beauty, and he remembered that window as a great work of art as well as craft. Its destruction was of course an assault on religion, but more than that, it was a desecration of what sane people regarded as civilisation. It had been beautiful, and now it was lost for ever.

He turned right into Dean Street and continued across Old Compton Street, where the bitter east wind gouged his face like broken glass. Not for the first time, he resented the course his life had taken. Trying to build a property empire, however modest, in the two decades of economic crisis, political instability and depression that followed the Great War had been an uphill struggle at the best of times, but the outbreak of war all over again in 1939 had put the curse of death on it. Since the beginning of the Blitz nearly four months ago, he'd lost two shops and the flats above them, and a third property had been severely damaged. Hitler had a lot to answer for. In the absence of the hated dictator, however, Thompson's rage of frustration turned instead onto Samuel Bellamy, the tenant from hell.

What irritated him most about Bellamy was his constant quibbling about the rent, and his uncanny talent for breaking fittings in the flat and damaging its fabric – always, he claimed, by accident. Yesterday he'd rung to complain that his toilet wouldn't flush and had threatened to withhold his rent until it was fixed.

Thompson's regular plumber was generally unavailable these days. There was so much demand for his services across the area that he could afford to pick and choose, and if he should deign to honour you with his presence even his oldest customers would find his rates grossly inflated. Rental incomes for property owners, of course, were not.

Thompson was adamant that he wasn't going to fork out good money for what was probably just a faulty ballcock – or more likely one that Bellamy had somehow managed to wreck – and that was why he had in his bag a small collection of tools with which he would do the job himself. His day of rest would go out the window, but he'd stop Bellamy's whining and make sure he collected the rent at the same time.

He checked his watch as he approached Bellamy's home in Peter Street. It was just coming up to eleven o'clock. With a bit of luck he'd get the ballcock straightened, extract the rent from Bellamy's wallet, and be in time for a pint and sandwich at The Intrepid Fox on the corner of Wardour Street. He'd rung Bellamy to say he was coming but told him he'd arrive at twelve. He knew Bellamy's tricks: at midday he'd be unexpectedly out, called away on some unspecified but urgent business to escape Thompson's wrath. But by arriving at eleven Thompson stood a chance of catching him at home and getting what was due to him. And if for any reason Bellamy proved to be out when he arrived, he'd brought along his own key to the property, so he'd fix the ballcock and then wait for Bellamy to return. At least there'd be something to read while he waited: with the number of books the man had crammed into that flat, it was a wonder the whole place hadn't collapsed under the weight of them years ago.

He arrived at number 37 and pressed the bell button beside the street door. To his left, the boarded-up door and windows of the small travel bureau that used to occupy the ground floor silently goaded him with another reminder of lost rental income. Four months ago the couple who ran it had decided to decamp to Oxford to avoid the bombing, and since then he'd had no takers for the lease. To his right were some vacant premises and then a gramophone record shop, from which came the sound of raucous jazz music. There was no response to the bell, so he banged loudly on the door knocker and waited, resenting the chill seeping through his overcoat. Still no answer. So, Bellamy had contrived to be out after all: it was typical of the man.

Thompson pulled the key from his pocket and let himself in. He climbed the narrow staircase up to the flat and shouted a perfunctory 'Hello' in case his tenant was unavoidably detained and unable to get to the door, but there was no answer. He put his bag of tools down at the top of the stairs and went into the room that Bellamy called his office: it smelt musty, as usual, and to Thompson's eye it looked like nothing more than a dumping ground for dust-laden old books. The only sign of occupation was the coal fire burning low in the grate behind the mesh of a smoke-blackened brass fire guard. But of Bellamy there was nothing to be seen.

He moved towards the fireplace to warm his hands by the glowing embers, wondering idly where Bellamy might have gone, but as he rounded the large desk that stood in the middle of the room he stopped in his tracks. On the threadbare square of carpet surrounding it lay the body of a thin, middle-aged man with untidy dark hair. He was sprawled on his back, arms and legs akimbo, and his unbuttoned jacket had fallen open. The white shirt that it revealed might well have been clean when he put it on that morning, but now it was disfigured for ever by the spread of a grimly glistening red stain, at the centre of which was a small hole. A single glance was all Thompson needed to recognise the face. It was Samuel Bellamy, and he wasn't going anywhere.

CHAPTER TWO

The chilly draughts that blew into the Riley Lynx on all sides reminded Detective Inspector John Jago that winter was not his favourite season. He'd always wondered what it might be like to live in a warmer climate than London could offer, but his time in France in the army during the Great War had all been spent in the north, where it wasn't much different to home. The only other time in his life that he'd travelled outside Britain was in 1936, when he'd been seconded to Special Branch for six months. Civil war had broken out in Spain, and the Branch had sent him to liaise with the French police over cross-border arms smuggling, using the language he'd learnt from his French mother. That had taken him to the South of France, but he'd been disappointed to find that even down near the Spanish border at this time of year temperatures could drop to freezing point and below. Now, people here in London were saying that the current winter was the coldest in sixty years.

He and Detective Constable Peter Cradock were driving up Charing Cross Road towards Soho. The London Metropolitan Police was responsible for some seven hundred square miles of the capital city and its surrounds, so Jago made no claim to familiarity with every inch of it. There were parts he knew like the back of his hand, but Soho wasn't one of them. He'd spent time there, however, in the line of duty: long enough to reckon he could find his way about it reasonably well, and long enough to know it was the kind of place where even the most experienced police officer had to be wary.

The uniformed constable standing outside the front door of 37 Peter Street looked as though he too was feeling the cold. He was stamping his feet when the two detectives pulled up and got out of the car, but when Jago gave his name, he drew himself up to attention.

'Morning, sir,' he said.

'Good morning to you,' Jago replied. 'And you are . . . ?'

'Purdew, sir. From West End Central – they got the call about the body and told me to come straight over and make sure nobody interfered with the scene of crime.'

'And has anyone?'

'Not since I got here, no, sir. The photographer from Scotland Yard's taking photos of the body, and I've got the man who found it waiting for you in the living room. He's the landlord, apparently, and he says it's Mr Samuel Bellamy, a bookseller, and this is where he lives.'

'Very good. What's this landlord's name?'

'Thompson, sir – Eric Thompson.'

'And what time did he find the body?'

'He said he found it at about eleven – he called 999 at five past. Oh, and by the way, sir, I took the liberty of calling the exchange, and they confirmed that they'd received a 999 call from this number at five past eleven.'

'Thank you – well done. Right, you stay here now, and we'll take a look around. Tell the landlord we want to speak to him, and we'll be with him as soon as possible.'

'Yes, sir.'

'Has Dr Gibson arrived yet – the pathologist?'

'No, sir.'

'Well, send him up as soon as he does. What floor's the body on?'

'First floor, sir. Up the stairs and turn left at the top – there's a door there to Mr Bellamy's office, and that's where he is.'

'Thank you.'

Jago and Cradock followed his directions, found the door in question and went in. As they stepped into the office, Cradock's eyes widened. 'Blimey,' he said. 'He was a bit of a reader, then.'

Jago took in the scene without comment. All four walls of the room were packed from floor to ceiling with shelves – not the elegant fitted type one might expect to find in a rich man's study, but a hotch-potch of bookcases of various hues and sizes cobbled together unevenly to fill the maximum possible space. Every shelf was stuffed with books, most of them old-looking and leather-bound, but some with a more modern appearance. A dark wooden spiral step ladder with the air of a library relic salvaged from a junk shop offered the only visible means of reaching those on the higher shelves, and there were smaller stacks of books dotted around the floor. His nostrils caught a smell of pipe tobacco and old leather in the stale air.

The room was about ten feet by fifteen, and in keeping with the chaotic shelving was furnished in a variety of styles. A voluminous upholstered armchair of a contemporary style filled one corner, attended by a couple of Victorian caned chairs and a nondescript occasional table with ring stains on its once-polished surface, and in the centre of the room stood a cluttered and battered mahogany desk that looked as though it belonged in a much larger space. A couple of feet away, pushed back and turned to one side as if its occupant had just left the desk, was an old-fashioned captain's swivel chair with splits in its worn leather seat. Jago wondered idly whether its owner had been a seafarer, or perhaps had just fancied himself as the captain of this room. Whatever he'd been or done, he was now lying dead on the floor.

Nisbet, the photographer, was at work on the far side of the desk. He paused to greet them. 'Morning – I'm nearly done. Just got a few close-ups to do.' He adjusted his camera on its tripod so that it was pointing downwards and completed his work. 'There,' he said, 'all done. He's all yours now. Looks like he's been shot in the chest.'

Jago knelt down beside the body. 'Indeed it does,' he said, noting, but not touching, the small hole an inch or so to the left of the buttons on his shirt which appeared to mark the site of the entry wound. 'And no sign of a gun, as far as I can see.'

'So not suicide, then?' said Cradock.

'That depends – someone else could've removed the weapon, couldn't they?'

'Oh, yes – of course.'

'We'll see what the doctor has to say when he gets here. In the meantime, see what you can come up with in terms of prints.'

'Righto, guv'nor.' Cradock got the fingerprinting equipment out of its bag and began to explore the room, dusting for fingerprints with Nisbet accompanying him to photograph them.

Jago stayed with the body. He slipped his hand into the dead man's inside jacket pocket and brought out a leather wallet that contained an identity card and a couple of pound notes. 'Here we are, Peter,' he said, showing the card to Cradock. 'He had one of those new green ones, with a photo.'

Cradock looked up from his fingerprinting to examine it. 'They're the ones people have to get if they want to travel into protected areas, aren't they? Could that be significant?'

'Possibly – we'll need to check that. But in the meantime, it's in his name, Samuel Bellamy, see, and the address is 37 Peter Street, so that tallies with what the landlord says. The photo's him too, so I think we can safely say we've identified him. And here – date of birth. Eighteenth of June, 1897, so that makes him forty-three.'

Jago checked the dead man's other pockets: they yielded a handkerchief, a comb, a pair of Yale keys and a few shillings' worth of coins. Jago put all these personal items into a buff envelope, and his attention shifted to a scattering of leather-bound books that lay open on the floor as if they had fallen. 'What do you make of that, Peter?' he said, pointing to them. 'Signs of a struggle, perhaps?'

'Could be, yes,' Cradock replied after a quick glance. 'I don't suppose a bookseller would go chucking books around for no reason. Maybe he got into a fight and someone shot him. They have gangsters in Soho, don't they?'

'So I believe, yes, but we'll need to check whether Mr Bellamy had a gun himself.'

'For protection, you mean?'

'For any reason.'

The sound of a door banging came from the floor below, followed by that of footsteps bounding up the staircase. The door opened, and in came Gibson, the pathologist.

'Sorry I'm late,' he said, getting his breath back. 'We had a busy night at St George's – the hospital was taking in casualties from that terrible fire in the City. It was a case of all hands to the pump, and even I was called in to help out. I expect you heard about it.'

'The big air raid? Yes, I heard a bit about it this morning – it sounded dreadful.'

'It was – but now I'd better get started on this poor fellow, if that's all right.'

'Yes, please – it looks as though he was shot.'

Dr Gibson examined the wound on Bellamy's chest. 'Yes, I think you're right. Let's just see if there's an exit wound.' He rolled the body carefully onto its side. 'Well, there's no obvious sign of one, but I'll examine him more thoroughly when I get him back to the hospital. I've got a vehicle on its way to pick him up.'

'Is there any chance it was suicide? We haven't found the weapon here, but it's possible someone could've found him dead and removed it.'

'I think suicide's unlikely. People doing that usually shoot themselves in the right temple – or the left temple if they're left-handed. It's much less common to find the entrance wound in the chest like this.'

'I see – in that case I think we're looking at a suspected murder. Could you give me an estimated time of death?'

'Yes – just let me get my thermometer.'

He reached for his bag. This was not a procedure that Jago enjoyed watching, so he made himself busy examining the papers on the desk until the doctor had finished.

'Right,' said Gibson. 'On the basis of his body temperature, I'd say this man's not been dead for much more than an hour.' He checked his watch. 'It's half past twelve now, so I'd say his estimated time of death was between ten-thirty and eleven-thirty. If the post-mortem suggests anything different, I'll let you know. Now, I propose to get him back to the hospital as soon as possible so I can take a proper look at him – and if that bullet's still inside him, I'll find it for you.'

'Thank you,' said Jago, inwardly bemused by the cheerful manner in which Gibson approached his gruesome tasks. 'And when will you be able to let us know your findings?'

'Let me see,' the pathologist replied. 'Why don't you come over to St George's at about four o'clock this afternoon, and we can discuss my findings over a nice cup of tea. Would that suit you?'

'Yes, certainly. We'll see you then.'

Jago saw Gibson off the premises and returned to Cradock. 'Are you finished now?' he asked.

'Yes, sir, all done – I don't think I've found anything that's going to help us, though. Pity there's no cups and saucers or glasses on the desk – if he'd had a cup of tea with whoever killed him we might've got something useful. But it's just books everywhere. I don't think I've ever seen so many books in one little room like this.'

'Right, then – we need to talk to that landlord now, so let's go and find him.'

Thompson was waiting for them in the living room and got to his feet when they came in. 'You're the police, I suppose, are you?' he said.

'Yes, Mr Thompson – I'm Detective Inspector Jago and this is Detective Constable Cradock.'

'About blinking time, too. Do you think I've got all day to sit around waiting for you? I've got a business to run and rents to collect – my tenants don't come knocking at my door begging me to let them pay me, you know.'

'I'm sorry – we won't keep you for long. Please sit down.'

'All right,' said Thompson grudgingly as he resumed his seat. 'So what do you want from me?'

'I'd like to know what time you found the body.'

'That was eleven o'clock this morning. I could see straight away he was dead, so I picked up his phone and dialled 999. That would've been about five past eleven.'

'Did you see anyone leaving the building as you were arriving?'

'No – there wasn't a soul on the street. Must be the cold weather.'

'And I understand you're the landlord of this property.'

'That's right.'

'So you knew Mr Bellamy well?'

'I wouldn't say well – I'd say just reasonably well.'

'I understand you said he's a bookseller – is that correct?'

'That's right, yes – he's got a little bookshop called Bellamy's Books, over in Old Compton Street. It's just by the junction with Charing Cross Road.'

'What else can you tell me about him?'

'Not much – but I can tell you he was a landlord's nightmare. Always late with his rent, complaining about everything, untidy, careless with my property – you name it. All the things guaranteed to drive a landlord crazy. But don't get me wrong – that doesn't mean I'd kill him. You don't think I did, do you?'

'I'm not suggesting that, Mr Thompson. Why were you here this morning?'

'I came to collect the rent – and to mend the toilet. He said it wasn't working properly. When I got here no one answered the door, so I let myself in – and when I came upstairs I found him lying there, dead. It's as simple as that.'

'And where were you in the hour before you got here?'

'I was visiting another one of my tenants – up the other end of Denmark Street. I got there about ten o'clock and left about ten to eleven to come here.'

'Could you give me his name and address, please?'

'Yes – his name's Harold Jenkins and he lives at 32 Denmark Street. And just so you know, I was having a row with him.'

'About what?'

'His rent – he's another one who doesn't seem to understand what that word means. So if you go checking up on me, I expect he'll remember my visit. Anything else?'

'Yes. Do you happen to know who Mr Bellamy's next of kin is?'

'Yes, that'd be his wife – Marjorie Bellamy. She lives here with him, but she's in the book business too – got a little shop or office or something over near St Paul's. I suppose you'll be wanting to break the news to her.'

'Yes, that's right.'

'Sooner you than me, mate. I can give you the address if you like.'

'That would be helpful.'

Thompson took a pocket diary out and thumbed through it. 'Here we are – the business is called Hayle and Sons and it's in Paternoster Row. I'll write it down for you.'

'Thank you. And could you jot down your own address for me too?'

'By all means,' said Thompson. He scribbled on a page of his diary and tore it out. 'There you are,' he said, handing it to Jago. 'I've written her phone number down for you as well. Whether she'll be there or not's another matter – I heard they caught it pretty bad over that way last night.'

'Yes, I believe they did. That's all we need for the time being, Mr Thompson, so you can go now. And thank you – you've been most helpful.'

Thompson picked up his bag of tools and left. As soon as he'd gone, Jago moved back to the office and picked up the phone on Bellamy's desk. 'I'm going to try and get hold of Mrs Bellamy,' he said.

He dialled the number Thompson had given him and heard the familiar clicking in his ear as the dial slowly rotated back to its rest position, but there was no ringing tone, only the continuous high-pitched buzz that meant 'number unobtainable'. He put the phone down.

'No one there, guv'nor?' said Cradock.

'I don't know, Peter. It sounds as though it's not ringing at the other end. It may just be broken, but I think we'd better get over to Paternoster Row – after that air raid last night it's just as likely to mean a bomb's got it.'

CHAPTER THREE

Jago drove eastwards, in the direction of St Paul's Cathedral, with Cradock beside him in the car. From the little he'd heard that morning about the previous night's big air raid on the City, he'd assumed there'd be extensive damage, but the scene that met them defied his imagination. It was as though overnight the clock had been wound back three centuries to the Great Fire of London, and everything he remembered from before the war had gone. The rabbit warren of narrow streets on the north side of the cathedral had been known for generations as the heart of the nation's book trade. Now all that remained was a jumble of ghost-like ruins. Walls here and there still towered two or three storeys high over the streets, but behind them was nothing but disorderly heaps of broken yellow bricks and charred timbers that spilt out in a deluge onto the roads.

They left the car when they could drive it no farther and continued on foot. The first thing that struck Jago was the silence that hung over the area; the second was the air he breathed, still warm from the fires and laced with acrid smoke. There was a strange stillness about the place: it was the stillness of death. He stumbled on the rubble, and as he steadied his feet and gazed at the desolation around him a sudden flash of memory seared his mind like a tormenting wound. He knew what would follow, and it did. Somewhere deep within him a pain and a grief that he'd never tamed began to well up, and he turned away lest Cradock should see his face. He pressed on and fought back in the only way he could: pushing it back down, as all his adult years had taught him, back down to where it could not break the surface and overwhelm him. His tactic worked: it was like screwing down an armoured plate over his raging emotions. He'd won the skirmish again, but he knew it was never the end of the battle.

Jago composed himself and forced his mind back to the job in hand. He could see firemen in the distance fighting a fierce blaze, while others nearby were spraying water onto smouldering debris. He approached one of them, a man who looked exhausted, his face black with soot and his uniform soaking wet. 'Excuse me,' said Jago, his voice calm and professional. 'We're police officers, and we're trying to find a place called Hayle and Sons, in Paternoster Row. Can you point us in the right direction?'

'I can tell you where Paternoster Row is,' the fireman

replied. 'You're standing on it – or what's left of it. I don't know where that particular business is, but I suggest you look down that way.' He gestured with his head to their right. 'There's some bits and pieces still standing and a few people poking around in the remains, so you might be lucky. But you can see for yourself there's not much left of anything round here. We've been here since nine o'clock last night, and it was all well ablaze by then – it was a windy night, and the flames were going wild. There was so much of it, we've had to pump water all the way up here from the Thames. I reckon we've got the worst of it under control now, though – I just hope we can get home soon, if we've still got homes to go to.'

The fireman shifted his stance so he could direct his hose towards another patch of smoking ruins. Jago thanked him for his help, and he and Cradock made their way down the street, clambering over the debris until they found the shell of a building with a scorched sign on which they could make out the first three letters of what might have been *Hayle and Sons*. A woman in a dirty overcoat was sitting on a pile of shattered masonry, her head in her hands.

'Excuse me,' said Jago, approaching her. 'Is this Hayle and Sons?'

She lifted her head to see who was speaking to her, and he could see her grimy face was streaked by what might have been tears. Her eyes seemed to look through him as if he wasn't there, as if she was struggling to drag her mind back from some other place to register his presence. Jago waited as she visibly pulled herself

25

together. She stood up, brushing some of the dust off her coat in a gesture of businesslike determination, and gave him a polite smile. 'You're not going to tell me you're a customer – if you are, we're closed.'

'No, we're police officers and we're looking for Mrs Marjorie Bellamy – we understand she works at Hayle and Sons.'

'She certainly used to, until last night – now I'm not sure what she's going to do. But I can help you with that – in fact you've found her. I'm Marjorie Bellamy.' She extended a hand to shake his. 'Perhaps you can tell me why you're looking for me in particular.'

Jago looked around for somewhere more suitable to break the news of her husband's death to her, but there was nothing but the aftermath of the night's destruction to be seen. 'I think perhaps we should sit down, right here.'

She sat down again, and he joined her. She looked at him anxiously. 'This is going to be more bad news, isn't it?' she said. 'What is it? What's happened?'

Jago hesitated. He was about to add more anguish to this poor woman's suffering, but there was little he could do to soften the blow. 'I'm afraid it's your husband, Mrs Bellamy,' he said. 'There's been an incident.'

'An incident? What do you mean?'

'I'm sorry to have to tell you this, Mrs Bellamy, but Mr Bellamy's been killed.'

She stared at him, wordless. She looked stunned. 'But I was with him . . . We had breakfast together . . . It's not possible . . . What happened?'

26

'Your husband was found dead in your home this morning, with a bullet wound to his chest. The wound was fatal.'

'You mean somebody shot him?' She paused. 'You don't mean he shot himself, surely?'

Jago shook his head. 'We don't believe he shot himself, no – we're treating it as a case of suspected murder.'

'Murder? But that's . . . Why? Who would want to murder Samuel?'

'We don't know, Mrs Bellamy, but we're going to find out.'

She looked down and shook her head as if not hearing him, then raised her head sharply. 'Where is he? Can I see him?'

'He'll be at St George's Hospital by now.'

'Is that the one at Hyde Park Corner?'

'Yes, it is. In a case like this there has to be a post-mortem examination.'

'Do I need to identify him for you?'

'It's not essential – he had his identity card on him, with his photograph in it. And the landlord also confirmed it was him. But if you want to see him, we can take you over to the hospital.'

'Thank you. I think I'd like to do that.'

'Very well – and then we'll take you back to your flat in Peter Street if you wish, or do you have to go elsewhere?'

'No, Peter Street will be fine. But you said just now the landlord confirmed it was Samuel – how did he get involved?'

'I believe he was there to collect the rent.'

'Ah, well, I leave that to Samuel – it was his flat before we got married, so after the wedding I moved in, but he was always the one who dealt with the landlord. That was fine with me – I've always had quite enough on my plate with the business.'

'You mean Hayle and Sons?'

'Yes, that's right – we're a small ecclesiastical publisher. I've worked here all my life. My grandfather started the business in 1870, publishing things like bishops' collected sermons. He had two sons – my father and his brother, who carried it on after him. My uncle died, but my father kept the name "and Sons" as a mark of respect. There were no more sons after him – I was my father's only child, so when he died it all came to me, and I left the name unchanged too. I say "it all", but it actually wasn't a lot. Times have changed, and there isn't the same demand for thick volumes of bishops' musings as there was, but I managed to keep things ticking over. But then this confounded war started, and that's made things very difficult – especially when the government brought in the paper restrictions. You only get six pages in your newspaper now, and we're not allowed the paper we'd need to publish even the reduced amount of books we were managing before the war.' She glanced around them and took a sharp breath. 'And now look at it – last night the German air force turned our offices to dust, and I've discovered this morning that the warehouse we used round in Ivy Lane was burnt down too, so we've lost all our stock. It means the entire business has been destroyed.' Her voice caught, and she sobbed. 'And now you say I've lost Samuel too. Everything's gone – my whole life.'

Jago said nothing, but waited. Within a minute or so she had regained her composure. 'So,' she said, 'is there anything else you need to know?'

'I'd appreciate it if you could tell us what time you last saw your husband.'

'Of course – that would have been at about nine-thirty this morning. As I said, we had breakfast together, and then I had a phone call about all this.' She swept her arm round to encompass the destruction surrounding them. 'I came straight over here to see what the damage was to our property . . . I never imagined it would be as bad as this.'

'But your husband didn't come with you?'

'No, he had someone coming to see him, and besides, this is – or was – my family's business, so he's never got very involved in it.'

'Do you know who that someone was?'

'No – he just said he couldn't come with me, because he was expecting a visitor, and it was important.'

'Do you know what time he was expecting this visitor?'

'Yes, it was at ten o'clock, I think.'

'Could you be more definite? It could be an important piece of information.'

She furrowed her brow for a moment or two. 'Yes, I'm sure he said ten o'clock.'

'And did he happen to say he or she?'

'No, he didn't. Look, do you think you could take me to see Samuel now?'

'Of course. We'll go straight away – we just need to go back to the car. It's parked not far away.'

They returned to the car and set off for the hospital. Mrs Bellamy lapsed into silence in the back seat of the Riley, and Jago didn't disturb her. She was on her way to see the body of the husband she'd had breakfast with this morning, and he wasn't going to burden her with questions: there'd be time for that when they got back. His mind revisited the picture of her sitting in the ruins of her grandfather's business in Paternoster Row, and he thought what a strange job he had. He'd never met this woman before, but now, suddenly, circumstances had forged a connection with her, obliging him to invade her privacy and if necessary probe every secret corner of her life. He wondered how he'd feel if the shoe was on the other foot.

The sights he'd seen in Paternoster Row brought Dorothy to mind. Her job was reporting the war to the American public, and he was sure she would have visited that area, barely a mile from her temporary home at the Savoy, to see the effect of the bombing for herself and craft it into words for her editor back in Boston. She might even have been there when he and Cradock were talking to Mrs Bellamy – in whatever remained of the next street, perhaps. That same war had suddenly and unexpectedly forged a connection with her too, but in a different way. She had become the most agreeable part of his life, and spending time with her the most agreeable of activities. He was surprised to feel something akin to sadness at the thought of possibly having been so close to her without bumping into her and decided to call her in the hope of meeting up sometime soon.

He had rung Gibson from a call box on the way to check that the body was suitable for viewing, and the pathologist had assured him that by the time they got there he'd have everything arranged appropriately so that she would see nothing unnecessarily distressing. When they arrived, the room was neat and tidy, and the body was covered up to the chin with a clean white hospital sheet, concealing any signs of the post-mortem examination.

Marjorie Bellamy needed only a brief look before pronouncing, 'Yes, that's my husband.' She stood and stared at him for a few moments before murmuring a brief farewell and planting a single kiss on his cold forehead, then turned away and buried her face in a handkerchief. The three men waited in silence until she signalled with a nod of her head that she was ready to go. Jago stepped to one side to let her leave first, looking for any outward sign of her inner thoughts or feelings as she passed him, but her face was expressionless.

CHAPTER FOUR

The journey back to Marjorie Bellamy's home in Peter Street was as subdued as the one to the hospital, but once they were in the flat, she seemed to force herself back into action. 'I'm going to make a cup of tea,' she said with an air of determination. 'Would you like one too?'

'Thank you, yes,' said Jago. 'That would be very kind. And would you mind if I asked you one or two more questions?'

'Very well,' she said, pushing her shoulders back. 'I know you have a job to do. I'll do my best.'

'Thank you. We'll take a look at your husband's office, if that's all right.'

'Yes, of course. I'll bring the tea in there when it's ready.'

When she had left them, Jago and Cradock returned to the office, where Jago began to peruse the books on the shelves. Most of them were works he'd never heard of. Before he could get very far in his examination, however, Mrs Bellamy returned with a cup of tea for each of them.

'Thank you,' said Jago, taking a cup and saucer from her. 'I understand your husband had a bookshop in Old Compton Street. Would these books be part of his stock, or is this his personal library?'

'It's a bit of both, I think,' she replied. 'Storage space is always a problem for booksellers. Samuel sold all sorts of books in the shop – new and second-hand, anything he thought there was a reasonable chance of someone buying. I suppose that was the bread and butter of his business, but he was more interested in what they call antiquarian books – that means old and rare ones, like these – because that was where he said the real money was to be made. He sold those in the shop too, and as far as I know most of these are stock he didn't have room for there. Booksellers tend not to collect books themselves, but I believe Samuel kept a few in here that he was particularly fond of. He had some private clients too, who collected particular types of book, and anything he'd acquired with them in mind he'd keep here too. I don't know anything more about those, though.'

'Can you tell me more about the shop?'

'There's not much to say, really. It's his business, and I haven't got very involved in it – as you know, I have my own to run, or at least I did until this morning. Besides, we only got married a couple of years ago, so what with the war and everything we've both had our hands pretty full just keeping our own businesses afloat.'

33

'What'll happen to the shop now?'

'Well, he's had a woman working there for a while, so I imagine I'll just keep her doing that until I've had time to think about the future.'

'What's her name?'

'Oh, she's called Judith Langley – Miss.'

'Thank you. And your husband's work – was it the sort of thing that might've made him enemies?'

'No, I don't think so. I know there were the usual business rivalries and the odd difficult customer, but not the sort of thing anyone would kill him for, if that's what you mean.'

'Are you aware of anyone else who might've wanted to cause him harm for any other reason?'

'No. I mean, I know what kind of place Soho is. It's full of shady characters and out-and-out crooks, and some of them are quite vicious, so I was a bit concerned about coming to live here when I married Samuel, but he was a bookseller, for goodness' sake. Who wants to murder a bookseller? And in his own home, too. It doesn't make sense.'

'Did many people know he lived here?'

'Yes – he made no secret of it, and he did most of his business from here, not the shop, so everyone he had any dealings with would know his address. Anyone could have got hold of it.' She glanced distractedly round the room. 'Do you think it could have been an intruder, like a burglar?'

'We've found no evidence of a forced entry.'

'So it must have been someone Samuel knew.'

'Possibly, but it could equally have been a stranger he let in for some reason, or someone who'd obtained a key to your home. Can you think of anyone that would apply to?'

'No. The only other person who has a key is our landlord. But what about that visitor he was expecting?'

'We need to know who that was – can you remember anything more?'

'No – as I said, I don't even know if it was a man or a woman. Since you asked me I've racked my brains, but I'm certain Samuel didn't mention anything more about who it was. All I know is he said it was important, but I don't know whether that was in a good sense or a bad sense. I'm very sorry, Inspector.'

'Don't worry, Mrs Bellamy. You mentioned just now that your husband kept books here that he'd acquired for collectors – would I be right in thinking some of those would be valuable?'

'Oh, yes – some of those collectors are quite wealthy. That's what made me think perhaps it was a burglar, and that Samuel had disturbed them or caught them in the act. But even so, do many burglars carry a gun?'

'Did your husband own a gun?'

'No. I'm sure he'd have told me if he did.'

'And do you?'

She looked at him with wide-eyed astonishment. 'A gun? Me? That's absurd – of course I don't.'

'I'm sorry, Mrs Bellamy, but I have to ask. By the way, we also noticed that your husband was carrying a green identity card. Those are usually issued to people who want to travel into prohibited places within the meaning of the Official Secrets Act, or protected places or areas within the meaning of the Defence Regulations. Do you know why Mr Bellamy had such a card?'

She shrugged. 'I think it was because he might need to go to a country auction in one of those areas, to buy books, or visit someone with a private library who was thinking of selling – he'd have to see their books where they were. I'm sure there wasn't anything suspicious about it, if that's what you mean.'

'Thank you. Now, did your husband have any family or close friends that we should inform about what's happened?'

'Well, the only family he has is his sister – she's called Christine Edison, and she lives with her husband, John, in Broadwick Street. I'd appreciate it if you could let them know – they're not on the phone, but the address is number 75, flat 2. As for close friends, I believe his oldest friend is a man called Ron Fisher, but I don't have his address. And there was another man he used to spend time with – I think they were quite pally. He's called Frankie Rossetti, and he runs a cafe in Frith Street called Frankie's Cafe. Not a very imaginative name, I know, but Samuel liked the place – he used to eat there quite a lot before we were married, and I think he still used to go round there sometimes in the evenings, especially when I was busy with work, but he didn't always say where he was going. We both had our own lives, you see. I think that's what happens when you marry later in life – you've got used to doing a lot of things on your own or with old friends, and you don't necessarily give all that up just because you've got hitched. We didn't – Samuel had his friends and I had mine, and we didn't spend all our time together.'

'And what about business associates?'

'I'm sure I don't know all of them – as I said, I didn't get involved in his business affairs – but there are two men whose names came up in conversation quite often. One's called Charles Abingdon – he's a collector who's bought quite a few things from Samuel. The other's called William Quincy – I think he buys and sells books, and sometimes buys things from Samuel. They're both quite well-to-do, I believe. Samuel said they were both posh, although he also used to say William Quincy was more posh than was good for him.'

'What did he mean by that?'

'I don't know – probably just some private joke, I should think. I don't know where they live, unfortunately, but they must be in London because Samuel used to say he was going to pop round and see them. I expect they'll be in the phone book – shall we check?' She opened a drawer in the desk and pulled out the two volumes of the London telephone directory, found the relevant entries and jotted them down on a scrap of paper. 'Here we are,' she said, handing it to Jago. 'Will that be all?'

'Almost all, thank you,' Jago replied. 'But just one more question. Can you tell me whether any book of particular value is missing from this room?'

'I can't, I'm afraid, no. Samuel had his own way of protecting his valuable books – he called it the wildebeest system.'

Jago raised his eyebrows in an unspoken request for elucidation.

'I know,' she continued, 'it sounds funny, doesn't it? I don't know the first thing about wildebeest, but he explained it to me once. He said they're hunted by lions and other predators, but they protect themselves by moving around in huge herds. He reckoned that if he had a valuable book, the best way to protect it from being stolen was to hide it amongst all the hundreds he's got in this room. No burglar would be able to tell what was worth pinching, and they certainly wouldn't be able to cart the whole lot away.'

'But how would your husband remember where the valuable ones were?'

'Ah, yes – he had a little trick for that. You'd never know, but there's a bit of loose skirting board over there.' She pointed in the general direction of the fireplace. 'And Samuel kept a special piece of paper behind it. I'll show you.' She crossed the room and knelt down, keeping herself between the hiding place and the detectives as if needing to protect the secret even from them, and then turned back to them with the paper in her hand. 'Here, you see,' she said.

Jago examined it: all it showed was a short handwritten list of what he took to be book titles, some of them crossed out, along with a jumble of letters and numbers and what might have been dates.

'I'll have to explain it to you,' she continued. 'The letters refer to the bookcases and the numbers to the shelves. When Samuel wanted to conceal something valuable, he made a note here of where he'd put it. The bookcases are in alphabetical order, but of course you have to know which one is A and which way to count round the room from there. The shelves are counted from the bottom up. Samuel reckoned that a burglar wouldn't find the list in the first place, and even if they did, they'd still have to work out what the letters and numbers meant. I suppose it wasn't foolproof, but he reckoned it was better than putting them in a safe or somewhere else that would be obvious.'

Jago nodded. 'And these numbers here,' he said. 'Are they dates?'

She took the paper from him. 'Yes, that's right. He made a note of the date he'd acquired the book, and then when he'd managed to sell it he crossed it out. You can see there are only three items not crossed out, so if you bear with me for a moment I should be able to check they're still here.' She moved to the bookshelves and counted carefully, then turned back to him. 'All present and correct.'

'So there's nothing valuable missing?'

'You could say that, I suppose, but of course the fact that the remaining items on his list are still here doesn't necessarily mean there wasn't something else of value that he hadn't quite got round to adding to it, or even that he'd forgotten to add. He was always busy. So if I'm to answer your question truthfully and accurately, I'd have to say I'm afraid I haven't a clue.' She offered him a smile that suggested sympathetic helplessness and shrugged her shoulders. 'Very sorry, Inspector.'

CHAPTER FIVE

The bitterly cold air on the street assailed Jago and Cradock as they left the Bellamys' home. The traffic was sparse, and there were no pedestrians in sight: it was the kind of day to be indoors if you could manage it, and if you were a policeman, the kind of day when you knew you'd be outside for hours on the beat getting chilled to the bone because you had no choice. Jago was grateful that he no longer had to spend his time standing in the middle of the road directing traffic on point duty. The hours in CID might be longer, but at least some of them were spent out of the cold.

'Let's check the neighbours,' he said. 'I want to know whether any of them heard or saw anything this morning around the time Bellamy was getting killed.'

'Righto, guv'nor,' Cradock replied, glancing back at the building they'd just left. 'The places either side aren't very promising, are they? One's boarded up, and the other one looks empty too.'

Jago turned round to face the neighbouring properties and nodded to his right. 'That one there looks more promising – the record shop. I think I just saw somebody moving inside the window.'

He tried the shop door and it opened, setting its bell tinkling above them, and they went in. A man with untidy hair and wearing a crumpled suit came over to greet them. 'Good morning, gentlemen,' he said, 'and how can I help you today? If you'd like to browse around the shop, please do, or if there's something particular you're interested in, I'll see whether we've got it. And of course, if you'd like to hear a record I'll be happy to play it for you.'

'I'm sorry,' said Jago, taking his warrant card from his pocket and showing it to the shopkeeper, 'we're not here to buy records – we're making enquiries in connection with an incident that occurred near here this morning. And your name is?'

'Mayhew – Leslie Mayhew. I'm the proprietor here. What sort of incident was that?'

'It was a shooting, Mr Mayhew, in the property next door but one.'

Mayhew's expression was incredulous. 'A shooting?'

'Yes, that's right. Were you here this morning?'

'Yes, I've been here since about eight o'clock. But when you say a shooting, do you mean—has anyone been hurt?'

'I'm afraid that is the case. Do you know Mr Bellamy, the bookseller?'

'Yes, of course. Is it him?'

'I'm sorry to say it was, yes – he was shot dead.'

Mayhew's eyes widened. 'Oh, my goodness. Was it an accident?'

'We don't think it was.'

'Dear Lord, that makes it worse – you think someone deliberately shot him?'

'It looks that way at the moment, yes.'

'Dear, oh dear – I know this is Soho, and people who don't live here probably think there are gunmen on the loose all the time, but it's not really like that – not here in Peter Street, at least. What a terrible thing to happen. But how can I help you?'

'I'd like to know whether you heard or saw anything suspicious, especially between about half past ten and half past eleven.'

'No – I was busy sorting out some of the stock, so I wasn't looking outside at all. I haven't had a single customer today, either – people don't go out buying records on Monday mornings.'

'Did you hear a gunshot?'

'No – but then I don't suppose I would. I was playing records, you see, and quite loudly. I sell all the latest hit records here, of course, for the more general customer, and sheet music too, to keep my turnover up. But what I specialise in is jazz, and I like it with the volume turned up, so that's what I play when there's no one else in the shop – and the places either side of here are empty now, so I'm not going to be disturbing anyone. I was probably playing some Count Basie or Billie Holiday about the time you mentioned, but whatever it was, there was only me in the shop and I had it on nice and loud. I don't think I'd have heard anything happening outside.' He shook his head. 'Poor Samuel. He was a customer of mine, you know – he was a big fan of jazz.'

'Really?'

'Yes, he used to buy records here, and sometimes if I got something new in that I thought he'd like, I'd ask him round here to the shop to have a listen. We both used to go to the same jazz club too. Soho's had all the best jazz clubs for years – the Shim Sham in Wardour Street, the Nest in Kingly Street, Jigs Club, the Cuba, you'll find them round every corner. I have to say some of them weren't too popular with the Metropolitan Police – they reckoned they were dens of vice and iniquity, and some of them have gone now, but the Blue Palm's still going strong. That was Samuel's favourite, and we've often gone there together. I should mention that we only went there for the music, of course – I wouldn't like you to get the wrong idea. We've heard some great jazz musicians and singers there – not just British, but high-class acts from the Caribbean, and sometimes Americans too.'

'Where is it?'

'What, the Blue Palm? It's not far from here, over in Dean Street – just up a bit from the junction with Bateman Street. It's run by a chap called George Nicholson and his wife – he sounds English with a name like that, but he's actually Greek. They keep late hours, like most of the clubs round here, but it's in a basement, so it's probably safer than an Anderson shelter – unless you get a direct hit, of course, in which case you've had it. The Blitz hasn't stopped people going there, though – it's still very popular, especially with people who like their jazz served hot. You should try it – you might well learn a thing or two about Samuel if you go down there one night.'

CHAPTER SIX

The owner of the record shop was unable to provide Jago and Cradock with any more useful information about Bellamy or the shooting, so they took their leave and tried the other nearby properties. At most there was no answer, their inhabitants presumably being out at work, out shopping or out of London altogether, but eventually they found someone at home on the opposite side of the street. Jago rang the bell, and after a brief interval, the door opened a couple of inches on a chain and a short, elderly woman peered at them through the gap. Her voice was as frail as her appearance. 'Yes?' she said.

Jago held up his warrant card for her to see. 'I'm sorry to disturb you, madam, but we're police officers. May we have a word?'

She scrutinised the card. 'Yes, of course. Do come in.' She slipped the chain off, and they went in.

'May I ask what brings you here?' she said. 'It's just that I've never had the police calling at my home before. Have I done something wrong? If it's about leaving that light showing that the air raid warden told me off about, I assure you it was a simple oversight.' She paused. 'You don't think I was signalling to the Germans, do you?'

'No, madam, that's not why we're here. We've come because you might be able to help us.'

'I see. Well, in that case you'd better come up to the flat.' She led them up the stairs and into her living room. 'My name's Spencer, by the way – Mrs Irene Spencer. My husband sadly passed away two years ago, but we'd spent all our married life in this flat, so I couldn't bring myself to leave it. Now, sit down and make yourselves comfortable. Can I get you anything?'

'No, thank you,' said Jago. 'We won't be long. We're making enquiries into a suspicious death that occurred earlier today and we'd just like to find out whether you've seen or heard anything that might be significant.'

'I'll certainly help if I can. But may I ask who it is who's died?'

'It was one of your neighbours – Mr Bellamy, over the road at number 37.'

Her eyes widened as she reached out to a chair to steady herself. 'My goodness,' she said, sitting down carefully, 'that is a shock. He looked so fit and healthy the last time I saw him. What happened?'

'As I said, Mrs Spencer, we're treating his death as suspicious. We believe he died from a gunshot wound. Can you tell me when it was that you last saw him?'

'Yes, of course – I bumped into him on the street on Friday, on my way back from the post office. We said hello and he wished me a Happy New Year – in advance, he said, in case he didn't see me.' She paused again. 'I say – you don't think he knew this was going to happen, do you?'

'At the moment we've no way of telling – is there any reason you know of why he might've been thinking that?'

'Oh, no, not at all. I expect he was just being polite. He always was, to me at least, but then people usually are to old ladies like me – I've no idea how he was with other people.'

'How well did you know him?'

'I can't say I knew him well at all. We had what people call a nodding acquaintance, and he was always friendly, but I don't recall ever having a long conversation with him. He always gave the impression that he was very busy, in a hurry to get somewhere else.'

'Were you in this morning?'

'Yes, I haven't been out at all. I normally go for a walk, for the exercise, but I didn't quite feel up to it today. When you get to my age you begin to accumulate ailments of various kinds, and it can be difficult to be out and about all the time. This morning I've been catching up with some ironing – I had a cold last week, so I'd got a bit behind with it. I can't start too early in the morning, because I need enough natural light to see what I'm doing – I plug the iron into the electric light socket, you see, so of course I can't iron and have the light on at the same time. I did get one of those special adapters that mean you can plug the iron and a light bulb into the same socket in the ceiling, but it blew the fuse, so I stopped using it.' She paused. 'Oh, I'm so sorry – I'm sure you don't want to know about all that.'

'Don't worry, Mrs Spencer. So, you spent this morning ironing, yes?'

'Not the whole morning. When I'd finished the ironing I sat down for a while, doing some knitting and listening to the wireless. I knit comforts for the troops – I'm not very good at turning the heel on socks, so I've been unravelling some old jumpers and making them scarves.'

'Did you happen to look out of the window onto the street at any point?'

'Only when I opened the curtains – that would have been at about eight o'clock. But I'm not one of those old ladies who sit by their window watching everyone who comes and goes – I've always thought that's rather bad manners. Besides, it's pretty dead around here these days – not what it used to be – so there's nothing much to see. I certainly didn't see anyone creeping down the street with a gun.'

'Did you hear anything unusual?'

'You mean like a gunshot – someone shooting?'

'Yes, or sounds of an argument – anything out of the ordinary.'

'Well, that's a funny thing, because yes, I did. I don't mean yes, I heard a gunshot, because I didn't think that's what it was. But now you mention it, there was a sound that might possibly have been one.'

'Are you familiar with the sound of firearms?'

'Only in the sense that I grew up in the country, and my father used to keep a shotgun. This didn't sound quite like a shotgun, and not so loud, but it was still the kind of sudden, explosive sound you get from a gun. To be honest, I thought it must be a car or some other vehicle backfiring – there are no fields around here, and no farmers shooting rabbits, so it didn't occur to me it might actually be a gun, but if you're saying poor Mr Bellamy was shot, I think yes, perhaps it was.'

'Can you remember what time it was when you heard it?'

'Yes, I believe I can. I had the wireless on, as I said – I'd been listening to *The Daily Service*. The next programme after that is *Music While You Work*, at half past ten, as you probably know, and I heard the sound just as the orchestra was starting up for that. It wasn't entirely clear, because it was when those trumpets sound right at the beginning, and they're rather loud, but now you mention it I'm quite sure it could have been a gun.'

'Thank you, Mrs Spencer, that's most helpful. We'll let you get back to your knitting now – and speaking as an old soldier myself, I'm sure there'll be a man somewhere who's very pleased to receive a scarf from you.'

CHAPTER SEVEN

'I think we'd better see if we can find Bellamy's sister at home now, if she's the only other family,' said Jago as he and Cradock returned to the car. 'And after that it'll probably be time to go over to St George's and see what Dr Gibson's managed to turn up in his post-mortem.'

The address Marjorie Bellamy had given Jago for her sister-in-law proved to be a decaying property at the western end of Broadwick Street, and when a woman opened the door the inside of the building looked as dismal as the outside had led them to expect. Her own appearance was not much different: at first sight, the word that came to Jago's mind was 'careworn'. She was clothed in a dark, heavy-looking dress, over which was a shapeless knitted cardigan with elbow-patched sleeves that she kept pulling down towards her wrists. A faded and stained blue apron was tied round her waist. Her face was pinched, with prominent cheekbones, but the powder she wore on it, applied so liberally that it caught even his untutored eye, left him unable to guess whether she was older or younger than she looked.

'Mrs Edison?' said Jago.

'Yes, that's me,' she replied. She sounded tired.

'We're police officers, and we'd like a word with you please. I'm Detective Inspector Jago and this is Detective Constable Cradock.'

She gave a forced laugh. 'Blimey – a detective inspector. That sounds a bit grand for people like us. I've never met a detective inspector before. Are you from that fancy new Trenchard House place down there,' she said, jerking her thumb back towards the street they'd just driven down, 'where the old Lion Brewery used to be? That's police, isn't it?'

'It is, yes, but it's a section house – that's living quarters for unmarried policemen. We're not from there.'

'Well, I must say it looks very grand – makes this end of the street look like the slums. Not that it's ever been the most salubrious part of town, as far as I'm aware. This is where the cholera started in eighteen something, you know – you could probably see that bit of the street's a lot smarter than this end. Anyway, you'd better come in.'

They entered a dingy hallway, and she closed the street door behind them.

'Terrible times they were, by all accounts,' she said. 'My husband's grandad used to live round here when he was young, and he said it was famous because some doctor worked out the cholera all came from the water in the street pump down on the corner with Lexington Street – just outside the Newcastle-upon-Tyne pub. You probably came past it on your way here – it's about halfway between here and that Trenchard House.' They followed her as she stumped up the stairs. 'Sewage from the pub and houses getting into the pump water,' she continued, 'that's what the doctor said. Seven hundred people killed, apparently, and only twelve houses in the street didn't have someone die. Makes you think, doesn't it? Not everything was better in the old days.' She stopped at the top of the stairs, opened the door to the flat and ushered them into a cramped living room. 'The water's all right now, though – would you like a cup of tea?'

'No, thank you,' said Jago, hoping she wouldn't think he mistrusted her assurance. 'We can't stay for long.'

'Right. Sit yourselves down, then. You'll have to excuse the mess – I'm doing the washing and haven't had time to tidy up yet.'

'Don't worry about that, Mrs Edison,' he said. 'We're sorry to have to interrupt you.'

'So what's up, then?' she asked casually. 'This is my husband, by the way.' She swept her hand in the direction of a sour-faced man sitting on a sagging sofa by the fireplace.

'Morning,' said Edison, without getting up.

'These are the police, John,' she added, and he nodded without further comment. 'We're not accustomed to getting visits from coppers,' she continued, addressing

Jago. 'I don't think we've broken any laws, though, have we?'

'No, that's not why we're here, Mrs Edison,' Jago replied. 'I'm afraid we've got some bad news for you. Perhaps you'd like to sit down.'

She took a sharp, anxious breath. 'Oh, no . . . What's happened?' She dropped down immediately onto the sofa and stared at Jago apprehensively.

'We've just come from your brother's home,' he said, 'and I'm very sorry to have to inform you that he's been killed.'

She looked dumbfounded, struggling to take in what he'd said. 'Killed? No, he can't be.' She passed a hand across her forehead as if to wipe the thought from her mind. 'Not Samuel – no, there must be some mistake.'

'I'm afraid not. Your sister-in-law has identified the body for us.'

'But what happened? Was it an accident? A bomb?'

'No. I'm afraid we're treating it as suspected murder – he was shot this morning.'

'Shot? That's—oh, I just can't believe it.' She pulled her apron up to cover her face, and the sound of sobbing came through it. When this abated she rubbed her eyes with the apron and put it down again on her lap, then shook her head slowly from side to side. 'Who'd want to shoot Samuel?'

'We don't know yet, Mrs Edison. Are you aware of anyone who might've wanted to harm him?'

'No, of course not – I mean, I don't know all the people he might've mixed with, but shooting him? I can't think of anyone who'd do that.'

Her husband edged his arm towards her, but she shied away from him. 'You'll have to excuse us, Inspector,' he said. 'This is a terrible shock for my wife. Getting news like that about your brother, out of the blue, like – well, it's a bit much to take in, isn't it? It's dreadful. She'll be all right in a bit, you'll see, but I don't think she'll be able to answer many questions. Is there anything else urgent you need to know?'

'Just one or two things, if you don't mind, then we'll be on our way – we can come back later.'

'Much obliged, I'm sure – what is it you want to know?'

'First, when was the last time you saw Mr Bellamy?'

'Me? Well, I haven't seen him since before Christmas, but the missus did, didn't you?'

'Yes,' said Christine. She drew herself up and took a deep breath, as if she was pulling herself together, and looked Jago in the eye. 'It was on Christmas Day. I popped over to their place to say Happy Christmas. We don't do Christmas presents or cards – can't afford it at the best of times, unfortunately, and things are even worse now.' Jago gave a sympathetic nod, and she continued. 'John's a warehouseman, you see, but a couple of months ago he was bombed out of his job – he worked in a furniture warehouse round in Lexington Street, and it was hit in an air raid. The whole lot went up in smoke, and since then he's been on the dole. I do a bit of office cleaning to help out, but so many firms have packed up and moved out of town now because of the bombs, there's not as much work as there used to be. So, what with one thing and another we're just about scraping by, and things like Christmas have to take a back seat.'

'I'm trying to find another job,' Edison interjected, as if the police might need reassurance of his probity. 'I'm not a scrounger. I do an honest day's work for an honest day's pay.'

'I'm sure you do, Mr Edison,' said Jago. 'Things are very hard at the moment.'

'When you're our age, Inspector,' said Christine, 'you know that's how life's always been for most people – ordinary people, I mean. It was tough even when Samuel and I were kids. Our dad had a job that meant he never knew how much he'd be earning from one week to the next, and what he did manage to bring home wasn't very good at the best of times.'

'What job was that?'

'He worked in the book trade, but nothing as fancy as a bookseller, like Samuel. He was what they call a runner.'

Jago was familiar with bookmakers' runners, but that was to do with a different kind of book: they collected bets on horse races. He hadn't come across it as the name of a job in the book business. 'What is that, exactly?'

'It's someone who goes round all the places where you can buy old books cheap, looking for anything that might be worth a bit more than they're asking for it. Like all those bookstalls and barrows on Farringdon

Road – you ever been over there?'

'No, I don't believe I have.'

'Well, there's tons of books there that aren't worth a brass farthing, but a good runner can ferret out a few that he can sell on for a profit. You know Christina Foyle, that woman whose dad runs the bookshop in Charing Cross Road? She's quite famous, isn't she? Samuel told me she once said she'd found some old first edition in the Caledonian Road market for sixpence and sold it for two thousand quid. Can you believe it? I don't suppose that happens very often, but for our old dad that must've been the dream of his life. It never happened for him, of course, but he never stopped looking. He trained Samuel up to follow in his footsteps, and Samuel started out as a runner too.'

'But your brother moved up in the world?'

'You could say that, I suppose – I reckon runners are pretty much the bottom of the heap in the book business. Samuel said a lot of the time the booksellers would only pay him a shilling or two for a book he'd found, so it wasn't exactly a money-spinner. I think he saw how little Dad made out of it and decided he could do better, so he put whatever money he could aside and then he borrowed some more on top of that, and eventually he set himself up as a bookseller.'

'And was he a success?'

'I don't know – you'd have to ask people who know more about it than I do. I'm not sure he liked running a shop, though, and he never seemed to have money to splash about.'

'So how was Mr Bellamy when you saw him on Christmas Day?'

'Oh, he seemed fine, I suppose. I wouldn't say he didn't have a care in the world, but he didn't give me the impression he was in trouble or anything like that. But he's four years older than me, and I've always thought that made him a bit cagey about what was going on in his own life – he'd never admit to any weakness or being worried about anything. But maybe that's just men for you – I don't know. Anyway, he certainly didn't give me the impression that his life might be in danger.' She shook her head. 'It's all just too sad . . . I can't believe he's gone, bless him. Poor Samuel.'

Jago gave her a moment to compose herself. 'Thank you, Mrs Edison – we'll leave you now. But before we do, is there anyone else we should notify of your brother's death?'

'I don't think so – Marjorie probably knows more about that than I do.' She thought for a moment. 'Actually, though, there is one person I know of that you ought to speak to – Ron Fisher.'

'Ah, yes, Mrs Bellamy mentioned him, but she didn't have his address.'

'Really? Well, I suppose he was Samuel's friend, not hers. They've been pals since they were boys and they used to work together, so he'll need to know. Nice bloke, he is. Samuel used to say he was the kind of friend you'd want to have with you in a fight, someone you could rely on. I haven't seen him for years, mind – my husband doesn't approve of me visiting unmarried men – but if he hasn't moved you should find him where he's always lived, and his mum and dad before him. It's a little flat down the bottom end of Berwick Street, over an ironmonger's shop – number 107, I think. Don't try going down there in a car, though – it's always full of market stalls, and there's barely room to walk down it, never mind drive.'

'Very good. And I understand there's no one else in terms of family?'

'No, there's just the two of us, me and Samuel.' She paused and gave a quiet laugh tinged with self-conscious sadness. 'That's wrong, of course, isn't it?' She glanced at her husband, then looked back at Jago. 'There's just me.'

CHAPTER EIGHT

It was Dr Gibson's lab technician and general assistant, Mr Spindle, who met Jago and Cradock on their arrival at St George's Hospital. His face and voice were as funereal as they had come to expect, and were it not for his white lab coat they might easily have mistaken him for a misplaced undertaker. 'Good afternoon, gentlemen,' he intoned in his lugubrious manner. 'Welcome to the gates of Hades.'

'I beg your pardon?' said Jago.

'I beg yours, Detective Inspector – just my little joke. We used to have a surgeon here who called me Cerberus. A nice educated gentleman he was, but not having had the benefit of a classical education myself I had to ask him what he meant. He said in Greek mythology Cerberus was the three-headed dog that guarded the gates of the underworld – he let all the dead in and didn't let them out again. Not strictly accurate in my case, of course – I think the coroner would have something to say about it if I didn't release our guests when required to – but he seemed to find it amusing.'

'Yes, well, I trust you're still allowed to admit the living.'

'Of course, sir – Dr Gibson's expecting you in the post-mortem room, if you'll come with me.'

He led them down the harshly lit corridor at a measured pace that seemed in sombre accord with his ponderous manner. 'A shooting, then,' he said after a brief silence, 'and in Soho. We haven't had a shooting case in here for a long time, but Soho's no surprise. It reminds me of what that man in the Bible said – can any good thing come out of Nazareth? You could say the same of Soho – it's all nightclubs and gangsters, isn't it? Shocking business. A million men died in the Great War so that we could live in peace and freedom, and still a man gets shot dead in the heart of London – and I don't suppose it was a German who did it. Was it a gangster?'

'We've got no indications yet of who might be responsible, but we're keeping an open mind. We're hoping what you and Dr Gibson have found out may be able to help us.'

'I certainly hope so too, sir. We may not've had any shootings to examine here recently, but I think Dr Gibson probably had to treat enough bullet wounds in the Great War to last a lifetime.' He stopped at a door. 'Here we are.'

He showed them into the post-mortem room, where

Gibson welcomed them and offered them a seat.

'Shall I make you all a cup of tea, Doctor?' said Spindle.

'Yes, please,' Gibson replied, then, dashing Jago's hopes of adjourning to less morbid surroundings for their refreshments, he added: 'We can have it here while we talk.'

'So,' said Jago when Spindle had left, 'what can you tell us?'

'Well,' said Gibson, 'the first thing I can tell you is that I've managed to find the bullet – you can take it with you. I made a more thorough check of the body when we got it here, looking for any sign of an exit wound, but I found none, which indicated the bullet was probably still somewhere inside him. We had to X-ray him, but it showed up clearly on that, so I didn't have to do all the probing and groping around in the body that people in my line of work used to have to do in the old days. It looks as though the bullet entered his chest, penetrated his sternum and was deflected, with the result that it passed through his heart and came to rest in the latissimus dorsi muscle in the thoracic cavity. Death would have been almost immediate. I shall record it as death by cardiac arrest caused by catastrophic injury to the myocardium of the heart.'

'And the time of death?'

'I've found nothing to suggest my estimate at the scene was very far out, so between ten-thirty and eleven-thirty, as I said then – but it is only an estimate, of course. Have you found any evidence to challenge that?'

'No. We've spoken to a neighbour who says she heard what might've been a gunshot just as *Music While You Work* was starting on the wireless, which would've been at half past ten.'

'That would not be inconsistent with my estimate – and the BBC always starts its programmes on time. Given that he would have died almost immediately, it would be reasonable for you to proceed on the assumption that he was shot at ten-thirty.'

Their discussion was interrupted by the return of Spindle with cups of tea and a plate of biscuits that he handed round.

'Thank you, Spindle,' said Gibson. 'I was just telling our friends here how doctors used to have to grope around inside bodies to find bullets in the old days – days you remember, no doubt.'

'Oh, yes, sir, or at least I remember what some of the old doctors used to say about them. It wasn't just dead bodies either – if it was a case of a bullet wound, they'd have to do the same to anyone who'd survived and still had it inside them. They had to give the patient plenty of morphia and stick their fingers into the wound as far as they could and then go by what they could feel. If that didn't find it, they'd use metal probes, but if it'd gone in further than that there wasn't much they could do.'

Jago was beginning to feel queasy and changed the subject. 'Can you deduce anything about the actual shooting from your post-mortem, Doctor?'

'Yes,' said Gibson. 'It's quite a complicated business, but to keep it as simple as possible, the first thing I'd say is it looks to me like a handgun wound – whoever did this definitely didn't use a shotgun, and if it was a rifle fired at close range, I'd expect much more visible damage. The fact that the entry wound is small and round suggests that the bullet entered at right angles to the body, so for what it's worth I'd say the wound was consistent with the firearm having been discharged from a point directly in front of the victim.'

'Thank you. Anything else?'

'Yes. I detected some charring of his shirt where the bullet hit him – that's normal, and it's caused by the expanding hot gases and particles of powder emitted from the barrel when the gun's fired. I also found traces of blackening and burning inside the wound. The closer the weapon is, the more of this we'd expect to see, and in this case I'd say the evidence would be consistent with the weapon being a revolver, probably fired from two or three feet away.'

'What makes you sure it was a revolver?'

'I'm only saying the marks I found were consistent with those that a revolver would leave, because most of them use black powder in the cartridge. The alternative would be an automatic pistol, but they use smokeless powder, which doesn't typically leave so much blackening or burning at the wound. For practical purposes I think you can assume it was a revolver. I can't tell you what particular make it was, of course – you need to talk to Mr Cornwell about that.'

'The gunsmith with the shop in Irving Street?'

'The very man – Scotland Yard's favourite firearms

expert, or so I've heard. Have you used him before?'

'No, I've met him and know all about him, but I've never actually worked with him. Believe it or not, in all those years I was stationed at West Ham I never had to investigate a murder by shooting.'

'More chance of it in a place like Soho, I imagine.'

'Maybe, yes. Now, if I can use your telephone before we go, I'll call him and arrange a visit for this afternoon if he can manage it. But is there anything else you can tell us before we leave you?'

'No – I think that just about exhausts my knowledge and expertise on the matter of firearms. Now you can go and test the good Mr Cornwell's.'

CHAPTER NINE

The plate of biscuits that Spindle brought to them in the post-mortem room had been a welcome accompaniment to the cup of tea they'd been offered, but Jago had noticed the look of disappointment on Cradock's face. The sight of a biscuit had probably served only to provoke the boy's stomach into desiring some greater sustenance. A request for more would not have brought down the wrath suffered by Oliver Twist, but it would still have seemed to Jago impolite under the circumstances, and besides, the idea of chomping on a pork pie within feet of a corpse was to him, at least, unappetising. It did remind him, however, that the events of the day had deprived Cradock of his lunch, so before they left, he procured with Gibson's help the most substantial sandwiches the hospital refectory could supply. As soon as they got outside, he handed his colleague a brown paper bag. 'There you are,' he said, 'get that down you, and never let it be said I don't look after you.'

'Cor, thanks, guv'nor,' Cradock replied animatedly, opening the bag and examining the contents. 'That's the ticket!' By the time they got to the car he'd already made serious inroads into his delayed nourishment. 'So are we going to see that gunsmith now?' he said, wiping the crumbs from his mouth.

'Yes,' Jago replied, 'but I think we should stop off on the way and have a word with that man Samuel Bellamy's landlord mentioned.'

'What, his other tenant?'

'That's right – Mr Jenkins. We know Thompson called 999 at five past eleven, but we only have his word for when he arrived at Bellamy's flat, so we need to establish his whereabouts at the time of the shooting as soon as possible.'

They drove to Denmark Street and found Jenkins at home: he was an elderly-looking man who leant on a stick but eyed them with a steely gaze when they appeared at his door and introduced themselves as police officers. 'What do you want?' he growled.

'We just need to ask you a question,' said Jago. 'May we come in?'

'I suppose so.'

He opened the door wider and let them in but gave no invitation to go any farther into his home. 'What's it about?'

'We're making enquiries into an incident that occurred this morning,' Jago replied, 'and we just need

66

to establish the movements of Mr Eric Thompson. I understand he's your landlord.'

'Yeah, that's right, the old crook. What's he got up to now?'

Jago ignored the question. 'We understand he visited you earlier today. Is that correct?'

'It is.'

'What time was that?'

Jenkins thought for a moment. 'He must've turned up round about ten o'clock. I'm getting on a bit now, so I don't jump out of bed early like I used to, but I'd had a shave and some breakfast before he arrived. I was just thinking about going out and buying a paper when there he was, banging on the door. He was barely inside before he started having a go at me – he's nothing but trouble, that man.'

'In what way?'

'He's always losing his rag with me if I'm a day or two behind with the rent. You wouldn't think there was a war on – all he thinks about is his money. He can turn very nasty.'

'Do you mean physically violent?'

'Not with me – not yet anyway. I may not be as quick on my feet as I used to be, but I don't take any lip from his sort. I told him where to get off.'

'This was to do with your rent?'

'Not exactly, no. He was going on about sub-letting – said I'd broken the terms of my lease by sub-letting a room in this place, and if I didn't stop, he'd put my rent up to cover it. That was nonsense – all I've done is let a pal who's been bombed out use a room here until he gets back on his feet. He might slip me a packet or two of Senior Service to say thanks, but I'm not charging him money for the room. I told Thompson to his face, but he wouldn't have it. "That won't wash with me," he said, getting on his high horse. I thought he was going to clout me, but I just stared him in the face, and I reckon he had second thoughts. He stormed off and banged the door shut behind him.'

'And do you remember what time that was?'

'I do, yes – I was supposed to be going out to meet up with another mate of mine, so I checked the clock. It was just coming up to eleven o'clock – about ten to, I think.'

'Thank you, Mr Jenkins, you've been most helpful.'

'Really? I don't think a copper's ever said that to me before. Always happy to do you boys a favour, though. And if you happen to see that man Thompson, you could do me a favour back and tell him to keep a civil tongue in his head next time he comes round here.'

Jago did not feel inclined to accede to Jenkins's request, but gave him a polite smile as they left.

CHAPTER TEN

The afternoon light was fading when they arrived in Irving Street, close to Leicester Square, but there was still enough to find the gunsmith's shop. It was about halfway down the street and identified by the sign above it *Cornwell & Sons, Gunsmiths*. The only person in the shop was a bald man of medium height with a moustache who looked in his fifties, standing behind the counter. 'Good afternoon,' he said. 'Can I help you?'

'Yes,' said Jago, presenting his warrant card. 'I called earlier.'

Cornwell perused the card. 'Ah, yes, Detective Inspector Jago.' He inclined his head towards Cradock. 'And this is?'

'Detective Constable Cradock.'

'Very good. Well, I'm Ernest Cornwell, the proprietor here, and I'm at your service.' He gave them a broad smile. 'I'm only too glad to be able to help – as you can perhaps imagine, playing a small part in Scotland Yard's cases adds an interesting dimension to my working week. And if my assistance can help to ensure the guilty are convicted and the innocent acquitted, so much the better. So what have you got for me?'

Jago glanced at the door to make sure no one was about to interrupt them. 'A man was shot dead in Soho this morning, Mr Cornwell, and we're treating it as a case of suspected murder. The pathologist has recovered the bullet from the body, so I'd like to know if you can tell us anything helpful by examining it.'

Cornwell nodded. 'Let's see what we can do, then.'

Jago took an envelope from his pocket and tipped the bullet carefully onto the glass counter. The gunsmith picked it up and dropped it into the palm of his hand. 'Yes,' he said, 'if you can wait for a moment, I'll just pop downstairs with this – I have a workshop in the basement where I work on the guns I sell, but for jobs like this it also becomes my own little forensic laboratory, so I keep my micrometer and other tools down there. I'd be grateful if you could mind the shop for me for a couple of minutes, as it were – my assistant's not here at the moment, and I imagine the Metropolitan Police wouldn't want me to leave a gun shop unattended. If any customers come, give me a shout and I'll come up – my work for you is important, but these days one doesn't want any customer to find the place shut during normal trading hours, unless, of course, there's an unexploded landmine in the back yard.'

He went through a door behind the counter and closed it behind him. Within a few minutes he returned and handed the bullet back to Jago.

'There's your exhibit,' he said. 'So, what can I tell you about it? First of all, this is .442 calibre ammunition, which would typically be used in a handgun. Secondly, it's made by Webley, a name I'm sure you'll be familiar with if you served in the Great War.'

Jago nodded but said nothing: he'd been issued with a Webley revolver when he was commissioned as an officer after two years in the ranks with a Lee-Enfield rifle.

Cornwell continued. 'This bullet is of a slightly smaller calibre than the ones used in the British Army's revolvers, and it's relatively uncommon.'

'So can you tell us what kind of gun it was fired from?'

'I thought that would be your next question. Unfortunately, I can't tell you the make and model, but statistically speaking the most likely candidate is another Webley revolver known as the British Bulldog. It was first produced back in Queen Victoria's time, and it was copied by other manufacturers all over the Continent and the USA, so there are thousands of them still in use around the world. It's what we call a pocket pistol, because it's small enough to fit into your pocket, or for a woman to carry in her handbag.'

'Does that mean it's what they call a lady's weapon?'

'It certainly could be – it's the kind of thing you might see in an American film, but you shouldn't let that influence you too much. Men use them too – you remember John Dillinger?'

'The American bank robber?'

'Yes. When the police eventually arrested him five or six years ago they found he was carrying a gun small enough to slip into his sock. It was a derringer – only four or five inches long. It wasn't one of those that fired this bullet, though – the derringer fires .41 calibre cartridges. The British Bulldog's main claim to fame is that it was the weapon used – by a man – to assassinate the president of the United States in 1881, President Garfield, who I believe didn't succumb to his wound for several weeks, poor fellow. Interestingly, in his case too the bullet was found inside the body. It may also be useful to know the cartridge for this bullet uses black powder rather than smokeless.'

'Ah, yes – our pathologist said his post-mortem examination suggested that would be the case. Now, I appreciate that you can't tell us precisely which gun was used in the incident we're investigating, but if we find a weapon and have reason to suspect it's the one used by our killer, will you be able to establish whether it's the one that fired this bullet?'

'Undoubtedly. As I'm sure you know, when the bullet's fired, the inside of the gun's barrel leaves unique markings on it, so if you bring me a weapon I'll take it down into my workshop and test it. I fire several bullets of the same calibre as this one into a roll of cotton wool with a sandbag behind it to make sure nothing goes astray, and then I use a wonderful gadget I have down there called a comparison microscope. It's basically two microscopes linked together, so I put your bullet and one of the ones I've fired side by side and compare those markings. If they're the same on both bullets, it means they've both been fired from the same gun, and you've got your murder weapon. So if and when you find your gun, just bring it along to me, and if I haven't been blown to kingdom come in the meantime I'll do the comparison and let you know.'

'Thank you, Mr Cornwell,' said Jago. 'We'll do that.'

CHAPTER ELEVEN

Jago checked his watch as the gunsmith's shop door closed behind them. 'I think it's time to call it a day, Peter,' he said. 'But tell me, how would you fancy going to a jazz club this evening?'

'I don't know, sir – I've never been to one.'

'Neither have I, but we know Samuel Bellamy used to, so we might discover something interesting. Besides, it might make a pleasant change from playing billiards at the Ambrosden Avenue section house for you.'

'Oh, yes, definitely, sir. But the one that record shop man said he and Bellamy used to go to – would that be one of those, er, Soho nightclubs?'

'It's a club in Soho that's open at night, so yes.'

A look of apprehension crossed Cradock's face. 'They're a bit dodgy, aren't they, sir?'

'Some of them are, certainly – I expect we'll find out

whether the Blue Palm is when we get there.'

Cradock's unchanged expression suggested he was not entirely reassured by this response.

'Don't worry, Peter,' Jago continued. 'I feel a responsibility to your mother to make sure you're not led astray while you're in my care, not to mention that young girlfriend of yours. So, all you need to know is that if you're in Soho, you don't go into a club just because you're invited, especially if it's a stranger doing the inviting. There are men who'll accost you in the street and try to persuade you to visit a nearby club, but they're usually touts for some very sleazy dens that I'm sure Emily and her mum wouldn't approve of. From what I've heard, the blackout hasn't stopped them, and neither has that crackdown we had last summer, so if we run into anyone like that, we decline their offer. Understood?'

'Yes, sir. Are they as bad as they're made out to be?'

'All I can say is if you go into a place like that without your eyes open, you'll regret it – they'll take you for a ride. They have what they call "hostesses" who'll sit at a table with you and ask you for a drink, and before you know it you're buying a bottle of champagne. Only it's not champagne, it's just some cheap white wine you could buy outside for two bob, and suddenly you're getting a bill for thirty-three and six, if not more.'

'Right. Lucky for me that you know so much about it, sir.'

'Strictly in the line of duty, Peter. So if it turns out to be a more respectable type of joint I'll buy you a drink, but otherwise we'll abstain. Now, do you know anything about jazz?'

'No, not really. I've heard it on the wireless and I think it's American, and it's what Louis Armstrong plays, but apart from that I don't know a thing.'

'Neither do I, so it should be an education for us both. And if the proprietor's there, we might be able to combine a little business with pleasure.'

'That bloke called Nicholson, you mean? The one who's actually Greek?'

'That's right. I'd like to see if he can tell us anything about Bellamy, and given the hours these clubs keep, I suspect we're more likely to find him awake at night than we are in the daytime.'

They drove to Dean Street, parked the car near the junction with Bateman Street and continued on foot. It wasn't easy to locate the Blue Palm in the blackout, but after a short walk they came to a door with a sign on which they could just about make out its name. Jago tapped on the door, and it was opened by a burly man who admitted them through the folds of a blackout curtain into a dimly lit entrance hall. His lined face marked him as above the age for military service, but his general demeanour suggested that he was still fit enough to handle trouble. He looked them up and down and held out his hand, palm up. 'That'll be five bob each for admittance, thank you.'

Jago handed over a ten-shilling note, and the doorman summoned a young man who led them downstairs into the basement. This proved to be a more extensive area than Jago had expected. The walls and ceiling were painted dark blue, with palm trees and fronds picked out here and there in a paler shade, and the electric lighting was subdued. A glittering bar ran along the wall to their right, and straight ahead was a small low stage with a piano on it. He guessed the open area in front of it was a dance floor, but it was unoccupied.

He'd wondered whether their everyday suits might be out of place in a nightclub, but as they took a table in a gloomy corner towards the back of the room he could see that his concern was unfounded. About half the men present were in uniform, and the rest wore lounge suits: perhaps those in the know had decided that black tie wasn't quite the thing for listening to jazz music.

A waiter came to their table and took their orders for drinks. Jago was relieved to find that this wasn't the kind of establishment he'd warned Cradock about. If there were professional 'hostesses' in the room, they were being more discreet about it than those who populated the more disreputable venues. When the waiter returned, Jago said, 'By the way, we'd like to have a word with the proprietor. Could you fetch him, please?'

The waiter looked at him as if uncertain what to read into this request. 'I'll see what I can do, sir.'

A few minutes later a tall, well-built man with a pencil moustache and brilliantined hair, wearing a suit that looked decidedly more expensive than Jago's, arrived and introduced himself. 'I'm George Nicholson – I understand you asked to see me. And you are?'

'We're police officers – I'm Detective Inspector Jago

and this is Detective Constable Cradock.'

Nicholson sat down at their table. 'Now look here,' he said, 'I don't know what you're doing here, but I'll have you know this isn't some kind of cheap clip joint. It's all above board. So what are you doing here?'

'Don't worry, Mr Nicholson, we're not here to check your prices. We want to speak to you because we're making enquiries into the death of someone I believe you knew.'

'Really? Who's that?'

'He's called Bellamy – Samuel Bellamy, a bookseller.'

'Oh, yes, I know Samuel – he's one of our regular patrons. But you're saying he's dead?'

'That's correct – his body was found this morning.'

'So what happened?'

'He was shot, Mr Nicholson, and we're treating it as a case of suspected murder.'

'My word, that is a surprise. But I don't think I can be of much help to you. He was just a man who enjoyed jazz and used to come here to listen to it. He'd have a drink or two, but he was never any trouble. There's not much more I can say.'

'I'd still like to talk to you – and your wife too. I understand you run the club together.'

'That's right – me and Ivy. But you can't talk to her tonight – she's gone to Ealing, to see her sister.' He glanced round the room. 'Look, Inspector, I'm very happy to talk to you, and I'm sure my wife will be too, but this is neither the time nor the place – it's more than I can do to keep this club ticking over all night on my own. Could we make it tomorrow morning?'

'I imagined you'd be sleeping late.'

'Chance would be a fine thing. If you work in this business you have to get by without a lot of sleep – there's too much to do that's got to be done when the rest of the world's awake. Just don't turn up before breakfast. How about ten o'clock? You should find us both here by then.'

'OK, we'll see you tomorrow morning.'

'Thanks, Inspector, I appreciate that. But don't rush off – stay and enjoy the show. And in the meantime, let me get you gentlemen another drink – on the house.'

'That's very kind, Mr Nicholson, but we'd better pay for our own. Regulations, you know.'

'Of course, I understand. Actually it's my wife who has her name over the door as the licensee here, so I wouldn't want to get her into any trouble with the law. But do stay – we've got Ethel Rae singing in a moment. She's only a kid but she's quite a sensation – Bellamy was a big fan of hers. In fact I think that was the main reason why he used to come to this place – to hear her singing. She must've known him at least as well as I do, so if you like I'll ask her to come and introduce herself when she's finished. But if you want to talk to her you'll probably have to leave that till tomorrow too – she'll be singing on and off all evening and has to rest her voice in the gaps. I need to look after her – she's got talent.'

'Very well – I'd like to meet her and arrange to speak to her later.'

Nicholson left, and before long the singer came out

onto the stage and began her performance, accompanied by a young man at the piano. Jago watched them: it was the first time he'd ever seen a performance of jazz. He would have been at a loss to explain jazz to anyone, but there was no doubting Ethel Rae had an exceptional voice. The pianist watched her intently as he played, never too loud to dominate but always providing sensitive support. He seemed to be improvising, constantly changing to accommodate her free-ranging style – there was clearly a strong bond between them that needed no words. Jago glanced at Cradock: the boy looked stunned by the sight of this beautiful young woman in a glamorous full-length sparkling gown and long velvet gloves. 'Good, eh?' he said.

'Oh, yes,' Cradock replied. 'Interviewing her should be interesting.'

'You sound a little bewitched, Peter. I hope you're not being deflected from your devotion to Emily.'

'Oh, no, sir, I like Emily best, but that Miss Rae, she's quite an eyeful, isn't she?'

'What a delightful turn of phrase you have. You'd better not say that to her – I suspect you might get an eyeful of her fist if you do. But it'll be worth finding out if she's had any interesting dealings with Mr Bellamy.'

Twenty minutes later she finished her performance to loud applause from the club's patrons. She stepped off the stage and exchanged a few words with those at nearby tables who were clapping most enthusiastically, then strode confidently across the floor to Jago and Cradock. 'Mr Nicholson tells me you're policemen,' she said, pulling over a chair to sit with them, 'and that you're here because Samuel Bellamy's been killed. Is that true?'

'Yes. I'm afraid it is. We believe he was murdered.'

She looked surprised. 'Really? The poor man. How dreadful.'

'We understand you knew him.'

'Yes, a bit.'

'I'd like to ask you a few questions about him, but I think Mr Nicholson feels it might be better if we did that when you're off duty, as it were.'

'I'd prefer that, yes. I'm not sure I'll be able to focus on my singing tonight if we're discussing someone being murdered. Perhaps you could call on me tomorrow. Come to my home – I live at 42 Newport Court, in the attic flat.'

'Not too early, I assume?'

'That would be very kind of you.'

'Eleven o'clock?'

'That sounds perfect – thank you. Now I'd better go and get my voice ready for my next set.'

'Thank you – I hope the news hasn't been too upsetting.'

'No need for you to worry, Inspector – I'm not upset at all.'

With that she swept away, leaving a trail of perfume behind her.

CHAPTER TWELVE

The next day was New Year's Eve: just another working day for Jago, as it had been for the last twenty-odd years of his life as a policeman. But this year it was different. Instead of going home at the end of a long shift to his own company and dozing off before he could see the new year in, he'd be meeting up with Dorothy for what he hoped would be a quiet drink somewhere. First, however, there was definitely a full day's work to be done, starting with a visit with Cradock to Samuel Bellamy's lifelong friend, Ron Fisher.

He was glad of Christine Edison's tip about the market. They parked the car outside the Pathé Films building in Wardour Street and walked round the corner to Berwick Street, a long straight road lined on both sides with old buildings, most of which had small shops on the ground floor and another three or four storeys of anonymous windows above them. It was narrow and gloomy, and with two rows of market stalls jammed in outside the shops from one end to the other there was barely enough room left to walk up the middle. They found the ironmonger's shop without difficulty, however, and Fisher came to the door when they rang the bell for the flat above it. He eyed them warily, but once they'd identified themselves he let them in and led them up a creaking staircase to his home.

'Police, eh?' he said, offering them a seat. 'What's this all about, then?'

'We're here because we understand you're a friend of Mr Samuel Bellamy,' Jago replied.

'Who told you that?'

'His wife, and then his sister – Mrs Edison – said the same. She spoke warmly of you.'

'Oh – that's all right, then. She was always a good girl, that Christine – very kind.'

'She certainly did us a favour – she told us not to try driving here, and now we've seen it I can understand why.'

Fisher laughed. 'Yeah – a bit crowded, isn't it? Where did you leave your car, then?'

'Just round in Wardour Street.'

'Should be all right there, although you know what they say about Wardour Street, don't you?'

'No, I don't.'

'They say it's the only street in the world that's shady on both sides.' He laughed again. 'Berwick Street's much more respectable of course, but the market's always busy.

You can get anything you want, from ladies' stockings to Brussels sprouts, and it's here six days a week – every day except Sunday, which is funny considering the sort of place Soho is. There's no end of dodgy stuff going on all over it, what with all the clubs and bars and what have you, but Berwick Street Market keeps the Sabbath.' He chuckled again. 'Maybe that's just the council trying to clean the place up, though – I don't know. I dare say there's market traders that'd be very happy to turn a penny on Sundays too if they had the chance. I thought the blackout might cramp their style, but give them their due, when it started they all carried on working – put blue paper over the lamps and rigged up tarpaulins to keep the light in and all that. Trouble is, I don't think people are too keen to go out shopping in the dark these days – difficult times, aren't they?' He sighed, and his face clouded: he looked preoccupied. 'And now poor Sam's gone – it doesn't bear thinking about. And shot, of all things – who on earth would want to do that to Sam?'

'So you know about his death already.'

'Yes, I heard it on the grapevine last night. Bad news travels fast – that's what they say, isn't it? I didn't believe it at first – it really knocked me sideways. He was like a brother to me, you know.'

Jago nodded sympathetically. 'Yes. Mrs Edison told us you'd been friends since you were boys.'

'Oh, yeah, those were the days. We were always getting into scrapes when we were kids. It was pretty rough on the streets round here, and poor Sam had this way of annoying blokes who were bigger and uglier than he was. I was always having to step in and get him out of trouble, but then fortunately I was handier with my fists than he was. He was lucky to have me around, I reckon. Yes, we were good mates.'

'Mrs Edison also told us you used to work together.'

'That's right – Sam's dad taught us both how to be runners. You know what that is, do you?'

'Mrs Edison explained it to us, yes.'

'Well, I suppose he did us a favour – it's kept the wolf from my door for thirty years now, although never far away from it, if I'm honest. People in the book trade like going to country sales and auctions to see if they can pick up a bargain and make a few bob by selling it on, or if you're like me you nose around bookstalls in street markets. The thing about being a runner is it all depends on what you manage to find. Now, how's this for a story? I remember a few years ago some old gent sent a first edition of *The Pilgrim's Progress* in superb condition for auction at Sotheby's, and it sold for nearly seven thousand quid. Apparently, he just happened to find it among a lot of old books his wife had inherited. He had no idea what it was worth, and he only decided to find out because he'd sold some old maps that he'd found in the house – they'd fetched a few hundred quid, so he thought an old book might be worth a bob or two. Imagine if he'd died and some relatives had brought in the house clearance blokes – it might've ended up in a junk shop or in a ten-bob job lot at a country auction, and if I'd seen it I'd have picked it up for a song. Of course, if it was any other edition, even an old one, there are so many copies still around that it wouldn't have been worth much at all, but a first edition, well, that's worth a fortune. It takes someone who knows to spot it, though, and that's where I come in – only unfortunately on that occasion I didn't.'

'Have you ever found something really valuable?'

His laugh was tinged with bitterness. 'No, more's the pity – if I had, I wouldn't be sitting here talking to you. But you can always hope, can't you? That's the thing about being a runner – it's like hunting, it's all about the thrill of the chase. I sometimes wonder whether Sam made the right move starting that shop of his. I reckon deep down he was still just a runner – what he loved best was sniffing round old bookstalls and finding the odd little gem he could sell on. I don't think he enjoyed being tied down by things like paying the rent on a shop, employing staff, keeping accounts, and he didn't like the pressure of having to cover all those costs. He was always a good customer for me, though. Once he'd set up the shop, I used to offer him books I'd found, and he always gave me a fair price – he knew what it was like to be a runner, see. Maybe he'd have been happier if he'd never started that shop of his, but I think he wanted to make more money – he'd had enough of being poor from back when he was a kid.'

'Yes – Mrs Edison told us things were tough for the family when they were children, particularly because their father didn't earn very much as a runner.'

'Well, that's how it is sometimes. Sam was a bit of a dreamer, I think – he said to me once if it happened to

Jessie Matthews it could happen to him. Get rich and successful, I mean.'

'Jessie Matthews the singer?'

'Yes, and actress, and dancer – they call her the Gossamer Girl, don't they? She was born just a few doors down the road here at number 94, in a little second-floor flat like this over a butcher's shop. Her dad had a fruit stall in the market. And now she's a film star, isn't she. I told Sam that kind of lightning doesn't strike in the same place twice, but he reckoned it could. I said he was wrong, of course, and he'd have to put up with being a runner. And I can tell you myself that's not the road to riches. If you're a runner you'll have good days and bad days, depending on what you find. But you're living hand to mouth – no one's paying you regular wages, so you never know when you'll be in money or out of it. Christine's right – things always seemed to be a bit financially precarious, as you might say, for the Bellamys back in those days. So yes, it was tough for Sam and her, but especially for Sam, because he was older than her, and he was the boy. Him and his dad, they were always at each other's throats.'

'Why was that?'

'It's just the way it is sometimes in a family, especially when times are hard. You sometimes hear people saying some bloke was a disappointment to his father, don't you, but in Sam's case I think it was the other way round – his dad was a disappointment to him. It got worse too as we grew up, because Sam started to think for himself. They were both a bit pig-headed, and his dad always thought he was right about everything, even when he was wrong. He liked to lay the law down – you know, "This is my house and you'll do as I say" and all that. Trouble is, that sort of thing's exactly what'll drive a young fellow out, isn't it, and then you've got father and son at daggers drawn, which isn't the way it's supposed to be. I mean, we've only got one life, and who wants to end up with a son not talking to them? Sam started to kick against that kind of stuff when he was still a youngster, and they just seemed to rub each other up the wrong way.'

'And did that ever change?'

'Well, there's the thing, you see. When he was about sixteen Sam's dad died. They were hardly speaking to each other at the time, but old Mr Bellamy dropped dead with a heart attack, just like that. That was a shock to Sam, and I think he always felt bad about it. It sort of hung over him all the time – the fact that they'd been on bad terms when his dad died and he'd never be able to do anything to make things right again. Not that he'd particularly wanted to while his dad was still alive, mind, but it's different when they die, isn't it? I think it was on Sam's conscience in some way and he didn't know what to do about it. I think he was angry about it too. You wouldn't have known, just talking to him, but I could tell. After a while he went off the rails a bit, drinking and suchlike, and even though he managed to get through that in the end as far as I know, he seemed to struggle to live what I'd call a normal life.'

'Did getting married help him to settle down?'

'Not for me to say. I was pleased for him when he did

get married – I was his best man – but him and Marjorie, they both came to it a bit late in life. I've always thought she probably got more than she bargained for – he must've been a bit of a handful for her.'

'In what way?'

'Oh, I just reckon he was probably too set in his ways by then – used to doing whatever he wanted to, and no one to stand up to him if he was wrong. Just like his dad, really, if truth be told. It's sad when you think about it – if his dad hadn't popped his clogs like that, they might've made it up and been friends, and everything would've turned out differently. I expect that's why he got on so well with that foreign pal of his, Mr Dimitriou – have you met him yet?'

'No – Mrs Bellamy didn't mention him.'

'Really? Well, he's old enough to be Sam's dad, but he's completely different – a very easy-going old geezer who takes you as he finds you, doesn't get into a row if he doesn't agree with you, what you might call philosophical. Maybe it's because he's a foreigner – I don't know.'

'What's his name again?'

'Dimitriou. And his first name's Ioannis. Funny, isn't it? But they often have funny names, don't they? Foreigners, I mean. He's Greek, and Sam said Ioannis is what Greeks say instead of John. Bit of a mouthful, though, isn't it? He and Sam used to play chess together, and I reckon that was probably good for Sam – nice and calm, quiet, friendly, and a chance to talk. He was a bit like a dad for Sam, the kind of dad he never had – someone who'd listen to him and not judge him all the time for being wrong.'

'I'd like to meet this Mr Dimitriou. Can you tell me where he lives?'

'Yes, he's got a little flat in Greek Street. Well, he would, wouldn't he?' He laughed. 'No, seriously – there's always been a lot of Greeks in Soho, and I think they used to have a little church round that way, so I suppose that's why it got called Greek Street. He lives at number 63. He speaks English as well as I do, too – probably better. You should go and see him – he's a friendly old bloke, and I'm sure he'll be pleased to have someone new to talk to. He'll be cut up to hear poor Sam's dead, though – you might have to break it to him gently.'

'Thank you, Mr Fisher. Is there anything else you can tell us that might be of help?'

'I don't think so, but if I do I'll get in touch.' He paused. 'You know, it's going to be funny not having Sam around any more. I'll still be out there tomorrow morning, poking around some old bookstall as usual, but he won't be there. Still, life must go on, as they say. With or without him, I'll be working all day the same as ever, hoping for that moment when you suddenly spot a book priced at a shilling but you know for a fact that it's worth pounds, so you buy it and then sell it, and you've got enough to live on.'

'Do you ever feel guilty about that?'

'No – some of those blokes just buy old books in bulk and dump them on the barrow hoping someone'll give them a few bob for them. They haven't got the time to check them all and find out whether they're worth anything, and some of them haven't got the inclination either – it takes too much time to learn. If I spot something in their pile that takes my fancy, I'm free to buy it. I'm paying the price they're asking for it, and it's only because I've got more knowledge than them that I know it's a bargain, and I've only got that knowledge because I've put in the years of hard graft to get it. So it's all fair as far as I'm concerned. Besides, it doesn't happen all that often – you're never going to see a runner who can afford to run a car. But it's the chance of picking up a find like that that keeps you going. It's a bit like the Holy Grail – you can spend your whole life searching for it, and you know you might never find it, but you can't stop trying. That's how it was with Sam – always searching for his Holy Grail. It was like an obsession.'

'His Holy Grail – was that a particular book, or just something very valuable?'

'To tell you the truth I'm not sure. I don't know whether he told Marjorie, but he never told me. Mind you, the last time I saw him he did say he'd found a gem just the day before. Priceless, he said – worth a packet if he found the right buyer.'

'When was that?'

'Just before Christmas.'

'But he didn't tell you whether he'd found that buyer?'

'No – like I said, that was the last time I saw him, may he rest in peace.'

CHAPTER THIRTEEN

'That little gem that he mentioned,' said Cradock as they left Ron Fisher's flat. 'Could that've been what Bellamy was killed for? I mean, if it was worth a packet, like he said, and someone else knew he'd got it, they might've decided to nick it – and if Soho's full of vicious crooks like Mrs Bellamy said, they might've got violent too.'

'But they'd have to know he'd got it, wouldn't they – if they'd deliberately come to his flat to steal it, that is. And if Ron Fisher's telling us the truth, Bellamy had only bought it just before Christmas, so he hadn't had it for long. So who might he have told?'

'His wife?'

'Quite possibly, yes – we'll have to ask her. Anyone else?'

'Well, whoever he was planning to sell it to, I suppose.'

'That's right – well done. We'll have to see if those

two men Mrs Bellamy mentioned know anything about it – and if not, whether they can tell us who else might've been interested in buying whatever it was.'

'Could be either, I suppose – they both sound a bit posh.'

'Yes, but if Bellamy used to say William Quincy was more posh than was good for him, as Marjorie Bellamy claims, he might be the more interesting. We'll start with him.' He glanced at his watch. 'But first we have a couple of appointments to keep – we'll leave the car where it is and go and see if the Nicholsons have finished their breakfast yet.'

The Blue Palm Club at ten o'clock on a Tuesday morning presented a very different spectacle to what they'd seen the previous evening. The electric lighting was now fully on and harsh, and it showed up the marks and stains on the walls. The room was silent, with two glum-looking women in pinafores and turbans slowly sweeping up empty cigarette packets, match booklets and other debris from the night's entertainments and exchanging occasional comments in low voices that sounded bored and tired. One of them stooped to pick up a discarded evening newspaper from the floor, gave a cursory glance at the front page and tutted to herself, then tossed it onto a table already covered with empty glasses and bottles.

'Nothing very glamorous about these places when the show's over, is there?' said Jago.

'No,' Cradock replied. 'Bit miserable, really – but I suppose there's always something fake about glamour.'

Jago was surprised: for Cradock, that was quite a profound thought. Perhaps the boy was maturing.

A palm-adorned panel in the dark blue wall across the room from them opened, and George Nicholson strode forward to meet them. Unlike the previous evening, he was dressed casually in heavy corduroy trousers and a pullover. He was followed by a stout, grim-faced woman in a plain dark dress and cardigan who looked, like him, as if she was in her late thirties, or possibly older. Her no-nonsense expression suggested she didn't suffer fools gladly.

'Good morning, gentlemen,' said Nicholson. 'This is my wife, Ivy.'

Mrs Nicholson acknowledged them with a brief nod but said nothing. Jago had the impression, however, that when she had something to say she wouldn't hold back.

'Perhaps you'd like to come into the office,' said Nicholson. 'It's not very private out here, and those women are bound to start the vacuum cleaner up any moment now.'

He led them through the concealed door and into a comfortably furnished office, where he invited them to join him and his wife at a round wooden table. 'So how can we help you?' he began.

'We're talking to people who knew Mr Bellamy,' said Jago, 'and we're hoping you might be able to help us get to know a bit more about him.'

'Well, I know he was a bookseller, and he mentioned once that his wife's something to do with the publishing business, but that's all I know about her. To be honest I don't know much more than that about him either. I'd never met him before he started coming here to the club, and I didn't have any dealings with him apart from in here, so I don't know about his private life. Like I said last night, he was just a man who seemed to enjoy jazz and used to come here to listen to it. He'd have a drink or two, but he was never any trouble. There was just . . .'

His face clouded: he seemed uncertain what to say next.

'Just what, Mr Nicholson?'

'Well, it was something to do with Ethel – you know, the girl who was singing here last night. Beautiful voice she's got, isn't it? She came and had a word with me a week or so ago. I think I said Samuel Bellamy was a big fan of hers, didn't I?'

'You did. You said you thought hearing her sing was the main reason why he used to come here.'

'That's right, yes. I did – at least until something she said made me wonder whether there was more to it than that. She said he was getting to be a bit of a pest.'

'In what way?'

'Paying her a bit too much attention – you know, always wanting to talk to her after the show, that kind of thing. She said he'd bought her some chocolates as a present – apparently he said it was just to thank her for her singing, but he was making sheep's eyes at her too. She said he was like an infatuated kid. Now, I don't mind our guests giving presents to our singers, but I don't want them being pestered. I offered to have a word – you know, warn him off – but she said no, it was OK, she could handle it.'

Ivy Nicholson spoke for the first time, and her voice was scoffing. 'I think he was getting obsessed with her. But that's the trouble with girls these days – they think they can handle anything. They've got no idea, some of them. My husband's always been very protective towards his girls, haven't you, dear?'

Jago thought he detected a hint of a sneer in her last remark, and it made him wonder exactly what kind of establishment the Blue Palm was. 'Protective in what way?' he said.

'Just looking after them, you know. He's very paternal, very gallant – it must be the Greek in him, I think.'

'Ah, yes,' said Jago, turning to Nicholson. 'Someone told us you were Greek.'

'Who was that?'

'It was Mr Mayhew – one of Mr Bellamy's neighbours. He runs a record shop.'

'Right, I know him – he comes here from time to time. So yes, I was born in Greece and grew up there. I didn't come to this country until 1922.'

'In that case I must congratulate you on your English accent – it's excellent. My mother was born and raised in France and came here when she was an adult, and she always sounded very French when she spoke English.'

'Very kind of you to say so. But I grew up in an unusual family – my father loved all things English, like his father before him. He named me Giorgos, which is how we say George in Greek – after George, Lord Byron, who's quite a hero in Greece because he fought for us in our war of independence from the Ottomans more than a hundred years ago. My father taught me English from an early age. When you're little you just soak it up, don't you?'

Jago nodded: that had been his own experience, growing up with a mother who preferred always to speak to him in French. 'Why did you come to England?' he said.

'Well, you may not know this, but when the Ottoman Empire collapsed at the end of the Great War, there was another war between Greece and the Turks. I was young and didn't really understand what it was all about, but I was talked into going off to fight. I got wounded, but I don't know – maybe that saved my life. I'd seen some terrible things when I was a soldier, and when I got out of hospital I just wanted to get away and start all over again, somewhere else. So that's why I came here. And the only person I knew in England then was my uncle Ioannis, and he was living in Soho, so that's how I ended up living in Soho too. My name then was Giorgos Nikolaides, but that's a bit of a mouthful for English people, and besides, it marks you out as a foreigner. So I changed it to George Nicholson, which is very English but quite close to my original name. I settled down here, became a naturalised British subject and married Ivy, and here we are still.'

'And your uncle – did he have the same surname as you?'

'No – his is Dimitriou. Ioannis Dimitriou. He was very good to me – he let me stay with him when I first arrived here, and later he put up the money to get me started in this business.'

'Hang on a minute, someone told us Mr Bellamy was friends with a man called Ioannis Dimitriou. Is that the same man?'

'Yes, it is.'

'But you just said you didn't know anything about his private life. That's not true, is it?'

'I suppose you're right, but look, my uncle's an old man. He doesn't do anyone any harm, and I don't want him getting dragged into a murder inquiry and having the police breathing down his neck. I was brought up to respect older people, especially when they're family, and I don't want him getting distressed. So yes, maybe I should have mentioned it – maybe my wife's right, I'm too protective. I'm sorry.'

'Right, well, I'd appreciate honest answers from now on – it's a very serious matter to hide anything from me that's relevant to my enquiries.'

'All right – I said I'm sorry.'

Ivy Nicholson leant forward in her chair and made a show of peering intently at Jago's face. 'You're not from round here, are you, Inspector?' she said. 'I've never seen you down at Vine Street. Or perhaps I should say West End Central – that's what the new nick's called, isn't it?'

'That's right. But no, I'm not based here – I'm at Scotland Yard. So are you a frequent visitor to your local police station?'

'Only when your mates there insist.'

'I see.'

'Yes – and while we're on the subject of assisting you in your enquiries, I don't want you getting it into your head that I've got anything to hide either, so I'll save you the trouble of looking me up in whatever files they've got round there. Mind you, they probably all got destroyed when the place was bombed, didn't they? Anyway, just in case any of your pals there happen to mention previous convictions, I'll tell you now – I've got plenty. But they're all trivial offences – not the sort of thing you trouble yourself with, I'm sure.'

'What offences would they be?'

'Just the usual sort of things,' she replied, affecting a bored tone. 'Selling drinks without a licence, fined ninety quid, not having a music and dancing licence, fined sixty quid, not having a refreshment house licence or tobacco licence, fined twenty-five quid.'

'Ah, yes, your husband mentioned you were the licensee for this place. So you're the one who takes the rap, as they say, right?'

'Yes, and what of it? Like I said, it's all trivial stuff. Besides, what does it matter if we break a few pettifogging regulations when Hitler's over there on the Continent enslaving millions of people and trying to bomb us to pieces every night? Anyway, the government's done its big clean-up, hasn't it – that new Defence Regulation they dreamt up in the summer to close down undesirable premises, whatever that means. A friend of mine owns the Stork Club in Regent Street, and she got closed down for twelve months. She appealed against it, but then someone decided to do the magistrates' work for them – old Hitler came over and bombed it. He obviously thinks the same way as them.' She paused.

Jago wondered whether she was expecting him to chide her for this impertinent equation of the local magistrates with the Nazi dictator, but he said nothing.

'We haven't been bombed yet,' she continued, 'but we don't want to be closed down, so we're a bit more respectable now. You won't find anything dodgy going on here. We decided to get properly registered and all that, so now we're all above board and legal.'

'I'm glad to hear it.'

'Yes, well, I've got a business to run, and needs must, as they say. I don't mind admitting I've got a few minor convictions to my name, but I'm not ashamed of it. The fact is, this world doesn't do us any favours, and neither does the government, and I have to bend the rules sometimes to keep us afloat. And if that means I break them, I'll take the punishment too. I don't care how many convictions I've got on my record. To me they're badges of honour – if you want to be in a tough business, you have to be tough and take the rough with the smooth.'

'Right,' said Jago once her diatribe appeared to be over. 'I'm glad to hear you're keeping on the right side of the law. I think that'll be all for now. We'll leave you to get your club tidied up, and I hope you keep it that way – in every sense.'

He looked her in the eye to reinforce his point and stood up.

'I'll see you to the door,' said Nicholson, and led them back to the stairs. 'Look, Inspector,' he said once they were out of earshot, 'Please don't think harshly of my wife. She speaks her mind, and that can sometimes make her sound a little abrasive.'

'That's all right, Mr Nicholson,' Jago replied. 'All I'm

interested in is the truth, and as long as I get it, I don't mind how it's packaged. Good day to you.'

'I think we should go and have that word with Ethel Rae now,' said Jago as they emerged from the Blue Palm Club. 'I want to get her version of that story they told us about Bellamy pestering her. And what do you make of the Nicholsons? An interesting couple, don't you think?'

'Yes,' Cradock replied. 'Especially her – I was a bit surprised by the way she owned up to all those convictions without us even asking.'

'Well, I suppose she thought it'd make a better impression – you know, woman with chequered past turns over new leaf, that kind of thing. She'll have known we might check her record, running a place like that, so perhaps it was a sort of safety precaution. But she struck me as the kind of woman who knows what she wants and how to get it – and her husband the same.'

'Do you think he was hiding behind his wife's skirt, though, sir?'

'Maybe – there are certainly men in that kind of business who'd be happy for their wife to be the one who carries the can. But she's no pushover, is she? As she said, if you're in a tough business you've got to be tough.'

'Hmm . . . That singer seemed a bit nicer, didn't she?'

'In looks, or in character?'

'Oh, character, of course, sir.'

'We'll see. She's in a tough business too, so maybe there are fists of steel under those nice long velvet gloves of hers. Let's go and find out.'

CHAPTER FOURTEEN

Dean Street was bleak and cold when the two detectives emerged from the Blue Palm and set off walking eastwards in the direction of Newport Court, where Ethel Rae lived. The only outward reminder of the nightclub's daytime tawdriness was a scattering of litter around its entrance and a discarded newspaper that fluttered in the wind, caught in a drain grille in the gutter. A road sweeper was working his way down the street towards them, stolidly clearing the pavement of other detritus and tipping it into his barrow, and five or ten yards away a down-at-heel middle-aged man in a woollen hat and a shabby army greatcoat that looked old enough to have seen service in the Great War was trying to sell matches to the passers-by. He was wearing dark blue glasses and had a white stick under his arm, and when they got closer Jago saw a pair of round medals pinned to his chest, the same as his own. Putting two and two together, he stopped.

'Good morning,' he said.

'Morning, sir,' the man replied, turning his head slightly to where Jago's voice had come from.

'Old soldier, are you?'

'That's right, sir.'

'War invalid?'

'Yes, sir. I was at Ypres, 1917. Went up the line seeing everything on the way – sun shining, lovely summer's day. Came back next day and couldn't see a thing.'

'Mustard gas?'

'Yes, that's right – first time they used it, apparently. The Germans had it, but we didn't. We didn't know what it was, but we soon found out what it could do. Terrible, it was.'

'Yes, it was a dreadful weapon – but I thought the blindness was usually only temporary.'

'That's right, sir, but it turned out it could come back later – there's been quite a lot of cases in the last few years, and I'm one of them. The doctors are calling it "delayed action blindness", and it looks like if you get it again like that, it's going to be permanent.'

'I'm sorry to hear that.'

'Thank you, sir. I try and tell myself I'm lucky to be alive, but when you're blind and in the gutter it doesn't always feel like that. Still, there's plenty worse off than me. You an old soldier too, sir?'

'That's right. I got knocked about a bit, but I've still got my sight. I'll have a box of matches, please.'

'Certainly, sir.' The man fumbled through the flimsy tray that hung round his neck by a greasy string and handed Jago a box. 'That'll be a penny ha'penny, please. I apologise for the price rise, but it's that Chancellor of the Exchequer's fault, not mine – him and his budget. Who'd have thought he could find himself so short of cash he has to stick an extra ha'penny on the price of a box of matches? Just shows how much it must cost to keep a war going, eh?'

'Not much you can do about that, I'm sure.'

'Too true. Anyway, sorry I've had to put the price up – it costs me more to buy them in, so I've got no choice, I have to pass it on to the poor customer.'

Jago reached into his pocket and pulled out a coin. 'Here, keep the change,' he said quietly. Cradock noticed it was a silver half-crown.

'Thank you, sir,' said the match-seller as he felt the coin in his palm and ran his thumb over it to identify it. 'God bless you.'

Jago wished him well and said goodbye, and he and Cradock continued on their way.

'That's sad, isn't it?' said Cradock. 'I mean, you see blokes like that all the time on the streets, with an arm missing, or a leg or an eye, but there's so many you don't particularly think about it. It was all a long time ago.'

'Not so long ago if you were there, Peter. Not if you were there.'

Jago fell silent, and Cradock knew that he should too.

CHAPTER FIFTEEN

Five minutes later they arrived at Newport Court, and Jago snapped out of his pensive mood. He rang the doorbell for the attic flat at number 42.

'Good morning, Miss Rae. I hope we haven't arrived too early for you,' said Jago when Ethel Rae opened the door to them. He'd checked his watch before ringing the bell, and it was just before eleven.

'No – your timing's perfect,' she replied. 'Come in. I must apologise for the stairs – it's a long way up to the attic, but it does mean the rent's cheap.'

She led them up several flights of stairs to the top of the building and showed them into a chilly little sitting room. 'Would you like me to put the electric fire on?' she asked. 'It's no trouble.'

'No, thanks,' Jago replied. 'We'll be fine.'

'I'm sorry I couldn't give you more time last night

too – when I'm working it's not really mine to give. But I'm at your disposal now for as long as you like. Take a seat.' They sat down, and she continued. 'It's an odd way of life, being a singer in a club. It's like living upside down – you work in the night when everyone's asleep and you rest in the day when everyone else is out at work. I suppose you do that in the police as well, though.'

'That's true – we all start out as uniformed constables and have to do our share of night duty. But you get used to it, don't you?'

'Oh, yes – and it was my choice to be a singer, so I just see it as part of the price I have to pay to do what I want.'

'So how did you become a singer?'

'Well, how does any of us become what we are? It's just a matter of chance sometimes, isn't it? In my case it's probably because of a game with bats and balls – if it hadn't been for cricket I probably wouldn't exist, and I certainly wouldn't have been born here.'

'What's the connection?'

'My dad – he came from Trinidad, and he was a cricketer. He came over here with a West Indies touring side after the Great War, and that's when he met my mother – she was English. He used to say he fell in love with her the first time he saw her. The tour was only for about four months, but he was a very good cricketer, and he was spotted by an English team. They offered him a job, and he stayed. It was a dream for him to play here, but I think the real reason was my mum. Anyway, to cut a long story short, they got married, and that's how I came to be born in England.'

'That sounds very romantic. So who did he play for?'

'Not a county team – nothing as grand as that – but still a serious side that played in the Lancashire League. They could see his talent, and they offered him big money – five hundred pounds a season – to play for them. He was a player, of course, not a gentleman – I imagine you know how it is in cricket?'

'Yes, of course – if you have a private income and can afford to play for nothing, you're a gentleman, but if you don't and have to earn your living and need to be paid, you're a player.'

'That's right, and never the twain shall meet, except when you're on the pitch. Then it's your ability that counts, not your money. I like to think it's the same in my world.'

'You mean singing?'

'Yes. When I was little, of course, what I wanted to be was a cricketer, like my dad, not a singer. He taught me to play, and I loved it, and he even managed to get me into a school where the girls played cricket.'

'There aren't many of those, I'd imagine.'

'More than you might think – when the Women's Cricket Association was set up there were very few, but now there's well over a hundred, and it's growing. Anyway, it turned out I was really good at it – Dad used to say I could catch for England. Being a child, of course, things like having to earn a living never crossed my mind. I just knew that he once told me if you played for England in a Test match you got paid nine pounds a day – and a man would be rich even on nine pounds a week. To me it sounded like a king's ransom – but it was only when I was a bit older I discovered only men get to be kings.'

'So was that why you decided to be a singer?'

'No, that was just something I grew up with. My mum always sang around the house, and she used to teach me songs when I was little, so it became my party trick. I'd sing for guests, and they'd tell me I was wonderful, so I kept doing it. By the time I was thirteen or so I was quite passionate about it – it was as though singing was something deep inside me that wanted to break out. My dad had some jazz records, and I used to play them all the time on the gramophone – I learnt the songs, but most of all I was learning the way the women on the records sang them. The big change came when he took me to see Nina Mae McKinney singing – it was at the Alhambra Theatre in Leicester Square, where the Odeon cinema is now. She'd come over from America for two weeks and there she was, singing on the stage in front of my eyes. She was young, she looked like me, and she sang the way I wanted to sing. I was captivated, and from that moment on I knew – I wanted to be Nina Mae McKinney.' She smiled at him. 'Do you like jazz, Inspector?'

'Well, to be honest, Miss Rae, I'm more of an "After the Ball" man myself – my father used to sing that in the music halls when I was a boy.'

'Your father was a singer? How wonderful – was he a success?'

Jago smiled. 'I don't think he made a lot of money,

and he was never top of the bill – but I think he was happy to make any kind of living out of singing, because that was what he loved. So I suppose that's success, in a way, and it's probably the closest most singers get to it. Does it sound like success to you?'

'Oh, yes – I'd sing for nothing if I had an audience of more than myself. But that doesn't pay the rent, does it? I want to have the kind of success that makes money too. I want to make hit records, be a star – but to do that it's not enough just to have talent. You've got to look good as well as sound good, and that means buying fancy frocks. You have to get a record company interested, and that means paying for demonstration recordings, so you have to spend money before you can make money. It's not easy when you're a young woman without connections, so I'm trying to make some and find money to invest in my future. It's not just about having a nice voice, you know.'

'I do know,' said Jago, thinking of the ups and downs of his own father's career and the unfulfilled dreams he'd lived and died with. 'But someone has to be that success, don't they? And why shouldn't it be you?'

'Quite right,' she replied. 'But I'm not going to leave it to chance – I'm going to make it happen, just like my dad did with his cricket.'

'I wish you well, then. And what is it about jazz music in particular that attracts you?'

'I suppose the short answer's everything, but most of all it's the way it makes me feel free. The thing about jazz is that it comes from your heart, not your mind – in fact I think it comes from your soul, somewhere deep down inside. You don't have to be frothy and frivolous all the time – you can sing your pain. And that's what makes the audience connect with it – it's that old "deep calleth unto deep" thing. It's not like those stuffy old Victorian parlour songs people used to sing – you know, "Come into the Garden, Maud" and all that. To me that's like the musical equivalent of whalebone corsets – it's stiff and constricting and rigid. But jazz – well, the first time I heard it, it just sounded so free, so playful. You sing around the melody whatever way you want to – it's like you're weaving above it, below it, before it, behind it, as if your voice is dancing with the music. You just sing what you're feeling right there and then. And the rhythm's not fixed, like in those old tunes – it's syncopated, so it makes you want to tap your feet or get up and dance – and it sounds like a completely different type of music. When you're singing or playing jazz, you can improvise – it's never the same thing twice. It takes skill, but if you've got it, it's simple – you just have to let yourself go and follow what you feel.'

'Thank you – that's very illuminating. But how do you find the reality of working in a place like the Blue Palm? Soho nightclubs are quite notorious, aren't they?'

'Oh, boy, that's an understatement if ever I heard one. I could take you to some terrible dives and basement drinking dens all round Soho – Greek Street, Gerrard Street, Lisle Street, just about anywhere you'd like to name. They prey on suckers, luring them in just so they can fleece them. When I first came to sing at the Blue

Palm, that's pretty much how it worked there too.'

'What did your parents think of that?'

'They didn't approve, obviously, but I told them I can look after myself – and I can. I was hired as a singer, and in my book that means nothing more and nothing less, so I didn't get involved in the racket the Nicholsons were running with the so-called "hostesses", and when they tried to persuade me I just gave them a flat no. You could say that working there completed my education in life – but I was looking up, to my career and my future, and I wasn't going to be dragged down.'

'Couldn't you leave?'

'Yes, and I nearly did, but then the government cracked down on joints like that last July, and you police were closing places down left, right and centre. I think the Nicholsons had already seen the writing on the wall, because they decided pretty quickly to go legitimate – got the club registered, paid for all the licences, and turned it into a halfway respectable establishment. Maybe not the kind of place you'd take your maiden aunt to, but legal – a proper jazz club, where people can come and enjoy the music without being diddled. I don't know how long it'll last, but it seems to be going OK so far – you saw how many people there were last night.'

'So would it be fair to say Mr and Mrs Nicholson had turned over a new leaf?'

She laughed. 'Can a leopard change its spots? I'd say they've changed their business strategy to suit the current situation – if they make more money this way, they might stick to it. But you being a policeman, I probably don't need to tell you that crackdown didn't work – every time a nightclub or bottle party got shut down, a new one opened up just round the corner, or even in the same building under a different name. And when a whole load of MPs got up in arms about it in parliament and wanted a new law to stop them, the Home Secretary said no. Those places are still running, so I reckon Mr and Mrs Nicholson are probably keeping their decision under review, as you might say, with an eye to the main chance. If they can make more profit going back to the old way, I wouldn't be surprised if they did. But in the meantime, I'd say the Blue Palm's definitely gone up in the world. It's a cut above those other places – you couldn't say it's ritzy, but it's got a bit of class. It's a jazz club, and people go to it because they want to listen to the music, not just spend their money on fake wine and women.'

'So there's nothing untoward going on in the Blue Palm Club?'

'No, not as far as I know. I'm not so sure about the place next door, though – there's something funny going on there.'

'What sort of thing?'

'I don't know, but sometimes I don't get out of the club until three or four in the morning, and I've seen people coming and going, even though it looks like it's empty, and cars and vans too, parked round the back. I don't know who it belongs to, but I wouldn't be surprised if it was someone starting up one of those dives again. If it's got a basement, like the Blue Palm, you can keep it going through the air raids and be all right, which must be good for business – unless you get a direct hit, of course, but then you probably won't know anything about it.'

'Indeed. Well, thank you – that's most enlightening. Now, I mentioned last night that I'd like to ask you a few questions in connection with the death of Mr Bellamy. We visited the club because we'd been told he used to go to it, and I think you said you knew him.'

'Yes, that's right – not well, as I said, but we were certainly acquainted. He'd been coming for quite a while – he was a jazz fan, and the clubs in Soho are really the place to be if you want to hear the best new jazz, even the disreputable ones. We get all sorts turning up – some become regulars, and some you never see again. We don't get to know most of them. But you said he'd been murdered, poor soul – what happened?'

'He was shot.'

'Oh, my goodness. And where was that?'

'In his home.'

'Do you know who did it?'

'We're still at an early stage of our enquiries – we're talking to people who knew him, who might be able to help us.'

'What sort of thing do you want to know?'

'I'd like to know what he was like when he was at the club. Did he ever give you any trouble?'

'Trouble? No – why do you ask that?'

'It's just that Mr Nicholson told us Mr Bellamy was paying too much attention to you – he described him as a bit of a pest.'

'Well, I suppose you could say that, but it was nothing I can't handle. The thing is, you see, when you sing professionally in a little club like the Blue Palm it's quite intimate. You're out there in the spotlight all dolled up and looking your best in a room full of men with more than a bob or two to spend at the bar, and if you're not careful it can get a bit out of hand, so you have to be able to keep your wits about you. I sing because I want to, and it earns me a living, but I don't want anything else there and I learnt long ago how to fend off any unwanted attentions, especially from middle-aged men who've had too much to drink.'

'Was that the kind of man Mr Bellamy was?'

'No, I'm not saying that. Mind you, he did enjoy the odd tipple now and again. I tried to persuade him once to lend me a bit of money to help me get my career going – on a strictly no-strings-attached basis of course, you understand. I reckoned if he thought I was so wonderful he might just do it, especially as he was a bit tipsy at the time. But he just laughed. He said, "If only I could, my dear, but business hasn't been going too well of late, and I'm in hock already – over my ears in debt." Then he came over all sad. I didn't pursue it – I clearly wasn't going to get any loans from him – but I felt sorry for him. No, he wasn't such a bad old stick. It was just that he used to make a fuss of me and sometimes he wouldn't take no for an answer. Look, to tell you the truth, he could be a pain in the neck – but if you think I'd shoot him for that, you're barking up the wrong tree.'

'Do you own a gun?'

She looked shocked. 'What? You're serious, aren't you? My goodness – of course I don't. I may have to discourage the odd wandering hand with some of those patrons, but I don't shoot them. If I shot every man who made a pass at me, Mr and Mrs Nicholson wouldn't have any customers left. Most of them are probably just hen-pecked husbands who are off the leash for the evening and get a bit carried away.'

'Was Mr Bellamy a hen-pecked husband?'

'I couldn't say – he never said anything to suggest he was.'

'Did Mrs Bellamy know about the interest her husband seems to have taken in you?'

'I don't know. He never mentioned it, and I've never met her. I don't recall her ever coming to the club with him – maybe she's not a fan of jazz, just like I'm not a fan of married men who chase after single girls. Don't get me wrong – I've got nothing against men, but right now I'm focused on my career. I like to think I might be married one day with kids of my own, but that's a long way off – and besides, it would have to be a pretty special kind of man for me to want to spend my whole life with him, not a man like him.'

'Did Mr Bellamy ever mention any concerns, anything that was worrying him?'

'No, not that I can recall.'

'Are you aware of anything else that might shed some light on why Mr Bellamy was killed – anyone who might've wished him harm, for example?'

She thought for a moment, then shook her head.

'No – very sorry, but I can't help you. I suppose someone must've had it in for him, but blowed if I know who. Now, will that be all? I do my voice exercises while the other tenants here are all out at work, so as not to disturb them, and I really should be making a start on them. But if I think of anything I'll be sure to let you know – and if you need me, you'll probably find me either here or at the Blue Palm.'

'Thank you, Miss Rae,' said Jago. 'That'll be all for now. We'll let ourselves out.'

He made his way back down the stairs towards the street door, followed by Cradock, and as they neared the bottom he paused to listen: the building was silent save for the silky tones of her voice soaring in the attic above.

CHAPTER SIXTEEN

The address Marjorie Bellamy had found for William Quincy in the telephone directory was 86 Brewer Street, and when Jago and Cradock arrived there they found that his home was a spacious and very comfortably furnished flat. Quincy, tall and slim, was wearing an elegant pinstripe suit with a handkerchief in the breast pocket, which he checked with a sideways glance into the mirror and adjusted as they went in. His wife's attire was similarly smart, and she looked as though she had just returned from the hairdresser. Their faces were confident and impassive, but they both registered shock when Jago explained the reason for his visit.

'Bellamy, dead?' said Quincy. 'I say – poor chap. And shot, you say? Do you mean he shot himself?'

'No – we believe he was murdered.'

'Oh, my word . . . I don't know which is worse.

Murdered? But who would want to do that?'

'Can you think of anyone who might've wanted to harm him?'

'No, I can't – but then I didn't know much about him or his private affairs. Ours was a purely business relationship, quite simple and straightforward.'

'And you, Mrs Quincy?'

'I'm afraid I can't be of any help there, Inspector. I know of Mr Bellamy through my husband's work, but I don't believe I've ever met him and I certainly can't imagine why anyone would want to shoot him. It's outrageous.'

'Indeed,' said Jago, turning back to her husband. 'Was there any reason why your first assumption just now was that he might've shot himself, Mr Quincy?'

'Not really – I suppose it was just because he was a bookseller, and to be perfectly frank, things have been pretty grim in the book business for years now.'

'I understand you're a bookseller yourself – is that correct?'

'Yes, it is. I've got a little shop in Bond Street – you get a good class of customer there. In fact you're lucky to catch me here this morning – I was about to go over there. Do call in any time – it's called W. Quincy and it's on the left as you go up from Stafford Street, just a bit past Yardley, the perfume people. But as I was saying, in recent years I've seen things in the book trade go from bad to worse. First there was the Wall Street crash, which hit us as hard as anyone else. It wasn't just property that people had been speculating on, it was books as well. People latched on to rare books as an investment, and the prices shot up – everyone was snapping up first editions because they thought they'd be worth more tomorrow. And for a while they were – until 1929, and then the crash came. It burst the bubble and sent the whole book market tumbling down – prices went through the floor, and they still haven't recovered. And now we've got this confounded war – it's very bad for business, especially if you're trying to sell books. People don't have as much money to spend on books as they used to, so sales are down, and it would have been even worse if the Chancellor hadn't changed his mind about putting that new purchase tax of his on books – sixteen and two-thirds per cent on the price of every book, it was going to be. He was even going to slap it on Bibles – the Archbishop of Canterbury himself got up in arms about that. I don't know whether it was thanks to him that books and newspapers were exempted in the end, but it was a narrow squeak, and a lot of booksellers would have gone under if it hadn't been for protests like his. I was just thinking that for a man like Bellamy the whole situation might just have been too much – might have pushed him over the edge, as it were.'

'You say a man like Bellamy – what do you mean?'

'Well, I mean I don't think he was particularly gifted at running a business, so I could easily imagine him not coping well in difficult days like these. I don't suppose that little shop of his made much money at the best of times.'

'I see. So you think Mr Bellamy's business would've been particularly at risk?'

119

'It's hard to say. I'm not privy to his accounts, but the whole trade's feeling the pinch these days, and he was operating at what I'd call the lower end of the market, where the margins are smaller.'

'The profit margins, you mean?'

'That's right.'

Jago cast a meaningful glance round the room. 'Would I be right in guessing you're not feeling the pinch quite so much yourself?'

Quincy smiled. 'Very observant of you, Inspector, although appearances can be deceptive, especially in these days of hire purchase. But I confess you're right. My business is more at the other end of the market – I tend to buy and sell the more expensive books.'

'And some people still have money to spend on more expensive books?'

'Not like they used to, I have to say – one regrettable effect of the war is that few of my private clients in this country are interested in buying antiquarian books at the moment. Fortunately for me, however, I have a number of wealthy clients in America who are collectors. They certainly have money to spend, and they're still spending it.'

'Good for your business, then?'

'Yes, and good for the war effort too – not many people know this, but the export trade in books is worth more than five million pounds a year, and sales to America are especially important because they bring in dollars, which are very valuable to the country. The government seems to have woken up to the fact at last, and now they've even added some bookselling jobs to the list of reserved occupations because of that.'

'So tell me please, what was the nature of your business association with Mr Bellamy?'

'He was a bookseller, but as far as I was concerned he was a supplier. Dealers in the book trade tend to sell to their private customers and to the trade, but I don't think Bellamy had much in the way of private customers, certainly not as many as me. So if he came across a book that was of potential value, he'd offer it to me – and if I knew of a customer who might be interested in it, I'd buy it and then sell it on.'

'Preferably to your wealthy American collectors?'

'Of course. The thing is, you see, there are many people who like to collect books, and the general public probably think that means first editions. That's true of course, but some collectors are much fussier than that. There can be different "issues" of the first edition – and sometimes the difference is just correcting a typographical error. With these books they want to know which "issue" of the first edition it is, because they want the very earliest, which is often much more rare.'

'And presumably the price goes up accordingly.'

'Naturally. I'm not just talking about the days of William Caxton, either – the same goes for some modern works. Take John Galsworthy, for example – in the twenties he was highly collectable, although prices for his first editions have gone down since he died. One of his early novels was called *The Island Pharisees* and it had a tiny misprint in the first issue of the first edition – the name of a man called Dolf was printed as Wolf, and it was corrected in the second issue. By the time Galsworthy won the Nobel Prize for Literature in 1932, just a year before his death, a fine copy of the second issue would be worth about fifteen pounds, but the first issue was extremely rare and might cost something like ten times that. I know several collectors in America who'd pay a fortune to get their hands on one. I realise that to a man who hasn't enough money to put butter on his children's bread it would probably count as madness, but for a serious collector that hunt for a rarity is a sort of quiet, rational obsession.'

'So your business is all about feeding that obsession?'

'I wouldn't put it quite like that. I see my job as helping people to fulfil their dreams and desires, and yes, sometimes even their obsessions, by connecting them with what they most covet and desire.'

'Is that only books, or anything else?'

'Anything that's within my power – but principally antiquarian books. It's all about supply and demand, you see. On the one hand we have here in this country many gentlefolk descended from old families that have grand houses they can't afford to maintain and often large libraries built up by their forefathers but now gathering dust. I can be a confidential bridge between them and, let's say, a wealthy collector in the New World who would very much like to acquire some of those books. As an English gentleman I'm well connected. I know people whose circumstances oblige them to part with their most treasured possessions but whose position in society requires they be disposed of discreetly. I offer that discretion and connect them with a purchaser, sparing them the vulgarity and embarrassment of auction rooms and advertisements. I act as the go-between for the person who has something of value to someone else but doesn't know who that other person is.'

'Was Mr Bellamy your only supplier?'

'No, not at all. I go to a lot of auctions myself and buy books that I think I'll be able to sell for a good price. Sometimes Bellamy and I would even be at the same auction in our respective capacities, but from time to time he'd turn up with something he'd discovered for himself and offer it to me.'

'How long have you had this association with him?'

'Oh, I'd say it goes back about four years.'

'And when was the last time you dealt with him?'

'Let me see, now. I think that would have been about a year and a half ago, when he offered me a first edition of Milton's *Paradise Lost* in remarkably good condition. That's a rare find, and I was able to sell it on to a gentleman in Texas who has an impressive library of English classics.'

'How had Mr Bellamy come by it?'

Quincy gave him a sideways glance of reproach that reminded Jago of his grandmother. 'I'm afraid I can't answer that, Inspector – like any good journalist, I protect my sources. Even policemen don't disclose the source of their information, unless it's evidence, do they? I'm sure you wouldn't disclose the identity of an informant to me, no matter how politely I asked. Correct?'

'Correct.'

'Well, all I can say is that I satisfy myself that any valuable book I buy has been legitimately obtained from a legitimate source – in other words, that there's nothing illegal about it. I take equal care to maintain confidentiality – in my line of business that's essential.'

'I see. So you've had no further business contact with Mr Bellamy since then?'

'No. We've kept in touch, of course, but we haven't had any specific business transactions.' He pulled back his jacket cuff to check his watch. 'Look, I'm terribly sorry, but if you'll excuse me I must keep my appointment – I'm seeing someone who wants to sell some books, and the beauty of this job is that you never know when the next one you find will be worth a fortune. Will that be all?'

'That'll do for the time being,' said Jago. 'We'll be in touch if we need to talk to you again.'

'Jolly good,' said Quincy. He gave his wife a peck on the cheek and left with a cheery wave.

CHAPTER SEVENTEEN

When they were back out on the street, Cradock pulled his coat tight around him and pulled a morose face. 'What's up, Peter?' said Jago. 'Feeling the cold?'

'Cold, sir?' Cradock replied. 'It's not cold, it's freezing – the sort of day a bloke needs to get something hot and nourishing inside him.'

'Ah, I see what you're getting at – you're thinking of food, aren't you? I should've guessed. Well, supposing just out of the kindness of my heart I bought you a spot of lunch?'

Cradock affected a theatrical shiver. 'That would be very nice, sir, now you mention it.'

'Come along, then. I want to meet that Mr Dimitriou, but Frith Street's just round the corner from where he lives, so perhaps we could look in at Frankie's Cafe and see what he has to offer. What do you say?'

An instantaneous transformation came over Cradock's face. 'I say that's a very good idea, sir,' he replied, beaming. 'Thanks.'

The inside of the cafe was as Jago had imagined it would be: decorated in a vaguely Mediterranean style with as many small tables crammed into it as possible to maximise income. If there had been a lunchtime rush, it was now over, because the place was almost deserted. He hoped the lack of customers didn't signify a corresponding lack of quality in the food. After surveying the room, he picked a table well away from any draughts of icy air that might surge in if someone else chose to patronise the establishment.

'Here we are, Peter,' he said, pulling out a chair. 'Well away from the cold here – I don't want you to perish, at least not before the end of your shift.' His comment was lost on Cradock, who had already settled in at the table and grabbed the menu card. Jago sat down too. 'See anything there you'd like?'

'I was just going to check, sir – I haven't been to an Italian place before, and to tell the truth I'm not sure I fancy that spaghetti stuff they eat. I tried some once in a Woolworths cafe, just for a laugh, and I couldn't work out how to stop it sliding off the blinking fork all the time – more trouble than it was worth, I thought. Do you think they'll have normal food too?'

'Don't worry, Peter – if they only do spaghetti, I'll ask them to make up a cheese and pickle sandwich for you as best they can.'

A man in a long white apron with a notebook in his

hand appeared beside them. 'Afternoon, gents. Can I get you something to eat?'

'Yes, please,' said Jago. 'I haven't looked at the menu yet, but my colleague here's a bit nervous about attempting to eat spaghetti, so have you got anything else that he might find less challenging?'

'Don't worry about that, sir. To be honest, no one round here wants to eat Italian food now – I think they'd see it as backing the wrong side in the war. Would egg and chips be in order?'

Cradock's face lit up for a second time. 'Oh, yes please,' he said. 'And a bit of fried bread with it?'

'I'll see what I can do, sir.'

'And a cup of tea to wash it down with?'

'Certainly.'

'I'll have the same,' said Jago. 'And before you go, could you tell me – are you by any chance Mr Rossetti?'

'I am, sir, yes. Have you heard of me? I don't think I've seen you here before.'

'Yes, someone told us about this place. It was Mrs Marjorie Bellamy – I understand her husband, Samuel, used to come here.'

Rossetti looked at him warily. 'That's right – so who are you?'

'We're police officers – Detective Inspector Jago and Detective Constable Cradock.'

'Right. Is this to do with what's happened to Samuel?'

'Yes – you know already?'

'I do, more's the pity – his wife phoned me last night. She said he'd been shot – murdered. Terrible business.

Are you working on it, then?'

'Yes, we're making enquiries into his death.' He looked round the almost deserted room. 'If you're not too busy, I'd be grateful if you could take a seat with us here and answer a few questions.'

'Of course – I'll just take your order to the kitchen and come straight back.'

He walked briskly to a door at the back of the cafe, disappeared through it and then almost immediately reappeared and returned to their table.

'Right,' he said, sitting down. 'The cook's making you the finest egg and chips you could hope to find in Soho. Like I said, orders for Italian dishes have dropped off lately, so we mainly make English food now. That's because we haven't got as many Italians here as we used to – up till last June there were hundreds of 'em in Soho, thousands probably, but then when Italy got involved in the war on the other side, your lot came round and took most of them away, including my dad – he's locked up with all the rest now in some internment camp on the Isle of Man.' He gave a snort. 'That's British justice for you.'

'But you weren't picked up yourself?'

'No. That's because as you can probably tell from my lack of an Italian accent, I'm not Italian – I was born here, so I'm as British as you are. I've never even been to Italy. Just because my dad's Italian it doesn't mean I'm a spy or a traitor, and neither is he. You should've seen what happened here in June – it was a disgrace. We had mobs shouting and screaming outside all the Italian businesses at midnight, breaking windows and making threats, just because all of a sudden they reckoned we were the enemy. I had to paint a sign up outside saying "This is a British cafe" to stop them wrecking the place, and when my dad was taken away I had to change the name from Rossetti's to Frankie's. He doesn't know yet, but I had to, to save the business.'

'I'm sorry to hear that, Mr Rossetti.'

'Thank you – but even so we're only just getting by. A lot of English people who knew this place when it was Rossetti's still haven't come back – you can see for yourselves how quiet it is. I'm glad my dad can't see it like this, but that's only because he's stuck out there in the middle of the sea. The only thing I'm thankful for is he wasn't on that ship that got torpedoed, the *Arandora Star*. Five hundred Italians died when it sank, and the only reason they were on it was because the government had decided to ship them out to be interned in Canada.'

He looked up as a young woman approached, carrying a tray. 'Ah, looks like your food's arrived,' he said, half rising from his seat as she put their lunch on the table before them. 'I'd better get back to work.'

'I'd like you to hang on for a moment, Mr Rossetti, if you don't mind,' said Jago. 'There's something else I'd like to ask you.'

'Righto,' Rossetti replied, sitting down again. 'Fire away, but don't forget your lunch.'

'I won't – pardon me if I eat while you're talking.' He picked up his knife and fork, noticing that Cradock was already shovelling chips into his mouth and hoping that the boy was sparing some of his attention to listen. 'I'd just like to know what you can tell me about Mr Bellamy.'

'Well, I first got to know him when he started coming here to eat. He was a bachelor, see, living on his own and busy with his work, so it suited him to eat out. Sometimes he'd come in for a sort of late breakfast, other times he'd come for lunch. Other days he'd just pop in for a spot of supper in the early evening, before we closed. I think it was just handy for him, being able to eat more or less any time of the day, whenever he wanted. We'd have a chat sometimes about the football, or politics. Then he got married, so after that he wasn't in here so often, but he still used to come round, sometimes to eat, sometimes just to have a cup of coffee and a chinwag.'

'Did he ever talk about his work?'

'Not much – I got the impression he was glad to get away from it.'

'Why do you think that was?'

'I couldn't say, really – he just seemed to be frustrated with it, as if things weren't going the way he wanted. He was a bit rude about some of the people in the bookselling business too.'

'Anyone in particular?'

'No – he might've mentioned some, but they were just names to me, in one ear and out the other, so I don't remember. I think he was just cheesed off with the lot of them.'

'Did he ever say anything that suggested he had enemies?'

'Well, the way he spoke about some of those people you might've thought they were deadly enemies, but that's what it's like in business, isn't it? There's a lot of rivalry, but that's what business is all about – I dare say that's how some of my competitors might talk about me if they thought I was getting an edge over them.'

'A competitive edge, you mean?'

'That's right. But if you want names and addresses, you've come to the wrong man. Samuel and I were just friends, not business associates.'

'I see – thank you. And speaking of friends, we're actually on our way to meet another friend of Mr Bellamy's right now. He lives just round the corner, in Greek Street, so you might know him.'

'Oh, yeah? What's his name?'

'It's Mr Dimitriou – Ioannis Dimitriou.'

'I know him, yes – old fellow, white hair. Bellamy brought him in here once or twice for a bite to eat, but that was back in the old days. I haven't seen him for a few months. Say hello from me, won't you?'

'We will, Mr Rossetti. Now, I see my colleague has finished his lunch, so I'll just eat the rest of mine up and we'll be on our way. How much will that be altogether?'

'One and eight,' said Rossetti.

Jago took a shilling coin, a silver sixpence and two pennies from his trouser pocket and slid them across the table. 'Thank you – very nice, and thank you for your help.'

'You're welcome – do come again.'

'If we need to, we'll know where to find you.'

Rossetti retired to the counter and stood there. Jago noticed he was watching them as they left.

CHAPTER EIGHTEEN

Five minutes after Jago and Cradock had left Rossetti's cafe in Frith Street, Ioannis Dimitriou welcomed them into his home. His white hair, grown long over his collar, and his slow gait betokened his age, and he spoke slowly and quietly, like a man who husbanded his breath. 'Sit down, please, gentlemen,' he said when they had introduced themselves. 'I shall certainly not be able to stand for long, and I shall get a pain in the neck if you do.' Jago and Cradock sat down on two chairs at the small dining table while Dimitriou took a worn but comfortable-looking armchair by the fireplace. 'So how can I help you?'

'We're here in connection with the death of Mr Samuel Bellamy.'

'Ah, yes, my nephew told me – a sad business, very sad. I liked him.'

'That's your nephew Mr Nicholson, yes?'

'That's right. I've got accustomed to using his English name now, but to me he's still little Giorgos.'

'Had you known Mr Bellamy long?'

'A few years – I don't remember how many. When you get to my age, the years pass more and more quickly, until in the end you can't remember when things happened. I've been in this country for forty years now, and yet sometimes it seems only yesterday I arrived.'

'So you were born in Greece?'

'Yes, in 1867, in Kerkyra – that's the place you British call Corfu, in the Ionian Islands off the west coast of Greece, right up next to the border with Albania. Did you know the British used to rule the Ionian Islands?'

Jago's knowledge of British imperial history was sketchy, but this old man was like a scholar teaching a pupil and was interesting. 'No,' he said, 'I didn't – when was that?'

'In my father's time – from 1815 to 1864, but then you gave them to Greece. Not very long really, but you must have had some impact, because people there still play cricket. My father was an Anglophile, and he brought up me and my brother to be the same. He loved our own language and used to say Greek was the language of truth, wisdom and civilisation but English was the language of freedom, and he taught me to speak it when I was very young. He loved your great Romantic poets, especially Byron, of course, for fighting for us, and William Blake for his mysterious prophetic vision. Have you read Blake?'

Jago opted for the honest answer. 'No, I haven't.'

'You should. I loved his poems, and the way things worked out, he came to play an important part in my life.'

'How was that?'

'There was something we had in common – when I was young, I wanted to be a painter, and so did Blake. But then something else happened. I don't know whether it was intentional on my father's part, but when I was fourteen he apprenticed me to an engraver – and that's exactly what happened to Blake when he was fourteen. He produced some beautiful engravings. Then later on I learnt to be a printer, just like Blake did. The only thing I didn't do the same as him was write poetry. And here's another thing – do you know where William Blake was born?'

Jago was beginning to feel conspicuously ignorant. 'Er, no, I don't.'

'Right here in Soho – at 28 Broad Street, over his father's shop. It's called Broadwick Street now. So when I moved to England years later I decided to live in Soho too.'

'When was that?'

'I came here in 1899. I worked as an engraver and set up a printing business, which did well enough for me to be able to invest in my nephew's business ventures.'

'And now?'

'I retired from that some years ago and now I'm a painter of icons. Like Blake, when I was young I wanted to paint, but I had to work for my living, so I've come to it late in life. Nowadays my most precious possession is my sight – without that, I could not create the works I want to and that other people ask me to.'

Jago could see an image of the Madonna and Child hanging on the wall behind Dimitriou. 'Is that one of yours?' he said, pointing at it.

Dimitriou glanced over his shoulder. 'Yes, it is. Growing up in Greece meant icons were part of my life. People who don't know much about the Greek Orthodox faith sometimes say we have them in our churches because we worship them, but that's not true – we revere them, because of our reverence for who is depicted in them. We create them to help us worship the one who created us.'

'Do you paint them for churches?'

'Some, yes – mainly for churches in Greece, of course, so I made it into a little export business to supplement my pension. Others I sell in this country, but those are mainly for collectors.'

Jago raised his eyebrows, and Dimitriou must have noticed, because he gave a gentle laugh. 'You're surprised, Inspector? People collect everything these days. Ten years or so ago there was a small exhibition of ancient Russian Orthodox icons in a gallery in Brook Street here in London, and the Queen went to see them. She happened to mention that she had a little collection of them in Buckingham Palace, and so of course it became rather fashionable to collect them. That was a business opportunity for me, and I became quite busy painting them.'

'But didn't the collectors want old ones?'

'Yes – the best icons are many centuries old and very valuable, so not all collectors can afford them, but they all like them to look old, so I learnt how to make a new icon look old. A lot of it's about adding grime, really, because the real ones have often spent hundreds of years in damp old monasteries and churches filled with the smoke of incense.'

'Wasn't that a betrayal of your art?'

'No – as I said, when I was young, I wanted to paint, but as I got older I learnt that a great artist has an original vision, and I don't have that – all I have is technique. I'm not an artist, Inspector, I'm a craftsman – but I've practised that craft for nearly sixty years now, and in my field I'm as good as any man alive.'

'I trust you told your customers those icons weren't as old as they looked.'

'Of course. They didn't mind, as long as they had something in the authentic style and appearance of the old icons to hang in their house.' He paused, labouring for breath. 'But you know, Inspector, this is a bad world, and there are bad people in it. The man I supplied my icons to in Greece was selling them, and when I told him what I was doing for the collectors here, he asked me to supply some for him too. He said the collectors in Greece knew more about these things than British people, so I'd need to make them totally convincing centuries-old icons. He even gave me some tips on how to do it.'

'You mean he was selling fakes?'

Dimitriou nodded silently, and Jago could see a sadness in his eyes. 'That's an ugly word, Inspector, but it's the truth. We live in a beautiful world made ugly by men, and the works I was creating as objects of beauty were being made ugly by him. But what could I do? It was my living. Am I guilty because he chose to do that with my work? Is the man who invented the gun that killed poor Samuel guilty? Is the man who made it?'

'No – in the eyes of the law it's the person who pulls the trigger.'

'That's right. But still, if no one had invented or made the gun, there'd be no trigger to pull. I was complicit in what that man in Greece was doing, because I didn't stop supplying him. Even though that was to prevent myself starving, I was carrying a burden of guilt.'

'So did you stop?'

'Eventually, yes, but it wasn't easy. And I've learnt that we never lose that burden entirely, because we can't undo the decisions we've made in the past. I play chess, you know, and I think that's why I like it – there are difficult choices, winners and losers, but nobody gets hurt.'

'Ah, yes – a friend of Mr Bellamy's told us you used to play chess with him. Is that correct?'

'Yes, we used to play from time to time.'

'What was he like as an opponent?'

'I enjoyed our games, because we both played at about the same level. When we were just chatting together, I always felt there was something of those old Romantic poets in him. Not that he ever wrote poetry, as far as I know, but he was a man of feelings. He could be emotional and introspective, impetuous even, and could get quite worked up if he felt strongly about something. It was the same with his chess. He'd get completely absorbed in the game, as if the only thing that mattered in the world was winning. But then he'd do something impulsive, as if he was so keen to win that he wouldn't make the long and careful preparatory moves that the game requires, and instead he'd do something rash to try to snatch a quick victory. That would be his undoing, and I would win.'

'How did he take defeat?'

'Sometimes he'd get angry with himself, which is understandable – but he was always ready to come back for more. And now he's dead, poor man. I shall miss our little chats.'

'Did he ever talk about his business life?'

'It did come up in the conversation sometimes, but I had the impression his time with me was a chance for him to get away from it. He didn't seem to find as much pleasure in his work as I used to in mine – I think it was more a pressure than a pleasure. But that's the case for most people, isn't it? Maybe I've just been lucky making a living out of what I love doing. I was able to help him from time to time, though – sometimes he bought old maps, and when he found out about my original training, he used to show them to me and get me to talk about the quality of the engraving. Maybe that was so he could impress his customers with his technical knowledge, but I think he was genuinely interested.

And there were times when he'd bought a job lot of old books at a sale somewhere and found some of them were in Greek. He'd bring them round and say "Can you help me? It's all Greek to me", and then laugh as if he was the first person in the world to make that joke. English people are always saying that to me, you know – it's very strange. Anyway, I'd have a look at each book and tell him who it was by, what it was about, and so on, and I think that helped him to decide what to do with it. He always apologised for taking my time, but for me it was a pleasure – I like helping people. I don't understand why people kill.'

'Do you have any idea who might've wanted to harm Mr Bellamy?'

'No. I've been thinking about that ever since I heard the news, but no one comes to mind. I think he led a quiet life – you know, books, chess, work and home – and I can't think why anyone would want to kill him. Could it have been an accident?'

'I don't think so, Mr Dimitriou. I'd like to ask you about something you said just now – you said you'd invested in your nephew's business ventures. Did that include his club?'

'Yes. It was what he wanted to do, although I tried to put him off the idea. You're a policeman, so I'm sure I don't have to tell you Soho has a certain reputation for gangsters, and in my mind at least, gangsters and nightclubs are like this.' He held up one hand with his first two fingers crossed. 'Like two sides of the same coin. Those clubs aren't children's playgrounds – there are too many people in Soho who make money out of other people's misery. Is it possible to run a nightclub here without being corrupted?'

'Would you include Mr and Mrs Nicholson in that?'

'It's not for me to say – I just think it's hard not to be tainted. I worry about my nephew – it may only be the years that have passed, but he's not the man I knew when he first came to this country. Then he was young, full of hope and ideals, willing to lay down his life for his country, but now . . . well, I just don't know. But I had to help him then, and I've always helped him since.'

'Yes, he mentioned that you were the only person he knew in England when he arrived. I'm sure you would've had a strong sense of obligation to help.'

'That's right – where I grew up, family was very important. If you didn't help someone in your family who was in need, you'd feel ashamed, so I helped him as much as I could. Although to be accurate, I wasn't the only person he knew here. There was that young English woman who nursed him so tenderly when he was in hospital in Greece. I believe you've met her.'

'Really? Who's that?'

'She was Nurse Hayle – Marjorie Hayle. She goes by her married name now, of course – Marjorie Bellamy.'

CHAPTER NINETEEN

'She's a dark horse, isn't she?' said Cradock as they walked down Greek Street away from Dimitriou's flat.

'Who is?' said Jago.

'That Mrs Bellamy – knowing Nicholson all those years ago and never letting on.'

'It might've been nice if she'd told us, but it's not as though she lied to us – we didn't ask her, did we? And besides, she might have her own reasons for not volunteering information about her private life unbidden.'

'I suppose so. Interesting that Nicholson hasn't mentioned it either, though, isn't it? Seems like it was something neither of them wanted us to know about. And what did his uncle mean? He didn't just say she looked after Nicholson, he said she nursed him so tenderly. Was he dropping a hint?'

'What kind of hint are you thinking of?'

'Well, you know, that there might've been something going on between the two of them.'

'It's the sort of thing that happens in life – we'll have to have a word with Mrs Bellamy about it. But first I think it's time we had a look at that little shop of Bellamy's, see what we can turn up there.'

'Apart from a load of dusty old books, you mean?'

'I do indeed, Peter – and first of all, we must see if we can find Miss Langley somewhere in the midst of them.'

Bellamy's bookshop in Old Compton Street had a narrow frontage, but it went back a long way: going into it was like entering a long, book-lined tunnel, and the atmosphere was musty. In the middle of one side was a small counter with a cash register, behind which sat a young woman in glasses, with her hair drawn back from her face and wearing a heavy home-knitted cardigan. A strong smell of paraffin came from the portable stove beside her.

'Miss Langley?' said Jago as Cradock shut the door behind them.

'Yes, that's right,' she replied. 'Can I help you?'

'Yes – I'm Detective Inspector Jago, and this is Detective Constable Cradock. We're here in connection with the death of Mr Bellamy.'

'Oh, yes,' she said. Her voice was strikingly earnest. 'Dreadful business. Mrs Bellamy told me what had happened – she said he'd been shot. I couldn't believe my ears – I mean, it happens all the time in books, but not here, in real life. It's shocking.'

'I know, and I'm sorry we have to trouble you. I'd just like to know whether you can tell us anything about Mr Bellamy that might help us in our enquiries. Is there anywhere here we can talk privately?'

'Not really, no. There's a little room at the back there that we call the office, but it's nothing more than a glorified cupboard, a shambles. It'd be a tight fit if all three of us tried to get in there at the same time, but in any case, my job's to stay out here and keep an eye on everything. You wouldn't believe how much stock gets pinched.'

'People stealing the books, you mean?'

'Yes – new ones, second-hand ones, cheap or expensive, whatever takes their fancy. It's a real eye-opener, I can tell you. They come in here looking like butter wouldn't melt in their mouths – or perhaps I should say margarine, now that butter's on the ration. They spend ages in here sauntering about, looking at all the shelves, like real book lovers, then slip a couple of choice volumes in their coat pocket and beat it. I caught some scruffy old ne'er-do-well at it the other week, and he said books shouldn't be trapped in shops, they should be out in the world, being read. He said he was releasing them from captivity so they could be free. A bit cracked if you ask me. I told him the only way the book in his pocket was going to be set free was if he paid nine and six for it like everyone else. He didn't like that. He slammed the book down on the counter and skedaddled before I could give him a piece of my mind, and he hasn't been back since. Anyway, you can see for yourselves that there's no customers actually in the shop at the moment, so if you don't mind, we can have a chat right here. What do you want to know?'

'Well, to start with, how long have you worked here?'

'A year or so – I started just before the war did. Mr Bellamy brought me in because he didn't have enough time to run the shop himself. To be honest, I don't think it was really where his heart lay – he wasn't a shopkeeper by nature. He liked being out and about at country auctions or in little antique and bric-a-brac shops looking for book bargains, whereas for someone like me, sitting in here all day surrounded by books is fine.'

'Was he not in the shop very often, then?'

'I wouldn't say that. He was in here a lot, actually, just not all the time. He liked to be here to deal with anyone who was interested in what they call the antiquarian books – that's the old and rare ones – because they're the most expensive, and he knew a lot more about them than I do. I think he liked to meet those customers too, because most of them are collectors, and if he could find out what sort of books they liked, he could go out and find other ones he might be able to sell to them. He wasn't bothered about the ordinary books, though – I think he did those just to bring a bit more money in, and he left me to run them.'

'What was he like to work for?'

'Not bad, I suppose, although in a job like this you don't expect to be treated with kid gloves. Being an assistant in a bookshop isn't exactly the best job in the world.'

'What are your duties?'

'I sell the books – mainly new and second-hand, but those old ones too, if Mr Bellamy's out. I have to keep a specially close eye on them – we don't want any of them to go walkies. Apart from that I have to dust all the books regularly, of course, to keep them clean, and generally keep everything tidy. And I run the lending library.'

'Like the ones in Boots the Chemists, you mean?'

'Oh, nothing as grand as Boots, but basically the same idea – a tuppenny library. The customers can borrow a book for tuppence, then bring it back when they've read it. The main difference is the Boots Booklovers Libraries are all in their big chemist's shops, while ours is just squeezed into that corner over there.' Jago followed the wave of her hand in the direction of some shelves that looked much the same as the rest of the shop but had a piece of card pinned to them bearing the words *Lending Library* written by hand. 'It's mostly fiction,' she continued, 'including a fair amount of tosh, but it's what our customers want. I don't know whether the Boots libraries make any profit, but in a place like this every square inch has to pay its way. Having a little lending library brings in extra customers.'

'Does the shop make a profit?'

'I don't know – Mr Bellamy tots up the takings at the end of each day, then he takes the money away and leaves a float for the next day, but whether he clears enough to pay the rent or not, I've no idea. The only thing I care about is whether he makes enough to pay me – not that that should be too difficult.'

'You mean the pay's on the low side?'

'You could say that, yes. Tell me, Inspector, have you ever read any George Orwell?'

Jago shook his head. 'I've heard of him, but I haven't read any of his books.'

'Well, he wrote one a few years ago called *Keep the Aspidistra Flying*, and it's about a young man who works as an assistant in a bookshop. If you read that, you'll find out what it's like – but to save you the time, I can tell you he finds it absolute misery. He works ten hours a day for two pounds a week, and by the time he's paid for his board and lodging he's practically destitute. He can only afford to buy single cigarettes and he hasn't got enough in his pocket to buy even one pint of beer.'

'And is that your experience too?'

'It's not far off. I work the same hours for the same money, and I live in a poky little bed-sitting room that costs me twenty-seven and six a week. No one could ever excuse me of being extravagant, but I find it nigh on impossible to make ends meet – the only consolation for all those long hours is that there's this little old paraffin heater and I don't have to pay for it. It's probably here to keep the books dry more than it is to keep me warm. You could say it's what happens to people who like books too much. I chose to work here because I find books irresistible – I love to read them and I like just being surrounded by them. And besides, to be brutally honest, I've got no qualifications for anything, so if I lost this job I'd be hard pushed to find another.'

'When did you last see Mr Bellamy?'

'Oh, that'd be last Saturday, when he popped in for the takings.'

'How was he?'

'He seemed pretty happy with everything – in fact he was in quite a jaunty mood, as far as I could tell.'

'Was that a typical mood for him?'

'No, I wouldn't say so. He often seemed like his thoughts were elsewhere – you know, preoccupied, sometimes even a bit anxious. But I suppose that's normal if you're trying to keep a business afloat.'

'Was it in danger of sinking?'

'No, I didn't mean that – although I wouldn't know, would I? I just mean sometimes he looked worried.'

'Are you aware of any specific trouble he might've been in?'

'No – he wouldn't have discussed anything personal with me. He wasn't that kind of man – he was the boss, and I was just a minion.'

'Do you know of anyone who might've wanted to harm him?'

'Certainly not – like I said, it was a real shock to hear what'd happened. He could be quite sociable and seemed to get on well with most people. The only thing he didn't like was when someone tried to cheat him – that made him really angry. He wouldn't even let anyone try to bargain over the price of a book. He priced every book in this shop himself, not me, and I wasn't allowed to sell anything for less than what he'd marked on it. That was an iron rule, as I soon learnt when I started working here. It didn't matter whether the book was two shillings or twenty guineas, he wouldn't have anyone try to beat him down. Maybe he made a song and dance about it so I wouldn't be tempted to give in when he wasn't in the shop, but I suppose it might've been because he'd had to buy the books in and knew what he needed to get for them to make a profit.'

'Do you think money was tight?'

'If what he paid me's anything to go by, I'd say yes, it must've been. I don't think he could've been making much profit, really – this place isn't exactly a roaring success, and I got the impression he wasn't too pleased about the way things were going. Not that I ever saw the books – the accounts, I mean, not the stock. Mr Bellamy took care of everything to do with the money, like I said. All I know is if he found anyone trying to put one over on him he'd come down on them like a ton of bricks. I remember once he was here and some bloke in a long overcoat took a book off the shelf and put it in his pocket. Mr Bellamy saw him walking towards the door, about to make off with it, and grabbed him by the lapels and started shouting at him. I thought he was going to knock the poor fellow's block off, but he just pulled the book back out of his pocket, shook him round a bit and shouted at him some more, then threw him out onto the street. It gave me a fright just watching, so Lord knows what it did to him. That's one customer I don't expect to see darkening our doors again, and I suppose from

Mr Bellamy's point of view it's a case of good riddance. But if you're asking whether someone like that wanted to harm him . . . Well, I suppose they might've wanted to get their own back, but shooting him? I don't know about that. All I do know is he definitely didn't like the idea of anyone getting the better of him.'

'Did Mr Bellamy ever give you any trouble?'

'No, he seemed to be satisfied with my work and he gave me quite a bit of freedom about how I ran things in here, but then again, as I said, I don't think the life of a shopkeeper was particularly close to his heart. I'm different. I'm a lot better off working in this shop than I might've been, and I'm grateful for small mercies – I'm indoors, I've got a bit of warmth, and I've got books. I'm learning a lot about the antiquarian ones too, and that might be useful for getting jobs in the future. Mr Bellamy may not've been a benefactor of mankind, but I reckon apart from Dr Barnardo he's the only man who's ever done me a proper good turn.'

'Dr Barnardo?'

'Yes, well . . . My mum, you see . . . But you don't want to hear about all that.'

'No, please – go on.'

'OK. It's just that . . . well, life deals everyone a different hand, doesn't it? I'm an orphan, you see, and by rights I shouldn't be here at all. Dr Barnardo's took me in, and they probably saved my life.'

'So you grew up in an orphanage?'

'Yes – they had a home for girls at Barkingside, over in Essex. It wasn't like a big institution – it was set up

149

as little groups in cottages, like a family, with a house mother. Mine was lovely, and it really was like a family to me.'

'That's not what you always hear about orphanages.'

'You're right, but they were kind. There was only one girl I didn't get on with – she wasn't nice. I always had my nose in a book, even then, and she used to call me a swot and bully me when no one was looking.'

'I suppose that was when you'd feel the want of a real parent?'

'Yes, but I was lucky – one of the bigger girls noticed and stepped in to protect me. I was shy, but she didn't seem scared of anyone. I don't know what she said to the bully, but it must've put the wind up her, because after that I never had any trouble.'

'And now you're working with books for a living.'

'Yes, I think I love reading even more than I did then. When I was a kid it was a way of escaping to other worlds, where girls went to boarding schools and played hockey and had fun. And when I grew up, I suppose it was the same – in a book I could spend time in nicer worlds than the real one. So now it never bothers me if there are quiet days when the customers are thin on the ground – I can just sit in here, cosy and warm, and read.'

CHAPTER TWENTY

From Bellamy's bookshop to his home in Peter Street was only a short walk, but the biting wind was buffeting them more strongly now as the afternoon light faded, and Jago had to pull his coat more tightly about him as they approached it. The cold must have shown in his face, because Marjorie Bellamy urged him and Cradock to come in quickly.

'Chills you to the bone, doesn't it, at this time of the year,' she said as they climbed the stairs to the flat. 'Come through here into the living room. You'll have to excuse me if I don't heap any more coal on the fire, though, what with it being so hard to get hold of – and now they're talking about putting it back on the ration list. I don't know – there never seems to be enough of anything these days, does there?'

'Don't worry about us, Mrs Bellamy,' said Jago. 'I'm

sure Detective Constable Cradock and I will be fine.'

'I've only just put the kettle on for a cup of tea, though, so perhaps you'd like to join me.'

'That would be very nice, thank you – we can warm ourselves up from the inside.'

'Help yourselves to a seat, then, and I'll be back in a moment.' She disappeared to the kitchen and returned a few minutes later with their drinks.

'Do you have any news?' she said. 'About Samuel, I mean – do you know . . .' She gulped anxiously. 'Do you know who did that terrible thing to him?'

'Not yet, I'm afraid, but we're beginning to gather evidence, and we're here because we think there's one or two things you might be able to shed some light on.'

'Well, of course, if I can . . .'

'Thank you. I've been wondering whether Mr Bellamy happened to say anything to you about finding some valuable item just before Christmas.'

She shook her head. 'No, not that I recall, and I think I would have remembered. What kind of item was it? A book, presumably.'

'We don't know, although that seems most likely, but Mr Fisher told us your husband described it as priceless and said it'd be worth a lot of money if he could find the right buyer.'

'Well, that would make sense if he had someone in mind – I remember Samuel explaining it to me when I first got to know him. He said a book dealer's work is obviously about finding books you know somebody will want to buy, but it's just as important to know who those people are, so you can offer it to them. But if you're saying he found it just before Christmas, it makes me wonder . . . I mean, there was nothing on that list of his I showed you yesterday dated as recently as that, so it's odd that he hadn't noted something that might've been so valuable – although as I said yesterday, he might not have got round to it. Whatever the reason, I'm afraid all I can say is I'm not aware of any specific thing he'd found.'

'That's all right. But if he had found something as valuable as that, would there've been any reason why he didn't tell you?'

'Plenty, I would think – if he managed to sell it for a lot he might have wanted to surprise me with the good news. He might have wanted to keep it under his hat until the deal was done, in case it didn't work out, or he might have just been intending to tell me later. There could be any number of reasons why he didn't mention it, but I'm afraid I don't know anything about it.'

Jago pursed his lips thoughtfully. 'There's something else I'd like to ask you. When I was here yesterday you told me a little about your own family firm, but we didn't talk much about your husband's business. I recall you mentioning that you'd both had your hands full trying to keep your respective businesses afloat, so I wondered whether you could tell me a bit more about that.'

'Well, as far as my business is concerned, Hayle and Sons has been struggling for years, and it wouldn't be an exaggeration to say that by the time we were bombed it was on its last legs. We may get a little compensation for the stock we lost, because of that new law the government brought in – you know, the one that makes it compulsory for businesses to take out insurance – but that won't save us. And in any case, the whole publishing trade then faced the problem of how to pay for the insurance without putting prices up. As you may have noticed if you buy books, that's when the seven-and-six novels went up to eight and threepence, and the eight-and-six ones to nine-and-six. For books like ours, putting the prices up just meant that sales suffered even more. To be perfectly frank with you, my business is dead on its feet, and I don't see it rising again from the ashes. Maybe Hitler's just put it out of its misery.'

'And your husband's business? Was that struggling too?'

'I think it was, yes. I helped him out as best I could with my own money, but I suspect there wasn't as much of that as he'd perhaps hoped. I may have inherited the family business, but my pockets aren't that deep.'

'I'd like to ask you something else about your husband's finances, Mrs Bellamy.'

'Go ahead. I must warn you, though – Samuel didn't necessarily tell me what he did with his money. He was a secretive man – I always felt there was a part of his life that he kept to himself and never opened up to me, and I suppose I've learnt not to ask if I'm not told.'

'Do you know why he was like that?'

'No. I think probably he'd been a bachelor for too long – too set in his ways, you know.'

'Yes, someone else has said that about him.'

'Who was that?'

'Just someone we were speaking to this morning. What I wanted to ask you was whether your husband was in debt.'

'Why? Has someone said that too?'

'As it happens, yes.'

'Well, it seems like everyone knows more about his finances than I do. The answer is no, he wasn't – or at least not as far as I know. But I have to admit he could have been, and I'd be none the wiser.'

'I see. Now, while we're on the subject of your husband's business, we've just visited the bookshop.'

'Really? I hope that was interesting for you.'

'It was, yes, and we met Miss Langley, of course.'

'Ah, yes – Samuel's little helper. She's been there for a year or so now – he was training her.'

'How do you find her?'

'Adequate for the job, I'd say. She's not particularly distinguished or talented, but Samuel took a shine to her and felt she was the right person, and I had no reason to disagree. It was an important decision, though, because when Samuel was out and about the shop was entirely in her hands, so a lot depended on her being active and conscientious.'

'Do you have any reason to believe she's not?'

'I'm not sure – I don't spend time in there. But on the odd occasion when I've popped in she hasn't struck me as being . . . well, let's just say I haven't seen her being overly busy. But maybe that's Samuel's fault for not paying her much.'

'And conscientious?'

'That's difficult for me to say too, for the same reason. She handles the money all day, for example, but there's no one supervising her.'

'Do you have any reason to believe she's dishonest?'

'No, I don't – not what you'd call evidence, anyway. It's just that the whole set-up must put temptation in her way. For example, there's the lending library. Every time a customer borrows a book, Judith has to take their tuppence and record the book in the register. But there's no way for us to check that she actually records every loan, so she could just be lending the book out and pocketing the money. I'm not saying that's what she does, mind – I'm just saying that she could, and we'd never know. Samuel was never one for putting watertight systems in place, and if you're running a business you really have to. I'm not suggesting he should have introduced something like the bizarre payment system they have round the corner at Foyles, but a little more organisation might have been a good thing.'

'Miss Langley said that your husband used to get very angry if anyone tried to cheat him. Does that ring true with you?'

'Oh, yes. He made a point of treating his customers fairly – said it was a matter of honour and reputation, and he told me hand on heart that he'd never knowingly cheated anyone. He expected his customers to be fair to him in return. He wasn't awash in cash, and he didn't like it if anyone came between him and a fair profit.'

'Yes, she mentioned that he took a dim view of

customers who tried to bargain his prices down.'

'Quite right too, I'd say – I think his profit margins were very slim at the best of times. It wasn't just the customers either – he took a dim view of some of his fellow booksellers too. It's a very competitive trade, and he told me it's not without its sharp practices.'

'Really?'

'So it seems. Samuel used to say that most booksellers were fair in their business, and had to be because their reputation was so important – but he also said there were rogues, the same as you'd find in any other line of work, I suppose, who'd get the rest a bad name if people knew what they got up to.'

'And what did they get up to?'

'I don't know – he didn't say. I expect Ron Fisher could tell you more about that if you ask him. Samuel did mention a thing called the ring, though – some sort of group who have a lot of power in the trade, and who make all the big money. I think they took a dislike to Samuel, for some reason. I don't know much about how it works, but that's something else I expect Mr Fisher might be able to explain to you. All I know is Samuel used to get very angry whenever the subject came up.'

'We'll have a word with Mr Fisher, then. Which reminds me, thinking of that priceless item he mentioned, he also told us Mr Bellamy had always been searching for something that he thought he might never find. Could that be what he'd finally come across?'

'I don't think so. You see, I think the thing he desired most in the world was certainly a book, but it wasn't a valuable one, let alone priceless. He was probably the only person who'd ever buy it if he found it. It was a very old book, written by a man called Pierre de Bellême, who Samuel said was an ancestor of his. The family was descended from Huguenots, you see.' Jago nodded, and she continued. 'I don't know exactly when it was, but his forebears came over here from France years ago, and loads of them came to live in Soho. I think this Pierre de Bellême was the first one in the family to move to England, and he changed his name to Bellamy so it would sound more English. He was a bookbinder, and he ended up writing some kind of book himself, about the history of his family and what had happened to them during all their troubles in France. Samuel was always looking for a copy of that book – it was like an obsession. But I don't think he ever found one.'

'Mr Fisher said the book or whatever it was your husband was searching for was like his Holy Grail.'

'Perhaps he found it then – although I don't think anyone ever found the real one, did they? But you said he'd talked about finding a buyer. I think if he really had found that Pierre de Bellême book, he wouldn't have parted with it for all the tea in China. I think it must have been something else.'

'Hmm . . . interesting. Just a couple more questions now, Mrs Bellamy. First of all, when we first met you in Paternoster Row you said you'd worked in your family business all your life. I just wondered whether you'd ever done any other work.'

'Really? Why are you so interested in that? I did

spend a little time in a different type of work, but that was all years ago.'

'What sort of work was that?'

'It was nursing, actually – I was young and idealistic, and didn't want to spend my whole life chained to heavy tomes of sermons. I wanted to go out into the world and do something to help people who were suffering.'

'And when was this?'

'Just after the Great War. I'd wanted to nurse in France during the war, but my parents didn't want me to go, and besides I was too young. When it finished I did some training, and then when I was twenty-one I came into a legacy from my late grandfather. I was an adult now, and so I went.'

'What year was that?'

'It was 1921, if you want to know, but really, this is all very trivial. I'm sure you must have better things than to excavate my past in such detail.'

'One more question, Mrs Bellamy – where did you go?'

She blushed. 'Well, er, as a matter of fact I went to Greece. They were at war with the Turks, and I volunteered to nurse wounded Greek soldiers.'

'I see – thank you very much. Now, when we were here yesterday we spoke to your neighbours, just to check whether they'd seen or heard anything that might help us with our enquiries. The gentleman who runs the gramophone record shop mentioned that your husband was something of a jazz fan.'

'Yes, that's correct. I can't say I shared his

enthusiasm, but he was very keen on it.'

'He told us that Mr Bellamy used to go to a jazz club called the Blue Palm.'

'Yes, he did – I've never been myself, though. I find jazz music unappealing, and I don't enjoy it.'

'Detective Constable Cradock and I went there last night, and we met the owner.'

'Yes?'

'Well, here's the interesting thing. He's called Mr George Nicholson, but it turns out he was born and raised in Greece and his name then was Giorgos Nikolaides. And even more interestingly, we've just been speaking to his uncle, who happened to mention that Mr Nikolaides moved here in 1922, and before that he was nursed in Greece by a young lady called Miss Marjorie Hayle. Is that the case? It's quite a coincidence.'

'Yes, it's true, but there's no great mystery about it. I nursed a lot of Greek soldiers when I was there – that was my whole reason for going.'

'And did you renew your acquaintance with this particular patient when he came to Soho?'

'Yes – he moved here because his uncle lived here and was willing to take him in and help him. I helped him a bit too, just to get him on his feet, as it were, but that's all.' She checked her wristwatch. 'I'm very sorry, Inspector, but I'm going to be late for an appointment if I don't leave in the next few minutes. There's really no more to it than that.'

'I'll be as quick as I can, then. The thing is, I just think it's an interesting connection. I also think it's curious that he's never mentioned it. Do you know why that would be?'

'Of course I don't,' she replied with a sudden petulance. 'You'll have to ask him yourself.'

'I shall do, Mrs Bellamy. Now, before you go, tell me please – did your husband know about your past connection with Mr Nicholson?'

'Well, I, er . . . I don't believe he did.'

'You didn't think to mention it?'

'No, I didn't – it was way back in the past, before I knew Samuel, and I didn't want him to go making a mountain out of a molehill. I wanted to avoid the risk of embarrassing Mr Nicholson, or myself for that matter.'

'Do you know whether Mr Nicholson ever mentioned it to your husband?'

'How would I know? Samuel never said anything about it, so I assume not, but I can't answer for Mr Nicholson.'

'No indeed. Thank you for that, Mrs Bellamy. And now I'm afraid there's something else I must ask you. I'm sorry to bring up what might be a rather sensitive matter, but someone's told us your husband had been paying rather too much attention to a certain young woman.'

'What do you mean by that?'

'I think the person concerned meant your husband had been spending time with her, and not in connection with his business. Getting obsessed with her – that's what someone else said. I wondered whether this was something you were aware of.'

'You mean he was having some sort of illicit affair? Certainly not. It sounds like pure tittle-tattle to me. Who is this woman?'

'I'm afraid I can't tell you that, Mrs Bellamy.'

'Who said this, then?'

'I can't tell you that either.'

'Well, I don't think you should pay any attention to idle gossip. The answer is no, I was not aware of anything of the sort.' She glared at her watch. 'And now, if that's all you have to say, I shall bid you good day.'

CHAPTER TWENTY-ONE

Jago noticed as they left Marjorie Bellamy's flat that Cradock was walking more slowly than usual, his brow decidedly furrowed. 'Something bothering you, Peter?' he said. 'You look puzzled.'

'Oh, it's not important, sir. I was wondering about that bloke Mrs Bellamy mentioned – you seemed to know him, but I've never heard of him.'

'Which bloke was that?'

'The one with the funny name – she said he was called Huge Nose. Was he some sort of villain?'

Jago affected an expression of pained pity. 'Do you know anything at all about French history, Peter?'

'No, sir.'

Jago smiled to himself. There was a lot Cradock didn't know, but if he had one redeeming virtue, it was transparent honesty. It made him think of Ioannis

Dimitriou, who seemed to have retained a childlike openness and naivety despite all his years of learning and experience, and he wondered what kind of man Cradock would be when he was seventy-odd years old. His imagination, however, was inadequate to the task, and he had to content himself with plugging one small gap in the boy's education.

'Mrs Bellamy didn't say "Huge Nose",' he explained. 'She said "Huguenots". They were French Protestants, and France was Catholic. I don't know how they got the name, but I do know thousands of them had to leave France a few hundred years ago when the king turned against them and there was a terrible massacre. Lots of them fled to England to find refuge. All she was saying was that Bellamy's ancestors were French.'

'Oh, I see,' said Cradock. 'I thought it sounded a bit funny when she said it, but I'm not very good at the old French stuff. Just as well I didn't ask her, I suppose.'

'I'm sure she wouldn't have minded explaining it.'

'Maybe not, but she was getting a bit prickly towards the end, wasn't she? I don't think she liked you asking about George Nicholson, not to mention what her husband might've been getting up to on the sly – not exactly Happy Families, is it? It really put her back up, I reckon – she definitely sounded annoyed.'

'Yes, an interesting response, but you have to remember it was only yesterday her husband was killed. She's bound to be feeling raw, and her emotions are going to be close to the surface. I think I might be a bit short if I were in her place.'

'So you mean we should give her the benefit of the doubt, sir?'

'No, not at all – all I'm saying is when someone's stressed they can react like that. So there may be nothing to it – but if she's hiding something, we need to find out the truth. Now, time's getting on, and I want to go and make the acquaintance of Samuel Bellamy's book-collecting associate Mr Abingdon, so let's go for a little walk.'

They headed north towards Oxford Street, crossed it and continued a short distance until they found the address listed for Charles Abingdon in the telephone directory. It was a strikingly grand block of Edwardian mansion flats, six storeys in a style of rich red brick and white stone bands that immediately reminded him of the Scotland Yard buildings, although in this quiet side street it spoke more of private power and money. A porter took them up to the Abingdons' flat.

'Can't be short of a bob or two if he lives here,' said Cradock. 'Looks very smart, doesn't it?'

'Indeed it does,' Jago replied, but any further comment he might have made was cut short by the heavy mahogany door in front of them opening. The anxious expression on the well-dressed woman's face made Jago wonder whether she'd taken him and Cradock for door-to-door salesmen who'd used some nefarious trick to worm their way into the building. Their coats, after all, were probably not as expensively cut as those to which the residents of such a place were accustomed.

'Yes?' she said cautiously.

'Mrs Abingdon?'

'Yes, that's me. I don't believe we've met.'

'No, we haven't.' Jago showed her his warrant card. 'I'm Detective Inspector Jago and this is Detective Constable Cradock, and we'd like to have a word with your husband, if he's in.'

'Ah, I see.' She sounded relieved to hear their official status, but added with a renewed uncertainty, 'He hasn't done something wrong, has he?'

'No, no – but we think he may be able to help us.'

'Very well, do come in.' She opened the door wider and called out, 'Charles – there are two policemen to see you,' as they crossed the threshold.

A tall man of athletic build who looked, like his wife, in his mid-thirties, strode towards them and shook their hands vigorously. 'Good afternoon, gentlemen,' he said in a bluff, self-assured voice. 'To what do we owe this unexpected pleasure?'

'I'm sorry to disturb you, sir, but we're investigating the suspected murder of a man in Soho yesterday – a man who we understand you knew.'

'Soho, eh? Hmm . . . rough place. Who was the unfortunate fellow?'

'It was a Mr Samuel Bellamy.'

'Bellamy?' Abingdon's manner changed in an instant as his face registered shock. 'My goodness – how awful.'

'So you did know him?'

'Yes I did – the book fellow. We weren't intimate pals, but we had what you might call a commercial relationship – one of my hobbies is collecting books, you see, and he occasionally used to find something of interest and sell it to me. But how the devil has he ended up murdered?'

'That's what we're trying to establish, sir, and we're hoping you can help us.'

'Well, of course – anything I can do.'

'Can you think of anyone who might've wanted to harm Mr Bellamy?'

Abingdon's face creased into a frown of concentration. 'It's difficult to say, really – I mean, I knew Bellamy, but I'm not sure that I knew any of his own circle, as you might say. As I said, ours was a commercial relationship. Could it have been a business dispute of some kind? I don't recall him ever talking about enemies, but then it's not the sort of thing that comes up in conversation very often, is it? If it was some personal matter, then I don't think I can help you – I didn't know him well enough. I could imagine him getting someone's back up, though – I always suspected there might be quite a temper lurking behind that calm exterior of his. But if you want me to name a suspect, I'm sorry – I don't think I can be of much use to you.'

'OK, thank you – if you think of anything else, though, please get in touch with me.'

'I shall. But look, I shouldn't keep you standing here. Let's go through to the library.' He turned to his wife. 'Perhaps you could lead the way, Edith.'

Jago was unaccustomed to the idea of anything that went by the name of 'flat' being big enough to include a library, but as they made their way to it his eyes widened. Their home was light and airy with high ceilings, fine plasterwork and large windows overlooking the street, and furnished with what looked like expensive antiques.

'Nice, isn't it?' said Abingdon, catching the look on Jago's face. 'All thanks to my grandfather's hard work, though, not mine.'

'He must've been very successful.'

'Yes – a self-made man. He made a lot of money in shipping. Have you heard of the Green Funnel Line?'

'Yes, it's quite a big one, isn't it?'

'It is, although not as big as it used to be – we have the Depression to thank for that, and now of course the war. We've lost quite a few of our ships to the U-boats, and there's no knowing how long that will continue. It's all very worrying.'

A longcase clock in the library was striking five as they went in.

'Excuse me,' said Mrs Abingdon, 'but I'd better draw the curtains – it's blackout time at five-thirty, and I don't want to get us into trouble.' She crossed the room and closed a pair of long, heavy-looking red velvet curtains. 'We had all our curtains lined with blackout material last year, when the war seemed imminent – it was an inconvenience, but I couldn't bear the thought of looking at dreary black curtains every evening.' She gave a final delicate – and to Jago's eye entirely superfluous – adjustment to the curtains and stepped back to admire them. 'There,' she said, 'that should keep us safe.' She turned to her husband with a smile. 'And before you get too far into the company's woes, darling, perhaps we should offer our guests a drink. Inspector, can I get you something – a whisky and splash, perhaps, or a jaggers and taggers? No slice of lemon, though, I'm afraid – you can't get them anywhere now.'

Jago preferred his Scotch undiluted with anything, and gin and tonic was not one of his favourite drinks, but in any case he couldn't say yes. 'It's still a little early in the day for me, Mrs Abingdon,' he replied. 'And besides, Detective Constable Cradock and I are on duty, so we'd better decline, but thank you very much.'

'Not at all. Do take a seat.'

The wing-backed armchairs in the middle of the room to which she motioned them were upholstered in the same red as the curtains. Jago was getting used to finding himself in rooms lined with ancient leather-bound volumes, so he didn't bother trying to read the titles on their spines before sitting down with his hosts. 'You were talking about the Green Funnel Line, Mr Abingdon,' he said.

'Ah, yes,' Abingdon replied. 'My grandfather started it. He had farming interests in Argentina – beef cattle, of course – and decided rather than pay a fortune to have someone else ship his meat over here he'd buy a ship and do it himself. He did very well and began to build up what is now the Green Funnel Line. So that's the family business. I don't actually work for the company, but I do retain a significant shareholding, and that provides enough to keep our heads above water, if that's not too inappropriate a metaphor, and to indulge my interest in books.'

'What type of books do you collect?'

'Mainly antiquarian works about travel and exploration in foreign parts.' He got up and moved to a globe, about a foot in diameter, mounted on a wooden stand. 'You see this? One of my most cherished possessions. It's what we call a library globe and it would have been one of a pair originally, but I only have the one. It must be more than a couple of hundred years old, but I picked it up for a song in a junk shop in Taunton about ten years ago. Come and have a look.' He beckoned Jago and Cradock over to join him. 'See there?' He pointed to the western hemisphere. 'Isn't that charming? It shows California as an island – that's what everyone thought it was in those days. And here – where the west of America and Canada should be it fades away to nothing and just says "Parts unknown". Fascinating, isn't it? History, right here in the room with us. I love it because it makes me think of all the great explorers and it reminds me of my own travels.'

'My husband has travelled very widely,' said Edith Abingdon, 'but I prefer to stay at home.'

'I think it must be in my blood,' her husband continued. 'When I was a boy, you see, I had a private tutor, and I used to go on voyages on the company's ships, sometimes with my parents, sometimes just with my tutor. My father hoped it would broaden my mind, and it did – I've had a love of travel ever since, and an abiding interest in the exploits of intrepid explorers in the past.'

He crossed the room and took a volume from one of its many shelves. 'Here's a book that inspired me.

It's about the travels of a man called James Holman. He was a lieutenant in the Royal Navy who was blinded in both eyes and pensioned off when he was still a young man. But despite being blind he travelled on every continent in the world.' He moved to another shelf. 'And here's something I acquired only recently. It's a first edition of Matthew Flinders' *A Voyage to Terra Australis*, and I bought all three volumes for thirty guineas. In 1801, when he was only twenty-seven, he circumnavigated Australia. He was the first man to do so, and got shipwrecked on the way home. Then he went to Mauritius, where the French accused him of spying and put him in prison for six years. The book was published in 1814, and he died the very next day, only forty years old. Fascinating fellow.'

'Was that something Mr Bellamy found for you?'

'No – I got this from someone else, but there are quite a few on this shelf that he supplied me with. He had a good nose for a bargain.'

'How did you get to know him?'

'Well, that was probably because there are three great passions in my life – books, cricket and jazz music.' He cast a glance in Edith Abingdon's direction. 'Apart from my dear wife, of course.' She smiled back at him, and he continued. 'I don't play as much cricket as I used to, but I was in the first eleven at school – that was Harrow – and then when I went up to Oxford I played for the university.'

'Charles is a Blue, you know,' his wife added.

Abingdon noticed that Cradock was looking baffled. 'I'm sorry, Detective Constable,' he said. 'All that means is that in my final year I played in the annual match against Cambridge. If you do that, you're entitled to wear a special blazer – it's highly prized and much-coveted. I got my Blue in 1925.'

Cradock opened his mouth and nodded sagely in a mute acknowledgement of this enlightenment, and Abingdon continued. 'I was a wicketkeeper – what the old-timers used to call a custodian of the gauntlets – but I had to stop playing when I got a dose of pleurisy. It made me quite ill, and it's likely to keep me out of this damned war too, more's the pity – I was born in 1904, so that means I'll have to register for national service in ten days' time, but I'm probably going to fail the medical, so it'll be no call-up for me, unfortunately.' He turned to Jago. 'Are you a cricketing man, Inspector?'

'I played in the first eleven at school,' said Jago, 'but nothing after that.'

'Oh,' said Abingdon, and hesitated.

Jago imagined the Harrow and Oxford man had realised there was no further conversational common ground to be found on the subject of cricket. There was significantly less chance, he thought, of a school like Abingdon's playing a cricket match against a school like his than there was of Heaven's first eleven playing against that of Hades. 'You were saying how you came to know Mr Bellamy,' he said.

'Ah, yes – well, Bellamy wasn't a great cricket man either, but he did share my other two passions. Books, of course, and jazz music – it was actually through the music that I first met him. I went to a jazz club in Soho and got into conversation with him there.'

'Was that the Blue Palm, by any chance?'

'I say, you're a good detective. Yes, it was – do you know it?'

'I know of it.'

'Well, it's an excellent place for jazz – one of the best in London. Of course, since you're a policeman I should add that in the past its reputation was, let's say, somewhat colourful, but more recently the proprietors have cleaned it up, and now it's quite respectable. Anyway, that's where I met Bellamy, and since then I've found him a useful supplier.'

'When did you last see him?'

Abingdon thought. 'That would be before Christmas sometime – I can't remember the precise date, I'm afraid.'

'Did he happen to say anything about finding a particularly valuable item?'

'No, I don't think so, although that was certainly the sort of thing he'd have talked about if he had. He could get quite excited when he found something valuable. And by the way, talking of excitement, have you been to see the show at the Blue Palm?'

'Yes, we have. We met a young singer there who has a cricketing connection too – her father played for Trinidad and the West Indies.'

'You mean Ethel Rae?'

'Yes.'

'I've met her too. Her father, you know, was Nelson Rae, a great batsman. And you might say he's where two of my passions meet – he and Learie Constantine were both part of the West Indies touring team that came here after the Great War, and they were known as jazz cricketers, so you can see what I mean.'

An image came into Jago's mind of a man in white trousers, shirt and sweater playing a trumpet, but he promptly dismissed it. 'I haven't come across that before – what's a jazz cricketer?'

'It's a term that Neville Cardus coined in one of his newspaper articles. He was reporting on a match that Cecil Parkin was playing in – you remember him? One of the finest bowlers of a cricket ball I've ever seen – I watched him take nine wickets in the Gentlemen versus Players match at the Oval in 1920, when I was a boy. He was bowling for the Players, of course. Anyway, when Cardus wrote his report, he said Parkin had become the first jazz cricketer, and what he was talking about was his style of play. He said Parkin's slow ball was a syncopation in flight. Now, if you know anything about jazz you'll know it's got a syncopated rhythm and it's all about improvisation, right?'

'I can't claim to know anything much about jazz, but that has been explained to me, yes.'

'Good. Of course, Cardus writes as much about music as he does about cricket, so he was saying a jazz cricketer isn't like those stodgy old-timers – he plays by instinct, not rules, and he's unpredictable, subversive, constantly improvising. The result is a spectacular style of play that's beautiful and exciting, but also ruthless – like some jazz singers I know.'

'Like Ethel Rae?'

'Well, there's no denying she's got a great talent, and she's the daughter of a jazz cricketer. She knows what she wants and she's determined to get it – and she won't necessarily stick to the rules. Who knows how far she'll go?'

CHAPTER TWENTY-TWO

Jago's conversation with the Abingdons came to an abrupt end when their telephone rang and Charles Abingdon was called away to deal with what his wife said was an urgent business matter that would take some time. Jago wondered briefly what this could be, given that Abingdon had indicated he was a shareholder in the shipping line but didn't actually work for it. But since he himself had never held shares in anything and knew nothing about the responsibilities of people who did, he was in no position to judge how genuine the interruption was. Perhaps it was a bookseller calling to offer their host a priceless travel book, or perhaps Mrs Abingdon had simply decided they'd given him enough of their valuable time. Whatever the reason, he had no further pressing questions on his mind for the couple, so he and Cradock took their leave.

By the time they were back outside on the street, the blackout was in force. There was something grim and faintly menacing about being surrounded by tall flat buildings shrouded in darkness, each with row upon row of windows but not one of which let slip even the faintest gleam of light. It was as if all of London had gone into hiding, and what was hidden would only be revealed by fire. Jago wondered how many of those blackened windows concealed people praying the fire would be elsewhere – and how many people elsewhere were praying, effectively, for it to fall here. If the bombs came tonight, by tomorrow London County Council would have some record of how many had fallen, but no one would have a tally of how many prayers had been answered, and whose. 'Nearly time to pack it in for today, I think,' he said. 'But I'd like to pop in on Bellamy's sister again before the sirens go off and see if we can find out a bit more about him. She might be feeling more up to talking now the news has had time to sink in.'

'Very good, sir,' Cradock replied.

'After that the evening's your own. Will you be staying up to see the new year in?'

'I don't know, sir. I don't suppose there'll be anything special going on at the section house. I might stay up for a pint with the lads, though. And you, sir?'

'I'm just planning to go out for a quiet drink. I don't imagine there'll be crowds out celebrating – it's a bit difficult to do that in the blackout, isn't it? But if there are, I'll probably be avoiding them.'

Cradock almost asked who Jago would be having his quiet drink with, but bit his tongue: it wasn't his place to ask, and besides, he could guess who it would be.

Christine Edison opened the door to them, and they squeezed into the darkened hallway by the light of a guttering candle that she carried in her left hand and that flickered in the draught coming in from the street. She led them up the stairs to the flat and blew the candle out as they entered the living room, which was bathed in the soft amber light of two gas lamps over the mantelpiece. Her husband was sitting by the small coal fire, reading a newspaper, and acknowledged their arrival with a brief grunt and a nod of his head.

'I hope you don't mind us calling this late in the day,' said Jago. 'Are we interrupting anything?'

'No, it's all right,' said Christine. 'We've finished our tea.'

'Right, well, we'll try to be quick. We just need to check something with you.'

'Of course – anything I can do to help.' She glanced at her husband. 'Is it something, er, private?'

Edison snorted. 'Don't mind me. If it's to do with her brother, there's nothing I know about him that she doesn't, so you just have your little chat and I'll get on with my paper.' Having issued his instruction in a way that didn't invite a reply, he buried his head in the *Daily Mirror* and left them to it.

'It's to do with something we heard this morning,' said Jago. 'We were talking to someone who claimed that your brother had said he was in debt. I wondered whether that was something he'd ever mentioned to you.'

'Well, he did and he didn't,' Christine replied. 'What I mean is, he didn't come straight out with it and tell me – not at first, anyway. I think maybe he didn't want anyone to know. But he did come round here one day and ask if he could borrow some money from me.'

'Parasite,' said her husband from behind his newspaper.

'Were you here as well, Mr Edison?' said Jago.

Edison thrust the paper down into his lap. 'No, I wasn't, but Christine told me later. My wife knows better than to have secrets from me, Inspector. She also knows I'd never allow her to give any of my hard-earned cash to a wastrel like that brother of hers.'

Christine gave an uncertain glance in Jago's direction.

'Please continue, Mrs Edison,' he said.

'Well, he asked, and I thought he must've been desperate, because he'd only to look round this place to know I wouldn't have any money to spare. And he knew I've always been the one who was hard up, not him.'

The expression on Edison's face was sour. 'It's not an honest working man's fault if he's exploited by his employers. We wouldn't be hard up if I was paid what I'm worth.'

'I'm not saying it's your fault, love,' said Christine.

'Yeah, right, well, what was he doing coming round here on the scrounge when he'd got a rich wife? She

179

must have pots of money.' He snapped his newspaper up again and disappeared behind it.

'So you didn't give him anything?' said Jago.

'No,' Christine replied. 'I'd got nothing to give him. But in any case, when it came to things like lending money, I'm sorry to say this but I didn't trust him. He was four years older than me, and when I was first working and saving up a bit of money he asked if he could borrow some. Like a fool I said yes and lent him my savings, but he never paid me back – he always had an excuse, and in the end I stopped mentioning it. I cried over that money, you know – I don't suppose it was much to him, but it was all the world to me.'

'So you weren't well disposed to help him, even if you'd had the money?'

'Well, I felt sorry for him, because he looked really scared, but there was nothing I could do, was there?'

'Did he tell you what he was scared of?'

'Yes, he said he owed money to some foreign bloke who wanted it back, and Samuel was afraid he might be mixed up with gangsters or something.'

'Did he say who this man was?'

'No, he didn't. He just said he thought they were mates, but it turned out they weren't. He said this bloke had threatened him. I didn't know whether he was just saying that to try and twist my arm, of course. I mean, how am I supposed to know?'

'Was your brother in the habit of lying to you?'

'I wouldn't like to say – I don't know, but like I said, I didn't trust him.'

Edison pushed his paper away, stood up and glowered at Jago.

'I told you, Inspector – he was a parasite. Give him money? I wouldn't give him the time of day. I may be out of work now, but at least I've had real jobs, where you get your hands dirty. That shop of his – that's not real work, is it? A pile of old books that nobody reads? What's the point of that? A butcher's or a baker's, that's what I call a real shop. You see people queuing up outside a butcher's to get in and buy themselves a pound of sausages, especially these days, but do you ever see a queue outside an old book shop like his? Of course not – old books are no use to anyone. And I've heard what he charges for some of them – it's more than I've ever had in my pocket. People who buy them must have more money than sense. And why have they got it? Because they're parasites too – parasites on society. They make a fortune out of exploiting men like me, then spend it all on fur coats and fancy cars, and fast women too. I think her brother sucked up to them because he thought he could prise some of their precious cash out of their pockets and have it for himself. He wanted to be rich, but as far as I'm concerned he was just a parasite on the parasites.'

Edison sat down again, seemingly having finished his diatribe, and Christine looked helplessly at Jago as if to apologise that he was beyond her control.

Jago resumed his questions in a voice that was markedly quieter than Edison's. 'Did Mrs Bellamy know about her husband being in debt?'

'No, I don't think so. Samuel begged me not to tell Marjorie – he was scared of what she'd think, and he was trying to get it fixed before she found out. So he was trapped, you see. I couldn't help him – I told him he'd have to tap one of his rich friends if he wanted money like that, not me.'

'And when exactly was this happening? Him trying to borrow money from you, I mean.'

'Oh, that was a few weeks ago, before Christmas. Next time I saw him was Christmas Day, and he wasn't going to say anything then because Marjorie was there.'

'Did your brother say anything else about this debt of his?'

'Only that things were getting desperate – he said if he couldn't find anyone who'd lend him enough to pay off his debts, he was for it. I said that's crazy – if you borrow money to pay off your debts you'll still owe someone all that money, however much it is.'

'And what did he say to that?'

'He said, "Yes, but if I don't pay this bloke off I don't know what he might do." He said if he could get a loan somewhere else it might give him time to work something out. I was scared – I even found myself wondering whether he might've taken out life insurance on Marjorie, that he might've only married her to fix that up and then do her in, God forgive me. It's a wicked thing to think about your own brother, but I didn't know what he might be driven to. He did say something about being in trouble with the ring, too. I thought maybe he'd gone and pawned Marjorie's wedding ring or something, but he said no, it's a bookselling thing – said I wouldn't understand. So I don't know what all that was about, but he looked very worried.' She shrugged her shoulders and looked at Jago apologetically. 'And that's about all I can tell you, I'm afraid. Very sorry.'

'Not at all, Mrs Edison. You've been very helpful. That'll be all for now, thank you – we'll leave you in peace.'

Christine Edison cast a sideways glance at her husband, as if unsure about this assumption, but he was still engrossed in his newspaper. She turned back to Jago. 'I'll see you back downstairs – just a moment while I get the candle.'

She lit the candle with a taper from the fire. 'Just seeing these gentlemen out, dear,' she said to Edison, who gave another grunt in reply.

Jago and Cradock followed her down the stairs.

'One last question before we go,' said Jago when they got to the bottom. 'You say your brother begged you not to tell Mrs Bellamy about his debt. Did you do as he asked?'

'Oh, yes. I'm not one to poke my nose in where it's not wanted. Besides, I like Marjorie, and I wouldn't want to hurt her by gossiping about her husband – it wouldn't seem right. She's been good to me since John got bombed out of his job. He gets angry if I tell him the housekeeping won't stretch far enough to buy the food we need, so she slips me the odd bit of cash from time to time when she knows I'm struggling – a pound here, ten bob there. She knows what John can be like.'

'Did your brother know she was doing this? I'm just wondering what he would've thought about the idea of his wife giving you money while he was desperately trying to borrow from you.'

'I never thought of that. Samuel never mentioned it, so I can only assume he didn't know what she was doing – and she didn't know what he was doing.'

'So they both had secrets from each other.'

'Yes, I suppose they did – but that's none of my business.' She looked back up the stairs. 'And by the way, you mustn't mind John. He can't help it – it's because of the job, you see, him getting the sack all of a sudden like that. It gets on his nerves, having to sit around the flat all day – it's not right for a man who's fit and strong to be doing nothing. Sometimes his temper just gets the better of him.'

She held the candle up so that its light fell on the door handle, and reached out her hand to open it. It was difficult for Jago to be sure in the flickering candlelight, but as she stretched her arm forward, the sleeve of her cardigan pulled back and he thought he saw bruises on her wrist.

CHAPTER TWENTY-THREE

The idea of finding somewhere for a quiet drink on New Year's Eve seemed, on reflection, to have been less than entirely realistic. Jago met Dorothy at the Savoy, where she lived with the rest of the American press corps, but she swiftly ruled the hotel out. 'The bar's jam-packed with American journalists,' she said. 'It'll be full of shoptalk – let's go someplace else. I know a little pub that's a bit off the beaten track, so shall we try that?'

'Fine,' said Jago.

The establishment in question was ten minutes' walk away in a side street near Aldwych Tube station, and was suitably uncrowded. Jago bought a lemonade for Dorothy and a pint of mild and bitter for himself, and they settled down in a quiet corner.

'So,' said Dorothy, 'have you been up to anything interesting since I last saw you?'

Jago smiled. 'Yes, I have, actually. I did something last night that I've never done before.'

Dorothy raised her eyebrows. 'Really? And what could that be?'

'I went to a jazz club in Soho.'

'I didn't know you were a jazz fan.'

'I'm not, but it was in the line of duty – it's to do with a case we're investigating. A man was shot dead in Soho, and it seems he was a jazz fan – and one of his favourite haunts was a nightclub called the Blue Palm. I took Peter there with me.'

'I hope you kept him on a tight leash.'

'Oh, yes, he didn't come to any harm. It was certainly interesting, though – we met a fascinating young woman there—'

Dorothy interrupted him. 'I hope you had yourself on a tight leash too.'

He laughed. 'It wasn't like that. She was a singer – a jazz singer – and she had the most beautiful voice. Interesting background too – her father was a cricketer from Trinidad and her mother was from Lancashire. She seemed determined to become a star, and judging by her voice I think she'd stand a very good chance of doing so.'

'That's quite a little story you've found there – what we journalists call human interest. It makes a change from air raids and bombs.'

'Yes – and speaking of which, did you write anything about that terrible air raid by St Paul's on Sunday night? I was there yesterday and could hardly believe my eyes.'

'I certainly did. What time were you there?'

'About midday – I was looking for the dead man's wife and found her sitting amongst the ruins of her business.'

'I was there too – I went over first thing in the morning, so I guess I beat you to it. I was in Paternoster Row, and it was horrific – there was nothing left of it. Someone said they thought Hitler had deliberately targeted that area to destroy your publishing industry because it represents freedom of speech and ideas. I don't know whether that's true, of course, but I used it in the piece I wrote because it's the kind of thing he would do – I mean, if the Nazis burn books in their own country because they don't want people to think for themselves, why wouldn't they try to burn books here too?'

'Maybe – who knows? What else did you say about it?'

'I was mainly trying to get across to readers at home just what a shocking sight it was – so much destruction. I don't think I'll ever forget it. It was difficult at first yesterday morning, because the bombing put our cable connections with the States out of action for a while, and in any case your censors wouldn't let us give even a hint of what buildings were hit or even which parts of the city had been most damaged, but then by the afternoon they lifted all the usual restrictions, so we could tell the whole story. I think it's had a big impact at home, especially with the President's speech.'

'What was that?'

'He made a broadcast to the nation on Sunday

evening just a few hours after the news broke over there about the air raid. It's what he calls a fireside chat, and he does it just once or twice a year when something big happens. He talked about the war and said the Nazis are not going to win it. He wasn't saying America's about to join in, but he said nothing must get in the way of us helping you – America was going to be the great arsenal of democracy. He sounded firm and determined, which must have given hope to your prime minister.'

'To all of us, I should think – we just want to get back to normal life.'

'That's what I was thinking down in Paternoster Row – would things ever be normal again? I walked round by St Paul's Cathedral, and you know that big Christmas tree they have every year on the steps outside the west door – well, it was still there, with its little lights on, so they were all twinkling right there in the midst of all that wreckage. I got our photographer to take a picture – it was a real symbol of hope, I thought.'

'Some might say it's more like whistling in the dark – Christmas tree lights don't stop bombs. But I have heard people saying it was a miracle the all-clear sounded at eleven o'clock or so on Sunday night. We've got used to seeing the incendiary bombs followed by high-explosive ones, but for some reason that second wave didn't come. I don't like to think what it would've been like if they had.'

'Some of my contacts think it may have been because of the weather, but they could be wrong.'

'They were right about Christmas, though, weren't they? You said on Christmas Day that they reckoned there might be some kind of unofficial two-day truce – no air raids, I mean. And it turned out we didn't have any bombs on Christmas Day or Boxing Day.'

'But the next day they were back with a vengeance – and then we had that terrible attack on Sunday. So it looks like we're back to business as usual, unfortunately. But at least we haven't had any raids today – maybe that's because of the weather too. If it stays that way for the rest of this evening, do you want to stay up till midnight and see the new year in?'

'To be honest, I don't usually bother. I know it'll be 1941 tomorrow, but I don't imagine anything else will change – we'll still have rationing and air raids and all the other things we'd rather do without. But do you? If you want to stay up, that's different. There's no one else I'd rather start the new year with.'

'Actually, it's not so much that I want to – it's more that I have to. My editor wants something from me on how Londoners celebrated it for tomorrow's paper. If the Luftwaffe shows up to spoil the party, of course, we could be in trouble, but at least we can try – where's a good place to go and see what's happening?'

'Well, traditionally the crowds gather outside St Paul's at midnight and sing "Auld Lang Syne", but after what happened on Sunday I think they may not be so keen tonight. The other traditional place is Piccadilly Circus, so why don't we go there?'

'OK, Piccadilly Circus it is – and may we both live to tell the tale!'

CHAPTER TWENTY-FOUR

'Got a couple of messages for you, guv'nor,' said Cradock when they met the next morning. 'The desk sergeant at West End Central said Detective Superintendent Hardacre wants to see us in his office at Scotland Yard at eleven-thirty sharp – to bring him up to date on the case. He also said they'd had a call from Mrs Quincy – she wants to have a word with us.'

'OK, thanks – we'll pop in on her later.'

'Actually, sir, she said she was going to be out most of today, so she'd come to the station at nine o'clock.'

Jago checked his watch. 'In that case, we'd better jump in the car and get straight round to West End Central and hope she hasn't arrived early. Oh, and by the way, Happy New Year.'

'Oh, yes, of course – it's today, isn't it. Can't say the prospects of it turning out happy look very good, though. Still, maybe we'll win the war this year, and it'll all be over by Christmas, eh?'

'I would agree, Peter, but I'm afraid I've heard that before and been sorely disappointed.'

'Things might be different this time, though, don't you think?'

'I don't have a crystal ball, unfortunately – and if I did I might not like what I saw in it. I fear we'll have to just wait and see what it brings, and hope for the best.'

'All right – me too, then,' Cradock replied cheerily. Jago said nothing, not wanting to burst his young colleague's bubble: one of the things the Great War had taught him was that hoping for the best didn't get you very far. A combination of grim determination to survive and dodging the attention of snipers and rats alike was a more realistic strategy.

He turned his mind to a more immediate and pleasant prospect. 'Speaking of messages, that reminds me – I found one waiting for me when I got back last night. It was from Rita, asking me to call her, so I did – she wanted to know if we'd like to meet up with her for a cup of tea.'

'What, over in West Ham, sir, at her cafe?'

'No, she said she was coming up to the West End today, so she suggested we make it somewhere round here, to save time. I said that was very thoughtful of her, and we'd be delighted to. I trust that meets with your approval.'

'Oh, yes, sir, definitely. Would that be a cup of tea with cake, do you think, sir?'

'We'll have to wait and see for that too, won't we? All I know is she'll be expecting us at four o'clock at the Oxford Corner House – that's the Lyons place by the corner of Oxford Street and Tottenham Court Road, so we'd better crack on if we don't want to keep her waiting.'

'Righto, guv'nor – crack on it is.'

They set off for West End Central police station. Jago was quiet. He'd always found New Year's Day an oddly unsettling time: it was just another working day, but it held a peculiar importance in people's minds, because the clocks ticked on from one year into the next. Now it was 1941, and 1940 was in the past. The only thing anyone could be pretty sure about was that the war wouldn't be ending tomorrow. Would the air raids go on? Would there be an invasion? Would he still be thinking the same things this time next year? If the future existed it was hidden behind a blank canvas, and whether it would prove to be glorious or terrifying was unknowable. That was perhaps all the more reason why the thought of having a cup of tea with a dear old friend like Rita was so reassuringly normal and familiar, if only for today. What might lie beyond that was anyone's guess: he'd just have to heed his own counsel and take things as they came.

The police station, a shiny new stone and steel edifice in Savile Row, had been the Metropolitan Police Service's showpiece when it opened in July 1940, but within little more than two months a German landmine had hit it, reducing it to a shell and killing three police officers. The divisional headquarters staff had had to move to Trenchard House in Broadwick Street until the ruined new building had been patched up and reopened in December, but when Jago and Cradock arrived, the station seemed to be back to normal. Daphne Quincy had indeed arrived early and was waiting for them.

'Good morning, Mrs Quincy,' said Jago. 'I'm sorry we're late.'

'That's quite all right, Inspector. I haven't been here more than five minutes.'

'Good. Let's go and find somewhere to talk.'

They took her to an unoccupied interview room and sat her down at a table.

'So,' said Jago, 'how can we help you?'

'Actually,' she replied, 'I'm not sure whether it's you helping me or me helping you. I called the police station because something odd happened to me recently, and what with Mr Bellamy being so horribly murdered, I thought perhaps I should tell you.'

'And this was something to do with him?'

'Yes, it was. You know he had a shop off Charing Cross Road?'

'Yes – in Old Compton Street.'

'Right. Well, I went in there a few weeks ago and bought a book as a Christmas present for a friend. It was a very nice edition of Longfellow's poetry, and it was three pounds – well, to be precise it was two pounds nineteen and elevenpence, but that's how they do it in shops, isn't it? I paid with a five-pound note and got two pound notes and a penny change. I remember being struck by how worn the penny was. You know how it is – those old Queen Victoria bun pennies you get in your change sometimes that have passed through so many hands over so many years that almost all the detail has been rubbed off. I remember thinking that you can't read the date on it, or the words, and even the Queen's head is so worn away you can't be sure which monarch it was. It's basically just a copper disc, and yet we all accept it because we believe it's a penny and it's worth a penny. It's just the same with the old silver, too.'

'And the odd thing you mentioned?'

'Yes, I was just coming to that. So I bought the book, and then I went on to another shop to buy some gloves and paid with a pound note, but instead of just giving me my change the shop assistant excused himself and said he'd have to check something with the manager. When he came back he said the manager was afraid he couldn't take it because he believed it might not be a genuine note. I offered him the other one and he took it away to the manager, but when he came back the second time he said they had doubts about that one too. He was very apologetic, but he declined to accept either of them. I've never been so embarrassed in my life.'

'Did you take them back to Mr Bellamy's shop?'

'Well, no, I couldn't, could I? The young woman who works in there always looks half starved, and knowing the kind of man he was I wouldn't be surprised if he only paid her a pittance. How could I suggest that she'd given me counterfeit notes in my change without putting her job at risk? She must have accepted the notes in good faith from an earlier customer, and if I complained, she might have had to reimburse me out of her own pocket. My husband and I are not short of money, and I thought it would be frankly less awkward all round if I just quietly forgot it.'

'Did you take them to a bank, to verify whether they were genuine?'

'No. I thought they might say they had to report it, and I'd have to tell them where I'd got them, and so on. And I certainly wasn't going to try to pass them off somewhere else, so I just kept them.'

'So what makes you mention this to us now?'

'Well, I don't suppose I would have thought anything more about it – I'd have just put it down to experience. But the funny thing is, I was talking to a friend the other day and she happened to mention that exactly the same thing had happened to her – and in Samuel Bellamy's shop too. The only difference was that in her case she'd paid with a ten-pound note and got a five-pound note in her change. Later on she tried to buy something in a different shop, but the shopkeeper wouldn't take it – he said he had doubts about whether it was genuine and would regretfully decline to accept it. Very polite of him, but even so, my friend said she felt like a criminal.'

'I see. Have you still got the two notes you were given?'

'Yes.'

'I'd like to have them, please, if you don't mind.'

'Of course.' She took the two banknotes from her handbag and passed them across the table.

'And if your friend still has the five-pound note,' Jago continued, 'could you ask her to bring it in to the station here and leave it at the front desk in an envelope marked for my attention?'

'Yes, I shall. Will that be all?'

'Yes – thank you. But before you go, tell me – when you mentioned Mr Bellamy just now, you said "knowing the kind of man he was". What exactly did you mean by that?'

'I meant I didn't regard him as an honourable man, and I didn't trust him.'

'But surely your husband did – he and Mr Bellamy were business associates.'

'They were, and my husband trusted him, but I consider that Mr Bellamy violated that trust.'

'In what way?'

'I don't know all the details, but I believe he went behind my husband's back and started selling books direct to one of William's clients. I'm not a businesswoman, of course, so I don't know whether that's illegal or not, but it seems to me to be underhand and vulgar. It's not the sort of thing a gentleman would do – but then Bellamy wasn't a gentleman, was he?'

Jago had no aspirations to be the arbiter of who was or was not a gentleman, so he gave no reply, and Mrs Quincy continued. 'In my book, it's simply not playing fair. But please don't tell my husband what I've said, Inspector. I believe in calling a spade a spade, but I'm afraid he's too well brought up to speak ill of the dead. He doesn't know I'm saying this to you, so I'd appreciate your discretion. He doesn't like me getting involved in his business, you see, so I try to keep out of it. Anyway, I really should be on my way now, so if you'll excuse me, I'll go. Do please let me know what you find out about those notes, though, if you can – it's fascinating. Goodbye now.'

Mrs Quincy slipped the strap of her handbag over her wrist, gathered herself together and sailed out of the room.

CHAPTER TWENTY-FIVE

'That all sounds a bit fishy, doesn't it, guv'nor?' said Cradock once Daphne Quincy had gone on her way. 'Fake banknotes, I mean – do you reckon there's some sort of racket going on in that bookshop?'

'There's certainly something fishy going on somewhere,' Jago replied. 'But whether it's a racket or a coincidence I'm not sure, especially in a place like Soho. I'll be interested to see whether we turn up any more evidence, but in the meantime I want to have another word with Ron Fisher – he says Samuel Bellamy was like a brother to him, but some of these other people we've been talking to have told us things that Fisher never breathed a word about. That might just mean he's a loyal friend, but I want to know what else he can tell us, so we're going back over to Berwick Street.'

* * *

Ron Fisher looked uncertain when he opened the door to them, but his face quickly broke into a jovial smile. 'Good morning,' he said brightly. 'I didn't expect to see you back so soon.'

'Good morning, Mr Fisher,' said Jago. 'I'm sorry to disturb you again, but there's a few things that've come to light since we spoke to you yesterday, and I'd like to talk to you about them, if you don't mind.'

'Blimey – that sounds a bit ominous. Not all my little secrets, I hope.'

'Actually I'm rather more interested in any possible little secrets of Mr Bellamy's that might be relevant to his murder.'

'I see – serious stuff, then. Come on up.'

They followed him up to the flat and into his living room.

'Here we are,' he said. 'Pull up a chair – take the weight off your feet. Now, can I get you something to drink? I've got some bottles of Bass in the cupboard if you want to wet your whistle.'

'Very kind of you to offer, but no thank you,' said Jago.

'So where do you want to start?'

'I'll get straight to the point, Mr Fisher. It's about Mr Bellamy's private life. The thing is, someone we were talking to yesterday suggested that your friend might've been paying rather too much attention to a certain young lady he'd got to know.'

'Not his missus, then?'

'No, not her. I wondered if you could tell us anything more about that.'

Fisher appeared to weigh up the question before giving his answer. 'Well, I think I said last time you were here that when you're a runner, out and about looking for books worth buying, it's all about the thrill of the chase, like hunting. It's like that for me, and it was the same for Sam. But if you want an honest answer, I reckon books weren't the only thing he liked to chase, if you get my drift.'

'I think I do,' said Jago. 'Carry on.'

'Okey-dokey. The thing is, see, when he got married he had to settle down, of course, but I don't think he ever lost that roving eye – I think he still loved the chase.'

'Other women, you mean?'

'That's it, yeah.'

'Do you know of any particular woman he was chasing?'

'Well, there were a few he happened to mention over the years – I think it was always the glamorous ones who turned his head.'

'But more recently?'

'It was just the same.'

'Was a young lady called Ethel Rae one of them?'

'Well, now, that'd be telling, wouldn't it?'

'Your loyalty is commendable, Mr Fisher, but this is a murder inquiry. I'd appreciate it if you could answer my question.'

'All right, then – yes, I think she was. I've never met her myself, though.'

'Did Mr Bellamy ever confide in you concerning any feelings he might've had for Miss Rae?'

'Well, yes, he did – a little bit. I mean, we've been pals since we were kids, and we always used to tell each other things we wouldn't tell anyone else. He told me a while back about this singer he'd met. He said she was something special and he fancied her. I called him a saucy old goat or something like that, and he said, "No, don't get me wrong – I'm a married man, aren't I?" I said, "Yes, and you'd better not forget it."'

'And what did he say to that?'

'Nothing. He just winked at me.'

'As if to say what?'

'I reckoned it meant he was feeling that old thrill of the chase again.'

'Was he unfaithful to his wife?'

'I don't know.'

'But surely with the close friendship you had with him, it'd be a question you might be expected to ask.'

'I didn't say I never asked him. I did, to his face – apart from anything else, I didn't want him to make a fool of himself and ruin his marriage. I like that Marjorie of his – she's a very nice woman.'

'So what did he say when you asked him?'

'He just laughed and said, "Mind your own business." I couldn't tell whether he was serious or just teasing me, but either way I didn't mention it again after that. I thought he might tell me one day if he wanted to, but that day never came, and now it never will, will it?'

'Have you told Mrs Bellamy about this?'

'Lord no – I'm not one to get between a man and his wife, any more than I'd get between two dogs having a fight. Far too dangerous. I like the quiet life, so I keep stuff like that under my hat. I don't suppose she knows anything about it, and as far as I'm concerned, now that poor Sam's dead, she doesn't need to.'

Jago cast an eye over the cosily cluttered little room. 'Is there a Mrs Fisher, by the way?' he asked.

'Well,' said Fisher, 'speaking confidentially, I decided a long time ago I'd like to spend the rest of my days with someone who'd be loyal and faithful and always have my best interests at heart. So I did – I live by myself, and we've been very happy together.' He gave a throaty, self-congratulatory laugh. 'Confirmed bachelor boy, that's what I am. Sure about that Bass, are you?'

'I'm sure, thank you.'

'So what's your next question, then?'

'I'd like to ask you something about Mr Bellamy's financial affairs.'

'Not sure I can help you there – I don't know anything about how he ran his business or his finances.'

'I understand that, but as you were old friends, this might be something he mentioned to you – we believe Mr Bellamy was in debt. Is that true?'

'Yes, he was, as a matter of fact.'

'Do you know who he was in debt to?'

'I think I do. Our Sam enjoyed a game of cards, see, and he was pally with this Italian bloke called Rossetti.'

'Frankie Rossetti?'

'That's the one, yes. He runs a cafe, but he also runs something else on the quiet. He gets together with a few blokes some nights and they play rummy – for money.'

'And Mr Bellamy got involved in these games?'

'Yes, and I think he got a bit more involved than was good for him. He thought he was a pretty hot card player, but he lost a lot of money – but then that's how it is with that sort of racket, isn't it? The sucker always loses.'

'You're talking about some sort of illegal gambling den?'

'I suppose that's what it was, yes.'

'Why didn't you mention this before?'

'I didn't think it was relevant – I was still getting over the fact that Sam was dead, and I wasn't thinking straight.'

Jago looked him in the eye, his head to one side. 'You struck me as someone who was thinking perfectly well, Mr Fisher. What else made you omit to tell us this?'

'Well, all right – it's just that these rummy games, they're all over Soho and they're all illegal. And a lot of them are run by people you don't want to cross – they're not just a bunch of loveable rogues who enjoy a game of cards, they can be very nasty blokes, and some of them are Italians. I don't know this bloke Rossetti, but round here you think more than twice about squealing on anyone with an Italian name to the coppers.'

'Thank you – I think we'll be having a word with Mr Rossetti.'

Fisher's voice was anxious. 'But you won't tell him I said anything, will you?'

'No, we won't. Now, while we're talking of rogues, loveable or otherwise, Mrs Bellamy mentioned that her husband had said there were a few in the bookselling business. Apparently he'd said they were the sort who'd get the other dealers a bad name if people knew what they got up to, but she couldn't tell us what that was. She suggested we ask you.'

'Well, yes, that's right – Sam certainly knew all about that. Speaking personally, I've always found most booksellers very fair in their dealings – they're jealous of their good reputations, you see, so they play straight with you. But having said that, it's a risky business to get involved in if you don't know your way around. If you're a bit wet behind the ears there's always going to be someone who'll try and take advantage. It's the same as anything else in this world where there's money to be made – you've got to make sure you keep your head screwed on right and don't take anything at face value. I always say don't believe the evidence of your own eyes, and don't trust anyone. It doesn't matter what someone's trying to sell you – it can be Renaissance art, antique furniture, or Cleopatra's love letters to Julius Caesar, there's always the risk that it's a fake, and if you fall for it, well, your money's gone down the drain. You have to keep reminding yourself – nothing's necessarily what it seems. It's the same with books – there's rogues out there who can't resist a bit of fakery, and if you're not careful you can get your fingers burnt. You have to be wise to their tricks so you can spot what you might call sharp practices.'

'For example?'

'Well, there's what we call "sophisticated" books.

When we say that in the book trade, we don't mean elegant or refined, we're talking about books that've been doctored. Let's say they've got a book with a damaged title page or frontispiece – they'll take one out of another copy and put it in so they can jack the price up. Basically they're cobbling things together from different sources to make one expensive book, and the whole idea's to deceive the buyer – it's the art of forgery, I suppose.'

'Was Mr Bellamy ever given to this kind of forgery, as you call it?'

Fisher narrowed his eyes into a knowing look. 'I wouldn't know about that, Inspector – you'd have to ask Sam.'

Jago took this to mean Fisher's lips were sealed, but whether out of loyalty or complicity he couldn't tell. There would be other ways to find out, though. He changed to a different tack. 'Mrs Bellamy also told us that her husband had run up against something to do with the book trade called the ring, and she thought you'd be able to explain what it is, so could you please enlighten us?'

'Yes, well,' said Fisher, 'I should explain that I'm not mixed up in it myself – I don't move in those kind of circles. But I do know a bit about what goes on. You remember I said how people in the book trade go to sales and auctions to try and pick up books they can sell for a tidy profit? Well, what the people selling the stuff don't know is that sometimes the dealers are all working together – they call it a bidding ring, or the ring for short. Some of those auctioneers, they just sell anything that comes along. They don't have any idea about books and what they're worth, and often the owners don't either, so the dealers can have a field day. They'll bid for the lots, but really they're all hand in glove – they're not competing with each other at all, so the goods get knocked down for a low price. They only bid against people who aren't members of the ring, so that keeps the prices down. Then afterwards they go off to a private room in a pub or somewhere like that round the corner and have their own little auction amongst themselves – it's what they call the settlement, or the knock-out, and the basic idea is they divide the difference between them.'

'What do you mean by "the difference"?'

'Well, let's say there's something in the sale that should be worth twenty quid. The members of the ring keep the bidding low, and one of them gets it for two quid. Now suppose there's ten people in the ring. When they go off for their own little secret auction, one of them – let's call him Smith – buys it for twelve. He can take it away and sell it for whatever he likes and make a profit, but the beauty of this racket as far as the ring's concerned is that the difference between the twelve pounds he pays for it and the two pounds the first bloke paid doesn't go to the original owner who sent it to auction, it gets shared out equally between the members of the ring – they call it their dividend. So the vendor only gets his two quid less auctioneer's commission, but our Mr Smith goes away with a book he reckons he can get more than twelve for

– maybe a lot more – and on top of that all the dealers in the ring get a quid each. Now, you don't have to be Einstein to work out that if there's a lot of books being auctioned at that sale and the ring's operating, by the end of the day every single member of it's going to be going home with extra cash in their pocket for doing nothing except making sure they only bid low or not at all in the official auction. And on top of that, because it's all done in secret, I don't suppose they'll be paying income tax on it. The long and the short of it's that the dealers are getting the money that by rights should've gone to whoever owned the stuff and sent it to auction.'

'So how much might this extra cash amount to?'

'Well, not being an insider I wouldn't know, but I've heard it said that if they're lucky, a dealer might make as much money from that secret auction as they would in a whole year without it – so that must be hundreds of pounds. No wonder they're keen on this ring thing – money for old rope, isn't it? It's been going on for years and it was perfectly legal until 1927, but then the law changed. That means now if your lot catch them at it they can get a hundred-quid fine or six months in stir, or both. I don't suppose any of them fancy being locked up for six months, but a hundred quid's nothing compared with the money they must make out of it. It doesn't matter what the law says, it still goes on – and what's more, people who know more about these things than I do say no one's ever been prosecuted under that law since the day it was brought in, mainly because it's so difficult for your lot to get hold of enough evidence.

A fat lot of good that is.'

'So was Mr Bellamy involved in this?'

'I think he wished he was, but I got the impression the dealers who led the ring were a bit sniffy about him.'

'Mrs Bellamy said she thought they'd taken a dislike to him for some reason. Do you know why that might've been?'

'I'm not sure, but I think it was that he'd got on the wrong side of one of the bigwigs in it, and they either kicked him out or wouldn't let him join it in the first place.'

'Why was that?'

'I don't know. It can't have been good for his business, though – being in that ring means a dealer can make easy money, but if you're not, you're going to have a hard time at those auctions and come home empty-handed. They can't trust you, see. And if you're kicked out and go into opposition, bidding against them, they're really not going to like you at all, because you'll be reducing their profits. There's been one or two dealers who were put out of the ring and then tried to get their own back by reporting them to the auctioneers or even threatening to go to the press and spill the beans. But that's a surefire way to make yourself some enemies. It can be a murky business.'

'Did Mr Bellamy ever talk about that?'

'No. All Sam ever said was that his face didn't fit, but he never said why. Maybe he'd put someone's nose out of joint. Or maybe he just didn't go to the right school – I don't know.'

'Do you know who this bigwig was, as you called him?'

'Can't say as I do, but it must've been a bookseller, because that's what they all are in that ring.' Fisher lowered his voice theatrically. 'All I can say is I reckon if you were an American collector and went into a smart bookshop, let's say in Bond Street perhaps, you might find him there. But remember – if anyone asks, it was a little bird that told you, not me.'

'I see,' said Jago. 'And if I went to this bookshop . . . might I perhaps find a queue outside it?'

Fisher thought for a moment, then gave a wheezy laugh. 'Indeed you might, Inspector,' he said with a sly wink. 'Indeed you might.'

CHAPTER TWENTY-SIX

'Excuse me, guv'nor,' said Cradock, loping along to keep up with Jago's brisk stride away from Ron Fisher's flat.

'Yes?' said Jago, stopping to face him.

'What did you mean about a queue outside that shop he was talking about? Fisher, I mean. Books aren't rationed, are they, so why a queue?'

'Ah,' said Jago, adopting a conspiratorial tone. 'Not a queue, Peter.' He drew a circular shape in the air with his finger and added a tail. 'A Q – Q for Quincy.'

'You mean—'

'Yes, I do mean, and I think Mr Fisher knew too, judging by his face. I think he's the type who doesn't like to get other people into trouble, so I spared him the embarrassment of naming our book dealer friend. We'll have to look into that later, but first I'd like to have another word with Mr Abingdon. I'm wondering whether he knows anything about that business Mrs Quincy referred to – about Bellamy going behind her husband's back and selling books direct to one of his clients.'

'Well, after all that stuff Fisher said about fakery and rings and what have you, I'm beginning to think he's right – you can't take any of this lot at face value. I don't trust any of them.'

'That's what you might call a policeman's lot, Peter – like it or not, we're paid not to take anything at face value. But that doesn't necessarily mean they're all lying to us.'

The mansion block where the Abingdons lived was even more striking in the full light of day than it had been in the fading afternoon light of their previous visit. It wasn't exactly a castle, but there was something weighty and impregnable about it that made it look as though it had been built to last for a thousand years. As they walked in through the imposing entrance porch, Jago recalled Churchill's speech the previous June after the Dunkirk evacuation. The Prime Minister had spoken of the British Empire lasting for a thousand years, albeit qualifying this with a significant 'if' to make it a hypothetical possibility rather than a prediction. The Edwardians who built this place, however, might well have considered such a lifespan their imperial destiny.

The entrance hall was silent, and the plush carpet beneath their feet absorbed the sound of their presence.

It was like stepping back into another, more settled age, Jago thought. The whole edifice might be demolished by a bomb before the day was out, but for the time being the luxurious residence known as Cordale Mansions was here to stay.

As before, the porter took them up to the Abingdons' flat, but this time Charles Abingdon was alone. 'I'm sorry my wife's not here to welcome you,' he said breezily as he let them in, 'but we weren't expecting you. She's out at one of her committees – I can't remember which one it is, but I'm sure it's to do with some very worthy cause. Can I get you a drink?'

'Very kind of you, Mr Abingdon, but no thanks,' said Jago. 'I just wanted to check something with you.'

'By all means – let's go and sit down, shall we?'

They followed him to the library, Jago hoping that this time their host would not digress into venting his enthusiasm for its contents.

'It's a simple matter,' Jago continued once they were seated. 'It's just that since we were here yesterday something's been brought to our attention concerning Mr Bellamy, and I wondered whether it might have anything to do with you.'

'Really? May I ask who you were speaking to?'

'Yes, it was Mrs Quincy. I believe you know her husband.'

'Yes, I do, although I can't say I'm acquainted with her.'

'You know him as a business associate?'

'Yes. That's right. Quincy deals in books, and I'm a

212

collector, as you know, so I used to buy the occasional volume from him if it was something that interested me.'

'You said much the same thing concerning Samuel Bellamy when we spoke to you before. So you bought from both of them?'

'Yes, that's true, although it was more in series than in parallel, if you know what I mean.'

'I'm sorry, I'm not sure I do.'

'I mean I used to buy from Quincy, but then switched to buying from Bellamy.'

'I see – and what was the reason for that?'

'Well, it's rather a delicate matter, so I'd appreciate it if you could be sensitive in how you handle what I say, but the simple fact is that when I was buying books from Quincy, Bellamy was one of his suppliers. I knew nothing of that, of course – Quincy would have obtained his books from a variety of sources. But it seems that Bellamy somehow found out how much Quincy had sold certain books to me for – books that Quincy had bought from him.'

'You say "somehow", but how would he have found out the details of a private transaction between you and Mr Quincy? Is it possible that you told Bellamy yourself how much you'd paid?'

Abingdon paused for thought. 'It's not beyond the bounds of possibility, I suppose. I used to see Bellamy at the Blue Palm Club, as I told you, and I must confess I have been known to overindulge in liquid refreshment on occasion there if the entertainment's hot and the company's agreeable. So it's possible that I may have been in my cups one night and let slip some comment in an unguarded moment – I simply don't recall. But be that as it may, what I'm saying is that Bellamy thought the price Quincy had given him for those books was far too low in comparison with what he'd sold them on to me for, and he felt cheated.'

'But isn't that how business works? Buying and selling and making a profit?'

'Yes – business is business, as they say, rather fatuously in my opinion, but it's got to be fair. Bellamy felt that Quincy was profiting at his expense.'

'And that's not cricket?'

'Precisely. Anyway, to cut a long story short, Bellamy approached me with a proposal that he sell direct to me instead of to Quincy.'

'So you mean cutting out the middle man?'

'I do, and when Bellamy started dealing direct with me I could see that the prices he was looking for were always more reasonable than what I would have expected from Quincy, even though Bellamy was presumably asking more than he would have got from Quincy.'

'So you and Mr Bellamy both benefited from the arrangement.'

'Yes, I felt I could trust him, and I think from both his point of view and mine it was a fairer and more equitable arrangement.'

'Did you ever discuss all this with Mr Quincy?'

'Certainly not – his dealings with Bellamy were none of my business. I don't know whether Bellamy ever took it up with him personally himself, but I wouldn't have wanted to be in Quincy's shoes if he had.'

'Why do you say that?'

'Well, it's just that Bellamy was a decent enough fellow, but he did have a tendency to fly off the handle if things weren't going his way. I don't think he was very good at controlling his temper – he could get very angry. But I may be wrong – I didn't know him very well.'

'Someone else who knew him told us he used to get angry when anyone tried to cheat him, so it sounds as though you're actually not far off the mark in what you say.'

'I see – I'm glad it's not just my own opinion, then. But forgive me – it's just that I don't like to speak critically of someone who's only just died. It somehow seems like bad form.'

'Would you describe Mr Quincy's actions as bad form?'

'I don't know, really – you can't be in any kind of business without getting your hands dirty from time to time, but I think there are still standards a gentleman should maintain, and fairness is one of them.'

'Would you describe Mr Quincy as a gentleman?'

'I'm not sure I should express an opinion on that. Why do you ask?'

'Because Mr Bellamy's wife told us he used to describe both you and Mr Quincy as "posh", but he also said Mr Quincy was "more posh than was good for him". Why do you think he might say that?'

'Did you ask her?'

'Yes, but she said she didn't know – that's why I'm asking you.'

'Well, I think it rather depends on what you mean by "posh". Some people think it's just about your manners and your money, but if you talk to the county set or the landed gentry they'd say it's all about breeding – who your family are, or were. Take me, for example. Most people would say I'm posh, and yes, I suppose I do have money and the right manners, but I don't claim any great breeding – I'm not descended from anyone with a title. I'm just a man who had the good fortune to be born to parents who'd done well for themselves, and I don't pretend to be anything more than that. But that chap Quincy . . . well, he's different.'

'In what way?'

'He's very much the suave man about town, and he puts on airs and graces that I think work a certain charm on his American clients, but I'm not entirely convinced.'

'Are you saying he's a fraud?'

'No, I'm not saying that – I'm not in a position to know. But if it's important to you, I'd suggest you ask him to tell you about his ancestry. I've heard he has quite an interest in genealogy.'

CHAPTER TWENTY-SEVEN

Jago ensured that he and Cradock arrived for their appointment with Detective Superintendent Hardacre at Scotland Yard not a minute after eleven-thirty. From what he'd seen of his new boss in Central Branch so far, Hardacre was a stickler about punctuality, and indeed about most other things, including in particular whatever happened to be occupying his attention at any given moment. One exception, however, was social niceties.

'Come in, then,' he said brusquely as he opened his office door. 'Don't stand around dawdling – I've got work to do even if you haven't.' He bustled across to his desk, leaving them to close the door behind them, and jerked a finger towards a couple of hard wooden chairs in a silent instruction to them to sit. He took his own seat, glared briefly at them across the desk, and pushed his wire-rimmed spectacles back up his nose. 'So, what have you established about this business in Soho, if anything?'

'We're making good progress, sir.'

'Yes, yes, I'm sure you are, but what have you actually established?'

'Well, no one we've spoken to yet has identified any particular enemies, although a woman who worked for him said he didn't like people who tried to cheat him.'

'Yes, well, none of us like that, do we, so that doesn't narrow it down much. Any family?'

'Married, but no children, and just one sister who lives nearby, married to an unemployed warehouseman.'

'Short of cash, then – that's always a motive. What about his wife?'

'She seems a pretty solid and reliable person – she runs an ecclesiastical publishing business.'

'Hmm – very respectable, I'm sure. Any trouble in the marriage?'

'Not that we know of. He did have connections with some possibly less respectable people, though – there's a Mr and Mrs Nicholson who run a nightclub and have a rather colourful background.'

'Nightclub, eh? That sounds suspicious, especially in Soho. Any record?'

'The wife's been up before the magistrates a few times and been fined for licensing offences and the like, but nothing major. The husband started the club years ago when he came to England after the war.'

'Foreigner, is he?'

'He was born in Greece and moved here as a young man in 1922.'

'Foreigner, then. There's a lot of foreigners in Soho, isn't there? A lot of foreigners in London, for that matter. Too many for my liking. Dodgy, is he?'

'Not noticeably, sir. I'm not sure I've got the measure of him yet.'

'You'd better get it, then, hadn't you?'

'Yes, sir.'

'Any skeletons in the dead man's closet?'

'One or two, sir, but we don't know yet whether any of them's significant. It seems he was paying a bit of unwanted attention to a young jazz singer at the Nicholsons' club, but she reckons it was nothing she couldn't handle. He had some gambling debts too, apparently, but we've only just discovered that, so we're still looking into it – we're planning to talk to the man he owed the money to today.'

'Right – always good to rattle a few skeletons. But you make sure you keep your wits about you in Soho and watch your step – there's a crook on every corner over there. Given half a chance they'd steal the shirt off your back as soon as look at you. And rackets too – you name it, you'll find it going on in Soho, and right under your nose as likely as not. I've nicked a few bad 'uns in my time, but that place, it's a villains' paradise. So keep your eyes peeled – I don't want you coming back here with a knife in your ribs.'

Jago found himself involuntarily thinking of the Bellamys' neighbour, the meek-mannered Mrs Spencer.

It was just as well it was he who'd had to call on her after the body was found and not Detective Superintendent Hardacre – five minutes with him briefing her on the local background of her home for so many years and she might never leave her flat again.

Hardacre's voice snapped him back to the present. 'Anything else to report?'

'Yes, sir. There's just one other odd little thing. Earlier this morning the wife of one of the dead man's business associates asked to see us, so we met her at West End Central. She claimed she'd got a couple of pound notes in change at a shop and when she tried to spend them elsewhere they were rejected as counterfeits.'

'And?'

'Well, the odd thing is she said the shop in question was the bookshop run by Mr Bellamy.'

'I don't see what's so odd about that. There's always someone trying to pass off fake coins and notes in shops, so why not in his? Listen, I don't want you wasting time on small fry when you've got a murderer to catch – understand?'

'Yes, sir.'

'I'm not saying turn a blind eye or anything, mind. If you want to know what I think about people who cheat honest shopkeepers, I'll tell you – I hate them. It's like stealing money out of their till. I'd lock 'em up as soon as look at 'em. I just don't want you taking your eye off the ball, all right?'

Jago added counterfeiters to his growing mental list of things and people the detective superintendent hated, and nodded politely. 'Yes, sir.'

Hardacre glanced at Cradock, who looked somewhat intimidated by the senior officer's tirade. 'Is he all right? Looks like he's seen a ghost.'

'He'll be OK, sir – he's been working hard. I'll take him straight to the canteen when we've finished and get a cup of strong tea into him. That should perk him up.'

'You do that. I've always believed in looking after my men, and I expect you to do the same.'

Jago assented with another 'Yes, sir', but reflected inwardly that if he followed Hardacre's example in caring for his men, poor Cradock might not live to tell the tale.

'So,' said Hardacre, 'is that all?'

'I believe it is, sir, thank you very much.'

'Right. Clear off, then, the two of you, and find that killer. I want to see someone swing for this.'

They escaped Hardacre's office and headed straight for the canteen, where Jago revived Cradock with a large mug of tea and had the same himself. They'd almost finished when a uniformed constable approached their table.

'Detective Inspector Jago?' he enquired.

'Yes, that's me,' Jago replied.

'Sorry to disturb you, sir. Chief Constable CID's compliments, and would you be so good as to call on him as soon as you can, before you leave?'

'Certainly – tell him we'll be straight up.'

'Thank you, sir.'

Jago drained his mug and marched off with Cradock, wondering whether Detective Superintendent Hardacre would ever send an emissary to present his compliments in like fashion, and concluded rapidly that he would not.

CHAPTER TWENTY-EIGHT

'Come in,' said Chief Constable Ford, rising from his desk to greet them when they arrived at his office. 'Good to see you, John.' He gestured towards a pair of chairs that looked distinctly more welcoming than Hardacre's. 'Make yourselves comfortable.'

'Thank you, sir,' said Jago as they took their seats. He glanced around the spacious room with its view over the Thames and wondered whether you had to rise to the dizzy heights of Chief Constable of the CID before the Metropolitan Police gave you a decent office. But he couldn't wish it on a better man than Ford. 'Happy New Year, sir.'

'Ah, yes, Happy New Year to you too, John. I'm not sure how happy it'll actually be, though, the way things are going at the moment. Still, there's plenty worse off than us in the world. Now, I expect you're very busy with this murder of yours, so I won't keep you – I just wanted a quick word with you before you head back to Soho. Detective Superintendent Hardacre's updated me briefly on your murder case. He mentioned in passing something about counterfeit banknotes turning up in the dead man's shop and assured me that he'd made sure to tell you not to get distracted.' He looked at Jago with eyebrows raised for confirmation.

'That's correct, sir. No need to worry about that.'

'Well, now, much as I respect Mr Hardacre – he is right, of course – on this particular occasion I'm going to politely disagree with him. The thing is, you see, counterfeit banknotes are precisely one of the things I am worried about, and if you've come across some of them in Soho, I'm interested. Not that it comes as any surprise to me – there's plenty of characters down that way who might take a fancy to dabbling in some forgery if it can make them money. So tell me, what have you dug up?'

'Well, sir, we've heard of a couple of instances of people finding counterfeit pound notes and fivers in their change, and I think there may be some kind of connection with Bellamy, the man who was shot.'

'Right, well, I'd like you to look into it a bit more if you can. The key question for me is whether it really is just a small-scale local operation or whether it's part of something bigger and more organised. We've seen a fair number of cases in recent years where it's a low-level business – the kind of thing where some man makes half a dozen fake pound notes in the spare bedroom at home and then passes them off in shops. It's usually quite straightforward – he goes into a tobacconist's and buys a shilling pack of cigarettes with one and gets nineteen bob change, so effectively he's turned a fake pound note into a packet of cigarettes plus almost a pound of real money. It's a way to make a bit of extra cash, and if his note's good enough to get past the shopkeeper, he walks away with his profit. When the victim banks his takings the bank might spot the forgery, in which case the shopkeeper's a pound out of pocket – and it's too late to try and work out which customer passed him the dud note. If that's what your man's got caught up in, it's probably not that significant.'

'Our case does sound slightly different, sir. It wasn't a customer taking counterfeit notes in, it was the shop handing out fake pound notes in the customer's change. The woman who told us said she bought something for three pounds with a five-pound note and got two pounds in change that turned out to be forged. She was very charitable – she said she assumed the shop must've accepted them in good faith from an earlier customer. I might've thought along similar lines myself, but then it turned out the very same thing had happened to another of Bellamy's customers. So I'm considering the possibility that he might've been passing off false notes to his customers, but I'm puzzled – what's in it for him?'

'That might be difficult to establish now that he's dead, but I suppose if he had access to counterfeit notes he could have been replacing a couple of genuine ones in the till with forgeries, then giving the customer the fake ones in their change and pocketing the real ones for himself. You'll probably have to dig a bit deeper if you want to find out exactly what he was up to, but you're right to be suspicious.'

'We think he was in debt too, sir, so all this makes me wonder whether he might've been tempted to pay off his debts with counterfeit banknotes. Does that sound possible?'

'A suitcase full of fake fivers, you mean? That would depend on how convincing they were and who he'd borrowed the money from, I should think. The kind of people you can get in debt to in Soho wouldn't take kindly to having the wool pulled over their eyes like that, and if they caught him trying to cheat them their retribution would be swift and violent.'

'Like shooting him?'

'It wouldn't be the first time.'

Jago reflected on this for a moment, making a mental note of what further lines of enquiry he needed to pursue. 'We'll look into that, sir,' he said. 'And what about the bigger type of operation you mentioned?'

'Well, that's really the other end of the scale – counterfeiting rackets that can affect the whole country. We know that shortly after the Germans invaded Poland the September before last, their bombers dropped heaps of counterfeit Polish banknotes on Warsaw, the idea being there'd be so many fakes in circulation the public would lose confidence in the national currency. That was reported in the press here, but there was something else happening that didn't get into the papers. What I'm going to tell you now is strictly confidential, and I'm sure I don't need to remind you what will happen to you if you communicate any of this information to an unauthorised person, as the Official Secrets Act puts it.'

Cradock sat up straight, like a schoolboy caught slacking.

'That means no blabbing, Constable.'

'Yes, sir,' said Cradock.

'Right. Now, in November 1939 our security services learnt from one of their agents on the Continent that the Nazis were planning something similar for us. It seems they've set up a large-scale operation somewhere in Germany to create counterfeit Bank of England notes and flood us with them, but probably in a more covert way than dropping them from the sky. We don't know what people they may've got set up in this country to help them, but I'm interested in any lower-level counterfeiters we come across, just in case. If we know who they are, there are certain people who'd like to keep a discreet eye on them.'

'And if there's something going on in Soho that's not as big as that but is more than just some bloke in his spare bedroom, presumably you'd be interested in that too?'

'Yes. If there's some organised operation to print large numbers of notes, the people who make them wouldn't be going into their local shops with a fake ten-bob note themselves. They'd be more likely to sell them to criminals wherever they can, for whatever they can get – maybe three and six for a pound note, maybe as much as five or six bob. Then the crooks who buy them use them in whatever way they want to turn their own profit.'

'I suppose that'd make life easier for the men who print the notes, because they aren't going to get caught trying to pass them off in a shop.'

'Yes, you're right. By the way, did this Mr Bellamy of yours have any German connections?'

'Not that we know of, sir. But he was acquainted with a man we've met who runs an Italian cafe in Soho – he's British-born himself, but his father's Italian and was interned in the Isle of Man in June. You'd still have been in Special Branch then, wouldn't you, so I suppose you know all about that.'

'I was, yes. What's the name of the cafe?'

'It's called Frankie's, but he told us it used to be Rossetti's – he changed it when Italy declared war.'

'Hmm . . . What street's it in?'

'Frith Street, sir. Is that significant?'

'Not necessarily. Soho's full of Italian cafes – they call it the Little Italy of London, don't they? But if I recall correctly, that's not far from Greek Street, isn't it?'

'It's the next street, sir.'

'That's what I thought – it's just that Greek Street's where the Italian Fascist Party used to have its London branch headquarters. Not now, of course, but that's where it was – they had a place at number 15 called the Italian Club, with the party office, the Italian Legion, the Italian Benevolent Society and an Italian library all in the same building, and they were printing an English-language propaganda weekly as well. Mussolini had some loyal fans round that way back then. That's all public knowledge, but we also came across some serious goings-on in Soho that weren't – for example, they were trying to take over all the Italian cafes and force their owners to buy their supplies from Italy.'

'Interesting.'

'Yes. Whether or not your Rossetti fellow had anything to do with that is another matter, of course, let alone any German plans to get fake currency into the country, but you never know – there may be something in it. Let me know if you come across any stronger evidence of a link.'

'Yes, sir. By the way, I should mention that I've never actually had to handle a counterfeiting case. Do you know much about how they do it? I mean making notes good enough to fool people.'

'That's an interesting question, and I'll answer it with another question – how carefully do you look at banknotes? That's an important element in the whole business. We see what we expect to see, so I'm never surprised when I hear of counterfeits being accepted. I suppose shopkeepers are more suspicious than most of their customers, but neither of them necessarily has the time to scrutinise every banknote that passes through their hands. The banks are the ones who spot them, because they're trained and know what to look out for, but by then the damage is done. I think you should pop down to the Bank of England – they can tell you more than I can about how it's done, although even when they're talking to a couple of police officers they'll probably keep their cards close to their chests – they won't want to give away all the tricks of the trade. I'll give them a call right now.'

He picked up the phone and got through to the bank, explaining the reason for his call, then slipped one hand over the mouthpiece. 'Would a meeting at two-thirty be all right for you, John?'

'Yes, sir, that'll be fine.'

'Good.' Ford removed his hand from the mouthpiece and spoke into the phone again. 'They'll be with you for half past two . . . Very good, I'll tell them that . . . Thank you . . . Goodbye.'

He replaced the handset in its cradle. 'That's all arranged. You go in by the main entrance and ask for Mr Jobbings. He'll do his best to be of assistance.'

'Thank you, sir.'

'OK. Off you go now, and good luck with your enquiries.'

CHAPTER TWENTY-NINE

Jago had parked his car on the Victoria Embankment, and as they walked towards it in the bright winter sunshine, with Westminster Pier behind them and the Thames slipping silently by on their right, it felt strange to be back outside in the everyday world of London. Just moments before they'd been inside, behind the inscrutable walls of Scotland Yard, discussing a Nazi plot to destabilise the entire British economy, while out here the passing citizenry knew no more about it than the birds in the riverside trees.

'That was a bit of an eye-opener, wasn't it, guv'nor?' said Cradock. 'What Mr Ford was saying about Nazi plots and what have you – it sounded like real cloak and dagger stuff. I was sitting there wondering what my mum would make of it – me getting mixed up in things like that. She'd have a fit.'

'Fortunately she'll be spared that fate, though, won't she, Peter – because you won't be telling her about it. Remember what he said – no blabbing, or you'll be for it.'

'Oh, yes, sir – I mean no, sir. You don't need to worry about that – my lips are sealed.'

'So I should think – I don't want to see you out of a job and selling matches in Dean Street.'

'Me neither, sir. So what's next?'

'Well, I don't intend to sit around here kicking my heels until some bloke at the Bank of England gets back from his extended lunch break, and we're certainly not paid to sit and watch the boats sailing by on the river, so I think we should go and see Mr Rossetti – I'd like to talk to him about rummy, and maybe kill two birds with one stone.'

'Right – so, er, what's the other bird?'

'Well, by the time we're back up in Soho it'll be lunchtime, so I thought while we're having a chat with Mr Rossetti we might take the opportunity to have something to eat too.'

Cradock smiled broadly. 'Very good idea, sir.'

The first person they saw when they entered Frankie's Cafe was the proprietor. 'Hello,' said Rossetti. 'What brings you back here?'

'We'd thought we'd catch a quick bite of lunch, if that's all right,' Jago replied, shutting the door behind him with a shiver. 'It's getting very cold out there.'

'You want to get some good hot food inside you,

then – take a seat.' Rossetti pointed to the nearest table and wiped it quickly with the cloth he was holding. 'I've got some nice pork sausages in today – would sausage, egg and chips suit you?'

Jago's enquiring glance in Cradock's direction produced an enthusiastic nod in response. 'OK, that'll do nicely,' he replied.

As on their previous visit, the cafe looked short of customers, and the speed with which Rossetti returned with their food suggested things were quiet in the kitchen too. 'There you are,' he said, putting their meals before them. 'And a jar of Hayward's Military Pickle for your sausages, if you like that.'

'Perfect,' said Jago. 'Won't you pull up a chair, Mr Rossetti – if you're not too busy, that is.'

Rossetti looked round the room. 'Sure – I'm not exactly rushed off my feet. I could do with a sit-down, though – didn't sleep well last night.'

'I'm sorry to hear that. Not because of the bombs, though, I assume – we didn't have any last night, did we? Quite a change.'

'Yes, I thought maybe Hitler had used them all up on Sunday night, but I doubt whether he's run out of stuff to drop on us yet. Maybe I've got so used to the noise that I can't sleep when it's quiet any more – who knows? I was lying awake worrying about when I'm going to get my customers back.'

'Yes, I'm sorry about the way the war's affected your business.'

'Well, it can't be helped, I suppose. It's so slack today

I've just sent the waitress home – there's nothing for her to do, so she might as well have the afternoon off. It'll save me having to pay her for standing round doing nothing, too. Mind you, she'll still be better off than all the Italian waiters at the posh West End places that lost their jobs – they just got sacked on the spot when Italy declared war.' He gave a weary sigh. 'But how's your own business going? Have you got any nearer finding out who bumped him off? Bellamy, I mean. Back in the old days he and I might've been sitting here chatting about the football – but that was before the war came and messed everything up.'

Jago noticed that Cradock had already got to grips with his lunch, so he started to eat his own. 'Yes, you mentioned the football,' he said as he cut into his sausage. 'He was keen on it, was he?'

'Oh, yes. Only trouble was he supported Clapton Orient, and they're not doing too well at the moment – bottom of the South Regional League, for their sins. I don't know why he bothered, but he was a bit of a romantic when it came to football – always thought they'd take the league by storm next season.'

'Aren't we all? It's funny you should say he was a romantic, though – someone else who knew him said the same thing this morning.'

'Really? Who's that then?'

'A man called Fisher. Do you know him?'

Rossetti shook his head. 'No. Did you go and see that other bloke you mentioned when you were here before – the Greek one?'

'Mr Dimitriou? Yes, we did.'

'Right, well, I hope it was worth your while. He's another romantic old fool, if you ask me – that's probably why he and Bellamy got on. Two of a kind, they were.'

'In what sense?'

'Well, Dimitriou's full of airy-fairy ideas about Lord Byron and all that noble Greece fighting for her independence stuff, but it's nonsense – if you're talking about reality, Greece is just a broken-down old country that was under the thumb of the Ottomans for hundreds of years and only got free because Britain helped them.'

'And Mr Bellamy?'

'He was no better – he's what I'd call a romantic of the British variety. You know – "my country right or wrong" and all that. He had that great gift of knowing that this country's superior to every other place in the world and it's always right. It's one of the worst things about the British – going round the world like polite gentlemen, making their little jokes about themselves, but only because they're so completely convinced of their own superiority that they don't need to brag about it. I'm no fan of Napoleon – he fought a war against Italy and then made himself the king – but he was right about the British. A nation of shopkeepers, that's what he said, isn't it? The British have never really had a great imperial vision, they just went out all over the world looking for a chance of making some money, and on the way they ended up with an empire. Everyone's always laughing at Hitler because he reckons his Reich's going to last for a thousand years, but Churchill said pretty much the same thing about the British Empire, didn't he, and now he's swapping bits of it in the Caribbean for old American destroyers. Just another shopkeeper. He'll be lucky if it keeps going for a thousand days at this rate, never mind years. But what do I know? I'm just an Italian.'

'Forgive me if I'm wrong, Mr Rossetti, but the way you're talking, it's as if you're not British yourself – but when we were here yesterday you were at pains to make it clear that you are. Has something happened to change your view?'

'It has,' said Rossetti, the scorn in his voice now shifting to bitterness. 'But it hasn't just changed today – it was back in June of last year, when my dad was interned. The British government had just decided overnight that he was an enemy alien. When I saw that mob shouting outside like a pack of animals, I felt sick – I wasn't so sure I wanted to be British after all. Don't get me wrong, though – I'm not a traitor. I just get fed up with the way people look down their noses at Italy and laugh at us – I don't see what they've got to boast about. I have to remind them sometimes that Rome had an empire when the people here were still living like pigs. It was Italians who civilised this country, and when they left, the British just slid back into obscurity and squalor. That Bellamy was typical – always making pathetic jokes to me about ice cream, in that stupid way Englishmen have about all Italians being ice-cream merchants. He thought it was funny, but that just showed what a Philistine he was. I

236

pitied him, really, but I found it grotesque. I mean, what did he ever do? Didn't exactly change the world, did he? He sold second-hand books from a tatty little shop in Soho, and that was about all you could say for him.'

'It sounds like you found him pretty annoying.'

'Well, he just had this way of getting on my wick. He was always having a go at Italy, and to me that felt like he was having a go at my dad.'

'Is that what you meant when you said the war came along and messed everything up?'

'Yes. It brought out another side to him, and I didn't like it – or perhaps it'd always been there but it took the war to show it up good and proper. He started going on about Abyssinia – he seemed to hold me personally responsible for the war there. But why shouldn't Italy have a bit of an empire? It's good enough for Britain and France, isn't it, so why not anyone else? He was always having a go at Mussolini, too, making out he's a mad dictator. But he's the man who saved Italy from anarchy at the end of the last war – he gave the country order instead of chaos and made it into a great power. No one seems to remember now what even the great Mr Churchill himself said just a few years ago – he said Mussolini was a Roman genius, the greatest lawgiver of all times. When I told Bellamy that, he called me a liar – but it was in the papers, wasn't it? He might've known something about old books, but apart from that he was a fool. He just parroted whatever the government said about Abyssinia and anything else Italy was doing. I don't think he was capable of seeing it impartially – he didn't have the intelligence. Now don't get me wrong – it's a terrible thing that he was murdered, but I just think if anyone could rub someone up the wrong way it'd be him. Do you know what he said to me when he found out my dad had been locked up? He said, "Well, that's too bad, isn't it? The government had no choice." And then he said, "When there's enemy aliens in our midst, we can't have traitors running around free on the streets – the only thing we can do is round them up and lock them away." That was the end as far as I was concerned. My father didn't betray Britain – this country betrayed him.'

By the time this unexpected outburst ended, Jago had almost finished his lunch. He ate his last few chips slowly, thinking it might give Rossetti a chance to calm down, then pushed his plate away. 'That was delicious,' he said. 'Thank you very much.'

'You're welcome,' Rossetti replied. 'Sorry to go on like that – it's only because I didn't get enough sleep last night. I run out of patience when I haven't slept. Now, would you like anything else?'

Jago got his reply in quickly, before Cradock could speak. 'No, thank you, Mr Rossetti, we've got a busy afternoon ahead of us. But there is just one more thing I'd like to ask you.'

'Oh, yeah? What's that?'

'I was wondering – was Mr Bellamy in the habit of playing cards with you?'

Rossetti looked surprised. 'He might've been,' he said warily.

'You sound as though you're not sure.'

'All right, then – we used to have the odd game now and then. Nothing wrong with that, is there?'

'Not necessarily. But the reason why I'm interested is that we've been told it was more than the odd game – in fact he owed you a substantial sum of money.'

'What are you getting at?'

'I'm getting at the fact that we have reason to believe you were running an illegal gambling den – the kind of racket that someone said to us was run by nasty people you wouldn't want to cross.'

'What? Are you suggesting I'm some sort of crook and I killed Bellamy because he owed me money?'

'So he did owe you money.'

'All right, a little bit maybe – but I didn't kill him. You're getting it all wrong.'

'It wouldn't be the first time a man's gambling debts got him killed.'

'No – listen to me, Inspector, you've got it wrong. He did owe me a bit, but he paid it all back. Why would I kill a man who repaid everything he owed me?'

Jago held Rossetti's anxious gaze for a moment, wondering whether this claim was true. 'All right, so he paid you back. How did he manage that?'

'I don't know – it's none of my business, as long as he did. All he said was it'd be OK – his wife had fixed it.'

CHAPTER THIRTY

The journey eastwards to the Bank of England took Jago and Cradock past the bomb-damaged ruins of shops and offices in High Holborn, then on into Newgate Street and Cheapside on the north side of St Paul's, where buildings burnt down to their foundations were a grim reminder of the devastation caused by the previous Sunday night's air raids. Finally they reached the Mansion House, where Jago turned right into Lombard Street and parked the car.

He'd never been inside the bank, but as they walked towards it past the war memorial outside the Royal Exchange building, he was struck by how grand it looked. The squat stone fortress-like structure that he remembered from before the rebuilding of the last fifteen years or so was still there, but it looked as though someone had planted a rich man's country mansion on top of it, and several new storeys now towered imperiously over Threadneedle Street.

The inside of the building was no less grand. The tall bronze doors through which they'd entered seemed appropriate for the institution that had guarded the nation's wealth for centuries, and the young soldier on sentry duty was a reminder that this was its role in war as well as in peace. Having identified themselves to a member of staff and waited for a few minutes, they were met by an elderly man with a stiff collar and a manner to match.

'Good afternoon, gentlemen. My name is Jobbings, and I understand you need some information about counterfeit banknotes.'

'That's correct,' said Jago. 'I'm Detective Inspector Jago and this is Detective Constable Cradock, and we're investigating a murder, but we're beginning to wonder whether there might be some connection with forged banknotes, so we're looking into that.'

'Very well. If you'll follow me I'll take you to the Issue Room – we can talk there.'

They followed him down long, elegant corridors until they came to the room in question.

Jobbings shut the door behind them. 'We're always very pleased to give the police any assistance in the matter of counterfeit currency,' he said. 'It's of the utmost importance to us that these people are put out of business at every opportunity. In the old days, of course, it was a hanging offence. We don't do that now, but we still take it very seriously indeed. So what exactly would you like to know?'

'Well, speaking as someone who knows very little about it, I suppose the first thing is how does their business work?'

Jobbings gave a thin smile. 'Their business, of course, is to make money – both literally and metaphorically.' He paused briefly, as if to give them time to appreciate his wit. 'If we leave to one side for a moment the technical means by which they create the forgeries, the financial benefit they derive from their work comes in various ways. At the lower end of the scale, the typical forger makes his profit by spending his counterfeit note in a shop and getting his change in genuine money. We also suspect forged notes are being used on the black market – unscrupulous traders in back alleys slipping counterfeit notes into their customers' change, for example. At the more organised end, a gang might create a large quantity of forgeries and then sell them to a number of criminal associates across the country. If they sold pound notes for, say, just a few shillings each, the criminals could then dispose of them however they chose and make their own profit.'

'I see,' Jago replied, 'And to take the technical side of the forgeries themselves, I'd like to know a bit about how to spot a fake note – just so that we know what to look out for if we find one. I don't expect you to share all your secrets with us, though.'

'Don't worry, Inspector, I shan't tell you anything you're not supposed to know. Spotting counterfeit notes is something we're trained to do, of course, and the bank takes a variety of measures to make the notes

242

difficult to copy. You'll be aware that we introduced new pound notes last March – blue instead of green – and then new mauve ten-shilling notes in April. That was partly to improve security, and we also announced that they were to have a new feature – a special thread woven into the paper on the left-hand side, just half a millimetre wide, which you can see if you hold the note up to the light. We haven't said what the thread's made of, though – that's one of our little secrets. The important thing is that it's a protection against forgery – and also, incidentally, against the old split note trick that counterfeiters are fond of.'

'Yes, I saw that thing about the thread in the papers at the time. Actually, the reason why we're here is because we've come across someone in the course of our enquiries who says she was given a couple of pound notes in her change in a shop, and then when she tried to use them in another shop they were rejected as counterfeits. They're both those new blue ones – I've got them here.' He took an envelope from his pocket and removed the notes. 'Can you tell us whether these are fakes?'

'Certainly.' Jobbings took the notes, felt them, scrutinised them briefly and then held them up to the light. 'Undoubtedly,' he said, handing them back. 'They haven't got that special thread I mentioned, and they're not as smooth to the touch as they should be.'

'Thank you. So, if you've added that thread as a security measure, was that because of a specific threat?'

'There's certainly been concern about the possibility

of large quantities of counterfeit notes finding their way into circulation, and that's because of the risk that public confidence in the currency might be undermined. But we also put the thread in because the new notes are cheaper to print, which is important in wartime. We've reduced the costs by moving to lithographic printing, but the quality's not as good as the plate and letterpress method we've used up to now, so without the thread we might have inadvertently made life easier for the counterfeiters.'

'You mean because a forgery's usually not as good quality as the real thing?'

'Exactly. We see notes produced by a whole range of people, from talented amateurs to skilled professionals, and I think I can safely say that wherever they are in that range, a forger will always make mistakes.'

'Such as?'

'I'm sure you'll understand when I say it's not the bank's practice to publicise defects in forgeries – we obviously don't want to help the forgers to improve their work, so I can't tell you any specific details. We prefer simply to examine suspect notes that banks forward to us for checking. Suffice it to say that we know exactly what to look for, down to the minutest microscopic detail, and we can spot forgeries that even your local bank might not notice, let alone shopkeepers and their customers. We also have another little trick up our sleeves. Do you know anything about Persian carpets?'

'No – not a thing.'

'Well, they're beautiful, and the finest specimens can be very valuable. But it's said that the people who weave them always include one deliberate mistake, because they believe only God can create something that's perfect, and if they made a perfect carpet it would be an insult to him. It occurred to someone here some time ago that we could perhaps take a leaf out of their book – we could include flaws in the design of our notes, and a forger wouldn't know whether they were intentional and should be copied, or accidental and should be corrected. Clever idea, eh, to keep them on their toes?'

'So that's what you do, is it?'

'I couldn't possibly say – and if we did, I most certainly wouldn't be able to tell you what any such flaws might be.'

'Of course. So are there lots of forged notes in circulation?'

'Not too many, I'm glad to say. With the higher denominations – five pounds, ten pounds and so on – in the past year we've only received a few dozen of each.'

'And the lower denominations?'

'We see more of those, but the numbers still aren't huge – in 1940 we received more than six hundred counterfeit ten-shilling notes, which was a couple of hundred less than in 1939, and there was a similar reduction in pound notes. And when you consider that there's more than six hundred million pounds' worth of banknotes currently in circulation, that's not much.'

'But that's just the ones you've received – presumably there could be lots more that haven't been spotted?'

'Yes, that's true, but of course we don't have a number for those.'

'And do you put those reductions down to the new designs?'

'We can't be sure – you'll understand if I say we don't have enough evidence to tell. So far the only attempts we've seen to forge the new pound note look as though they may be the work of the same person who produced some fairly good counterfeits of the old green note, but whoever created it hadn't made any effort to make it look as though it had the new special thread in it.'

'So what kind of equipment would someone need to forge banknotes?'

'It would depend partly on the quantity – if you wanted to print them on the scale we do, you'd need a lot of space and large machinery, but someone with the right skills and materials who only aimed to produce small numbers could still use the old method, creating the copper plates in a corner of a room and printing the notes on a small press.'

'What skills would they need?'

'Letterpress and plate printing, obviously – they'd need to know how to operate a press – and they'd also need someone who could engrave the plates and do the etching, which requires special tools as well as a lot of skill.'

'And the materials?'

'For the printing, they'd need the copper plates, some nitric acid to etch them, and of course the inks and paper. We use special watermarked paper for banknotes, made at a papermill in Hampshire, so that would be hard to get hold of, if not impossible. But some forgers manage to find quite convincing substitutes – we had a case only about eighteen months ago with a fellow in Swindon who said he'd bought some paper from a man in Cardiff and used it to make pound notes. It might surprise you to learn that the only way we have to detect bogus paper here in the bank is by feeling it, but on the other hand, of course, we are the experts. When the Swindon man was caught, my colleague who oversees our printing section examined the paper and said it was a very good imitation of the stock we use. I don't suppose that was much consolation to the forger, though – he got four years' penal servitude for his pains. He was what I'd call the talented amateur end of the range.'

'Has the war made any difference to all this?'

'You mean are people still trying it on? Yes, they are, but you won't read anything about it in the papers. The government's wartime regulations say the press isn't allowed to state that any banknotes are forgeries unless it has express authority from the government – and if it's reporting trials of people accused of counterfeiting, it mustn't give descriptions of any process involved that might assist foreign agents who want to destroy confidence in the currency. The whole thing's been hushed up on grounds of national security.'

'I see. Well, we'll certainly watch our step. We've also had a report of someone having the same problem with a five-pound note, but we're waiting for her to bring it in. Could you take a look at that too for us when we get it?'

'Of course – it would be a pleasure.'

'Good. Thank you for your help, Mr Jobbings.'

'And thank you, Inspector. We take counterfeit notes out of circulation, but if you can do the same with the people who make them, I can assure you your efforts will be appreciated all the way up to the highest level here in the bank.'

CHAPTER THIRTY-ONE

Having found out everything they needed to know, Jago and Cradock retraced their steps to the car. Jago slid in behind the steering wheel, glad that he was wearing gloves against the cold, and Cradock took the front passenger seat beside him.

'Most enlightening, wouldn't you say?' said Jago as he turned on the ignition and started the engine.

'That stuff in the bank, you mean?' Cradock replied. 'Definitely – I don't suppose many people get the chance to go in there and find out all about that. I'm going to be checking all my ten-bob notes very carefully from now on – and pound notes too, although not many of those come my way, more's the pity.'

Jago pulled away from the kerb and turned the Riley round to begin their journey back to Soho. 'At least what you've got is honestly earnt, Peter,' he said. 'It might not make you rich, but it does mean you can sleep at night – bombs and sirens notwithstanding, of course.'

'Yes, sir. And speaking of ill-gotten gains, what are we going to do about Frankie Rossetti and his gambling racket?'

'Good question. There's a few more stones to be turned over as far as that's concerned, but I think we can safely pass it on to the Vice Squad at West End Central and leave them to do the digging. We've still got a bigger fish to catch.'

Jago couldn't tell whether his metaphorical reference to fish had triggered some response deep in Cradock's metabolism, but something made the young detective constable suddenly jump. He pulled back his coat sleeve and checked his watch. 'Half past three, sir,' he said, failing to conceal the anxiety in his voice.

Jago's mind made the connection immediately: Cradock's must have jumped from fish to eating to cake and thence to their appointment with Rita. 'Are you thinking about cake again, Peter?'

'Just hoping, sir, that's all.'

'But you've only just had your lunch. Where are you going to put it?'

'Lunch was hours ago, sir – well, maybe two, but we didn't have any pudding, did we?'

'That is true. As I said before, you'll have to wait and see – and you'll have to hope you're in Rita's good books, too. But don't worry about being late – we'll be there on time.'

* * *

The place where they were to meet Rita was easy to find: an eye-catching five storeys of elaborately decorated stone-clad splendour with a large sign above its second-floor windows saying *Corner House*. The establishment was equally grand on the inside, with a sweeping staircase and huge marble mosaic landscapes decorating the walls, and when she took them up to the Mountview Cafe on the first floor they found themselves in a vast room that looked capable of seating hundreds of customers. It was busy, and across the sea of small tables a light orchestra was playing unobtrusively over the hubbub of conversation. Jago secured a table for themselves, and within moments a Nippy dressed in the company's famous uniform black dress with two rows of pearl buttons from neck to waist came to take their order. Rita took command and instructed the waitress to bring them tea and a plate of cakes, to Cradock's barely concealed delight. When the Nippy had gone, Jago tried to insist that he would pay, but Rita was adamant.

'This was my idea – I invited you, and I'm paying,' she said. 'Now you're working up here I don't suppose you can get away very much, so there's not much chance of me being able to feed you at my cafe. I thought you won't be dropping in, so I'd have to come to you. I wanted to wish you a Happy New Year, see – and you, Peter.'

'Thanks, Rita,' said Jago, 'and Happy New Year to you too.'

'Yes, thanks,' Cradock added hesitantly. 'Happy New Year.'

'Don't worry, dear,' said Rita with a smile, 'this isn't some sort of trick to mother you and make you feel all soft and obligated to marry my Emily.'

His eyes widened.

'No,' she continued sweetly, 'I prefer just to let love take its course. When old Cupid's got you in his sights there's nothing you can do about it.'

Cradock felt hot around his collar and suspected his face must be flushing, but feared that if he said anything he might embarrass himself even more. Fortunately Jago came to his rescue.

'It was a very nice idea to invite us, Rita,' he said. 'We don't get much time to stop normally when we're on a case, but we couldn't ignore an invitation from you.'

'Aw, thanks – you're too kind. There's another reason why I wanted to see you, too – it's because I've got a little present for both of you. But I'll tell you about that later.'

'That sounds intriguing – I can't wait.'

The Nippy returned with a tray, placed their tea and cakes carefully on the table, gave them a polite smile and departed. Rita took hold of the plate of cakes and drew it towards her, scrutinising its contents carefully.

'I think that's the biggest piece, Peter,' she said, turning it towards Cradock, 'so you'd better have that one. You look like you need feeding up – we can't have you wasting away, can we? What would Emily say?'

Nervous at the thought of any further discussion of Emily with her mother, Cradock took the only evasive action he could think of. 'Hmm, thanks,' he said, avoiding her maternal gaze and looking at the cake instead of at her.

Once again Jago intervened protectively. 'So what's happening to your cafe while you're here?' he said, sipping his tea. 'It's only Scotland that has the day off today, so have you shut up shop just for us?'

Rita took her eyes off Cradock and turned to Jago. 'No, I can't afford to do that. It's business as usual – or at least I hope so.'

'What do you mean?'

'I mean I've left Phyllis in charge. Head like a sieve, that girl's got – sometimes I wonder why I keep her on. But she managed not to set fire to the lunch on Christmas Day, so I'm giving her another chance to prove she's got something between her ears after all. I just hope I've still got a cafe when I get back – when her mind wanders I reckon she's more of a danger to me than Hitler is. And talking of him, I saw in the paper this morning that he's said for every bomb we drop on him he's going to drop ten or even a hundred on us. That's not very nice, is it? Do you think he means it?'

'I'm not sure even Mr Hitler's got that many bombs – and I get the impression he doesn't always stick strictly to the truth.'

'You're telling me. The paper said his mate Goebbels was having a go too – he said the German people were reverently bowing before the Almighty because he was so clearly blessing them. That can't be right, though, can it? I mean he's obviously on our side – that's God I mean, not Goebbels. But then what do I know? I didn't go to grammar school like you.'

'Even a grammar school education doesn't necessarily unlock all the mysteries in the universe. Speaking from my personal experience, I'm not sure God's on either side myself. And as for Goebbels, he's Hitler's Minister of Propaganda, so I reckon that means his job's lying like the devil to anyone he thinks might believe him.'

'Yes, well, I don't want to sit here thinking about people like that, so let's forget them for a bit and enjoy ourselves.'

'Good idea, Rita. So, what made you choose this place for our treat?'

'Well, I've been here before once or twice – just to see what the competition's doing, of course.' She laughed. 'That Joe Lyons did very well for himself, didn't he? Different league to me. Anyway, they said when I phoned up that you were working on a case in Soho, so I thought this'd be about as close as I could get without actually being there. My old mum told me stories about Soho that'd make your hair curl, so I prefer not to set foot in the place. I suppose you've got no choice, what with it being your job and all, but I have, so I thought we'd stay on this side of Oxford Street, thank you very much. I like these Lyons places – I have to admit, as cafes go they're a bit more classy than mine, but they serve good food, they make a decent cup of tea, and their prices are reasonable considering they're on smart streets like this.'

'It's certainly a smart location, but it takes me back, actually. This is where the old Oxford Music Hall used to be – I remember hearing my dad singing here when I was a lad, not long before he died. Strange to think it's all gone now, and they've built this place instead – makes me feel old.'

'You're not old,' said Rita. 'You're in your prime, and still a catch for any girl who's got her head screwed on right.'

Jago gave her an appreciative smile, as if to thank her for being charitable.

'So tell me,' she continued, 'what's brought you down into Soho – is it a murder?'

'Yes, it is – a man was found shot in his home. He was an antiquarian bookseller.'

'An anti-what?'

'He sold old books – hundreds of years old, some of them.'

'I see – like a junk shop, then?'

'Well, maybe about as tidy as a junk shop, but it's not junk – some of them are quite valuable.'

'Hmm . . . that's probably why we haven't got any anti-whatever you call it shops round West Ham way, then, isn't it? Not much cash to spare over there. What did you say it was called again?'

'Antiquarian.'

'Right, well, that's maybe the sort of highfalutin language people use up the West End, but I'll just call it old. Expensive old junk. I suppose up here there's more mugs with money who want to buy old books, right?'

'That's about it, yes. Some of them've got more money than the likes of you or me will ever see.'

'More money than sense, more like.'

'Maybe. Rich Americans like buying them too, so there's money to be made.'

'Nice work if you can get it, then. Trouble with my sort of work is if I charge tuppence for a cup of tea, it doesn't matter how rich the customer is, whether he's from America or Timbuktu, he only has to pay tuppence. If I could work out some way to charge Americans two quid a cup, maybe I'd get rich too, but I don't think they'd fall for it. And talking of Americans, how's that lovely lady of yours, that Miss Appleton?'

Jago laughed. 'She's not mine, Rita – if anyone's a free agent, it's her.'

'But are you taking care of her? She's one in a million, that one, but she needs looking after.'

'That was supposed to be my job when I first met her – I was ordered to make sure she didn't come to any harm around the East End, but she soon made it very clear she didn't need a chaperone. She does what she likes and looks after herself.'

'Yes, well, that's Americans for you, isn't it? Land of the free and all that. That's probably why they've got so much money, not like old stick-in-the-muds like me, eh?' She looked down to her side and ran a finger along the chair.

'What are you doing?' said Jago.

'Just checking – in my cafe you won't find a speck of dust on your chair, so I want to know what they're like here. It's all about standards, isn't it?'

'I've always understood the Lyons Corner Houses

pride themselves on their high standards of hygiene and cleanliness.'

'Yes, well, that's as may be, but I like to see for myself – appearances can be deceptive. You can have a very fancy outside to your shop and still have rats running round the kitchen where the customers can't see, and I don't hold with that, no matter what the name over the front window is. Mind you, these days you can wake up in the morning and find your fancy outside's been blown right off by a bomb, and the sign and window gone for a Burton too. Exciting times we live in, aren't they? Some of us could do with a bit less excitement, that's what I say, and I think our Emily feels the same way when those sirens get going.'

'How is Emily?'

'Oh, she's all right – just pining a bit, you know.'

'Oh yes? And what's she pining for? Or should I say who?'

Rita nodded in Cradock's direction. 'I don't think I need to say anything more about that.'

'Ah, that's probably my fault,' said Jago, noticing another blush appearing on Cradock's face. 'I make him work long hours – but unfortunately that's what it's like when you're in the CID. No such thing as regular hours when you're a detective. And actually, if you'll pardon me for being on duty for a moment, there's something I wanted to ask you.'

'Some police thing?'

'Yes. It's just that we've come across a shop in Soho having a spot of trouble with fake money – you know, forged. I wondered if you'd had anyone trying to use counterfeit cash in your cafe.'

'Not recently, no. There was some bloke two or three years ago who tried it on, but it was a pretty poor copy – didn't fool me for a minute.'

'Was he arrested?'

'Er, not exactly, no. He was a miserable little creature, short and scrawny, but when I said it was a fake and I wasn't having it he got abusive and swore at me. Well, I'm not having that in my own cafe, so I thought to myself what would my dear sweet old Walter have done if he'd still been alive? I thought yes, that's what he'd do – so I told the little chancer what he could do with his pound note and gave him a good smack in the chops. I said if he ever darkened my door again I'd get the law on him – meaning your good self, of course. He sloped off with his tail between his legs and I never saw him again. Good riddance.'

'Hmm . . . an interesting approach.'

'I like to think my Walter would've been proud of me,' she said with a wistful look in her tired grey eyes. She sighed quietly and gathered her thoughts, then perked herself up. 'And besides, I thought I was saving valuable police time.'

'Very considerate of you, Rita. But if you happen to get any more customers with fake notes, let me know, won't you?'

'Of course, dear – anything for you.'

Jago glanced at the clock on the wall. 'I think Peter and I had better be on our way now,' he said, starting to get to his feet, 'but thank you for treating us.'

'Hang on a minute,' she replied. 'You haven't had your surprise yet.'

Rita bent down to the floor beside her chair and brought up a shopping bag, from which she produced two brown paper bags. She placed them both on the table, one in front of Jago and the other before Cradock. 'Want to guess?'

'I don't think we could – you'd better tell us.'

'Oh, all right, then.' Rita lifted his paper bag from the table and opened it carefully, taking out a substantial package wrapped in greaseproof paper. 'There you are,' she said, unfolding one corner enough for him to glimpse what it contained. 'Rita's finest bread pudding – about three days' worth for each of you, I reckon. That should keep the wolf from the door when you're out and about. I used all the stale bread I had in the cafe, and I went round to West Ham police station and got some from their canteen – I said it was for you, and they said I could have it, so they haven't forgotten you yet. My Walter used to love my bread pudding, you know – he said there was nothing like it. And the government keeps telling us not to waste food, so I feel like I'm doing my bit for the war.'

'That's really kind of you,' said Jago. 'I'll look forward to having a bit of that later – and I'm sure I speak for Peter too.'

'Oh, definitely,' said Cradock, beaming.

'Good,' said Rita. 'I hope it'll be better than all that police grub you have to eat – I'm surprised it hasn't killed you yet. And if you can get your hands on a nice bit of custard it'll go down a treat.' She folded the greaseproof paper back over the corner of Jago's portion and put it back into his brown paper bag. 'There you are, Mr Detective Inspector. Off you go, then – I hope all your investigating goes well and you find out who killed that poor anti-whatsit man. And make sure this lad here gets enough food – we don't want him looking like a seven-stone weakling when he could be another Charles Atlas, do we? And I don't suppose Emily does either. Any time he needs to get a good square meal down him, you just send him over to Rita's cafe and I'll get him beefed up in no time.'

CHAPTER THIRTY-TWO

Jago and Cradock said goodbye to Rita and returned to the Quincys' flat. This time William Quincy appeared to be alone and was dressed in an expensive-looking suit. He glanced at his watch as he let them in. 'I'm afraid I have an appointment in half an hour from now, gentlemen, so I can't give you very long.'

'Don't worry, Mr Quincy, this should only take a few minutes, if you'd be so kind.'

'Very well, then. Tell me what you want, and I'll do my best to be of assistance.'

'Thank you. When we spoke to you yesterday, you said your business relationship with Mr Bellamy was quite simple and straightforward. But since then we've heard that he claimed you'd cheated him. I'd like to know whether that's true.'

'Who told you that?'

'As you pointed out yourself yesterday, Mr Quincy, I don't always reveal my sources. Is it true?'

'It sounds as though someone's got the wrong end of the stick. We might have had the occasional difference of opinion, but that's normal in any business.'

'You said you hadn't bought anything from him for about a year and a half. Why was that?'

'I only buy from someone like Bellamy if they've got something to sell that I'm interested in, and also if they only want a fair price for it. It happened that he didn't have much to offer during that period, and when he did turn up one day with a book in which I expressed a modicum of interest he wanted a price that I thought was unreasonable, so I declined to buy. He might have seen that as being cheated, but honestly, he could have taken it somewhere else and maybe got the price he was trying for – who knows, perhaps he did. To my mind that's just normal business – you offer me something for a certain price, I say no, and you go away. I was under no contractual or moral obligation to buy from him just because he had something to sell. Whether that's what he was referring to, if he actually said what you claim he said, I can't possibly know. All I will say is that he had a bit of a chip on his shoulder. Maybe he envied my success – who knows? As I told you before, we operated at different ends of the market, and mine is more profitable. The truth is, I don't think he could ever have done what I do – he didn't have the contacts, for one thing, and neither did he have the background.'

'He wasn't an English gentleman, you mean?'

'If you want to put it that way, then yes.'

'Someone else told us you had an interesting background – they said we should ask you about your ancestry. Would you care to enlighten us?'

'By all means. It's all to do with this unusual name I've been blessed with. Before I became a bookseller, you see, I worked in banking, and several years ago I was over in America on business. Somebody I met there commented on the name and asked if I was related to John Quincy Adams, one of the early American presidents. I said I didn't know of any direct connection with our family, but I thought a little honest speculation would do no harm, so I mentioned that my father was very interested in genealogy and had spent a lot of time tracing us back to a titled Englishman called Quincy, some of whose descendants had emigrated to the colonies, so perhaps we were related. What I hadn't expected was how many doors this would open for me in America when I started dealing in antiquarian books.'

'Because people were interested in meeting a member of the English aristocracy?'

'I think so, yes.' He shrugged, but Jago couldn't tell whether the sheepish grin that followed was genuine. 'In my defence, however, I must say I never claimed I was part of the aristocracy – not even the landed gentry. My father was just an ordinary chap, an engineer – not at all distinguished, although he'd had some success in the field of steam locomotive boilers – but he'd always been somewhat eccentric. It seems that before I was born he met someone in a pub in a village down in Somerset who told him there used to be a baronet who lived there hundreds of years ago called Sir Everard Quincy, but he had no male relative to inherit the title, and when he died the baronetcy became extinct. For some reason my father latched on to this and it became an obsession – he was convinced he was the lost heir to this baronetcy and had to prove it. He saw himself becoming Sir Arthur Quincy, and I would follow him as Sir William.'

'Which presumably never happened?'

'Quite. But as it happened, this quest of his was what first got me interested in antiquarian books. One day he came across a dusty old volume called *The Visitations of the County of Somerset* in an antiques shop and discovered later that it was very rare. It recorded all the families in the county who were entitled to a coat of arms – what they used to call the "gentle" families – and he found there was indeed one called Quincy. He employed a quack genealogist who obligingly supplied some no doubt spurious evidence to support his claim to the title. But these claims have to be assessed by one of those obscure British institutions most of us have never heard of. In this case it's something called the College of Arms, which I think was set up by some king hundreds of years ago, and the fellow in charge of it's called the Garter Principal King of Arms. Apparently, it's his job to consider a claim like my father's and decide whether to uphold it or not. Unfortunately, in our case he rejected it. It was a great disappointment to my father.'

'And presumably a lost business opportunity for you? I imagine some of your American book clients might've liked the idea of dealing with a baronet.'

'Undoubtedly, and I must admit that I did occasionally let slip that my father was pursuing the claim and expected it to be upheld. I felt I owed it to him – he'd invested a lot in equipping me for my future role in life.'

'What do you mean?'

'Well, as a mere engineer who got his hands dirty, to our gentry he remained irredeemably and unalterably "trade" to the end of his days, and definitely not part of the county set. But he poured much of his precious savings into sending me to one of the more minor of the minor English public schools in the belief that they would inculcate in me the overweening self-confidence and effortless superiority of the ruling class. In other words, they'd turn me into precisely what you just said – an entirely convincing English gentleman.'

'And they succeeded, I assume.'

'Oh, yes, without a doubt. People may not always like what they see, but they do have an unwavering tendency to believe what they see. Someone once said I was like a pound note. It's a curious fact that our whole economy is based on the fact that we all agree to believe a pound note is worth something. We'll happily exchange land, goods and services for those pieces of paper, and a forgery that's sufficiently convincing is worth just as much as a genuine one as long as people believe it's real. I'm just a man, but if people see and hear a gentleman, they'll believe that's what he is.'

'So are you saying that's what you're like – a counterfeit pound note?'

'I suppose I am, really – or perhaps I should say a perfect replica. The only difference between me and most of the gentry, even the peerage, is that they've sustained the illusion for more generations than I have. But questionable as it may be, it's kept me in a job and out of penury all my adult life. And I venture to think that through that job I make the world a happier place.'

'It sounds as though Mr Bellamy might not've described his working relationship with you in those terms.'

'What do you mean?'

'You mentioned yesterday that the book trade was going through hard times and that it was more difficult for someone like him than it was for you. But when he wanted to sell you a book you said no. Did that leave him with a grudge against you? You said he had a chip on his shoulder.'

Quincy looked thoughtful for a moment. 'I did, yes, but it's never crossed my mind that he might have a grudge against me personally.'

'Not even if he thought you'd excluded him from the ring?'

'The what?'

'The bidding ring – you know what that is, I assume.'

'I've heard of it, yes, but I have nothing to do with it. No, if he had a chip on his shoulder I think it was more to do with the general state of his own business, and I wasn't responsible for that. He wasn't the sort of man who wore his heart on his sleeve, though, so I always found it difficult to know what was going on inside him.

I don't like to speak ill of the dead, Inspector, but not to put too fine a point on it, I never really trusted the fellow.'

'Why was that?'

'I don't know – it was just a feeling I had. And now that he's gone, I find myself thinking I didn't really know him either.'

CHAPTER THIRTY-THREE

It was dark when they left William and Daphne Quincy's flat, and Jago drove carefully through the blacked-out streets. The car's off-side headlight had been deprived of its bulb to comply with the wartime regulations, and the near-side lamp was partially masked, so he was thankful for the local council's efforts to apply white paint to as many roadside kerbs, trees and lamp posts as possible in order to keep drivers in the road, where they belonged. The government's decision to allow some streets to offer the comparative luxury of so-called 'starlighting' meant that now, instead of the total darkness of the original blackout, motorists could at least hope to pick out the faint bluish glimmer of streetlights in the distance and gain some idea of the direction of the street ahead. As with some other aspects of the emergency regulations, Jago had at first been puzzled that this should be allowed, while striking a match to light a cigarette in the blackout was not. But the Home Office authorities had given their assurance that the new subdued lights could not be seen from the air, so that, he supposed, was that.

They retraced their route back along Brewer Street, with Cradock sitting forward in the passenger seat, straining his eyes to spot the junction with Wardour Street. 'Do you reckon he was lying about the ring, sir?' he said. 'Quincy, I mean.'

'Condemned out of his own mouth, I'd say. A gentleman's word may be his bond, but he's just told us he's a fake, so I've no reason to believe him. But we're not here to investigate bidding rings. Before we pack up for the day, I want to see whether Marjorie Bellamy's at home. She told us she didn't know anything about her husband being in debt, but now Rossetti says Bellamy told him he was going to repay the lot because his wife had fixed it. That sounds to me like she did know, so I want to find out what else she's been keeping from us. I don't like being lied to.'

They reached Wardour Street without mishap, turned left and then left again into Peter Street, and pulled up outside Marjorie Bellamy's flat.

'Hello,' she said when she answered their ring at the door. 'Come in – I was just about to make a flask to take down to the shelter with me when the sirens go off.' She led them up the stairs to the flat. 'Would you like a drink?'

'No, thank you. This is just a quick call, so we won't be keeping you for long.'

'Come into the living room, then, and sit yourselves down. How are you getting on with your investigation? How you any idea yet who . . . who did it?'

'We're making progress, but I'm afraid there's nothing I can tell you yet.'

'I understand – I'm sure you will when you can. It's strange, you know – I can't get used to the idea that Samuel really isn't here any more, that he won't come through that door any moment and say hello. I know that's what everyone says when they're bereaved, but it's true, and it's unsettling. I come home now and the place is silent – I put the wireless on just to have another voice in the room. I'm surprised, because I lived alone quite contentedly for many years before I married Samuel, but I suppose I've got used to him being here – and now I have to get used to being on my own again.'

'I'm very sorry, Mrs Bellamy – it must be a trial for you.'

'It's kind of you to say so, but I'm trying to be positive – that's something I've learnt in my business life when times have been hard. I'm thankful that Samuel and I found each other – we married rather late, so we didn't have much time together, but then there are no guarantees in life, are there? I try not to take anything for granted and remind myself that fairy tales are just that – and best left behind with the nursery rhymes. I suppose most of us grow up thinking one day we'll find somebody wonderful and fall in love, then get married and live happily ever after, but it's not always like that, is it?'

Jago found himself inwardly agreeing with her, but

his own immediate sense of thankfulness was for the fact that it wasn't a policeman's job to share his innermost feelings. He waited for her to continue.

'But you know,' she said with a sigh, 'when all's said and done, I think I've got a lot to be thankful for – yes, my own marriage was short, but at least it was relatively happy, and not everyone can say that. But that's enough about me – you don't want to hear about all my trials and tribulations. Was there anything you wanted from me?'

'Yes, there was – and it's rather a serious matter.'

She looked at him warily. 'Yes?'

'Mrs Bellamy, you told us you knew nothing about your husband being in debt, didn't you?'

'Yes, that's right.'

'We now have evidence from a witness that gives us reason to believe you did know. As you may be aware, obstructing the police in the execution of their duty is an offence. I believe you've lied to us, and I'd advise you not to try to cover that up with another lie. I'll ask you again – did you know your husband was in debt?'

Her face crumpled. 'All right, yes, I'm sorry – I should have told you. I did know, but it was his debt, nothing to do with me – it was none of my business.'

'But it became your business, didn't it – according to the man he owed money to, your husband said he was now in a position to repay it, because, as he put it, "My wife has fixed it." So why didn't you tell us the truth?'

'I don't know – I think I was just too embarrassed. I didn't want to get mixed up in it. You have to understand

– when I married Samuel I didn't know he gambled, and it was only when he got deeply in debt that he told me. I was shocked – my world has always been ecclesiastical publishing, not illegal gambling dens, and to think that my husband was involved in anything like that, well, I just didn't know what to think. All I wanted to do was get him out of it and make him promise he'd never do it again.'

'And did he promise?'

'Yes, he did. But I'm not a fool, Inspector. I know that gambling can be as addictive as drink, so all I could do was try to wipe the slate clean and implore him not to fall into the same trap again. But I keep my feet on the ground, and I knew if he had a vulnerability like that someone might try to exploit it again, or he might simply be too weak himself to resist temptation.'

'You must've been concerned about the potential financial implications of him slipping up a second time.'

'Of course I was – we'd be ruined. But if you think I'd kill him, you're making a big mistake. I can't be the first woman to discover the man they love has feet of clay, but that doesn't necessarily stop you loving them. It's just a situation you have to manage, and so I managed it.'

'Indeed – you fixed it. So how exactly did you do that?'

She looked first to Cradock, then back to Jago, like a cornered fox. 'I, er . . . I just had a word with someone I knew – someone with more money than us. I'd helped him in the past and I thought he might be willing to help Samuel out now for my sake.'

'Would this by any chance be someone you once nursed in Greece?'

She looked down into her lap and whispered. 'Yes.'

'So Mr Nicholson lent you the money to pay off your husband's gambling debts.'

'No, not exactly. I asked George if he could help, and he said he would, but he said I needn't get involved – he'd have a word with Samuel and make the necessary arrangements. I believe that's what he did. He said because of our past, er, association, he wouldn't mention to Samuel that I'd asked him – he didn't want to embarrass me. He'd just say he'd heard on the grapevine what had happened and he'd offer to help Samuel with a loan to cover that and any other debts he had.'

'And that's what he did?'

'Yes, as far as I know.'

'But that would mean now your husband had an even greater amount to repay, this time to Mr Nicholson. Is that correct?'

'Yes, it must have been.'

'And on what terms?'

'I don't know – I'm sorry, Inspector, I've never had any dealings with anything like this before. I don't know what went on between Samuel and George, and to be frank with you, I don't want to know.'

'I understand, Mrs Bellamy. Now, there's something else I'd like to ask you.'

'Yes, what's that?'

'Someone made an interesting comment to us

yesterday. They said that when you married Mr Bellamy, whatever money you had went into his business and never came back. What do you say to that?'

'I say it's nothing but idle gossip. How can anyone presume to know what went on between my husband and me in our marriage? It's preposterous.'

'You did say yourself, though, that you'd helped him out with his business difficulties with your own money. But then you said you suspected there wasn't as much of that as he'd perhaps hoped. Some people of a more cynical bent than me might interpret that to mean your husband had perhaps married you for your money. Is that true?'

'Certainly not. Look, Inspector, my husband knew I wasn't rich. I can assure you he married me for love – and I loved him too, for all his faults.'

'And apart from his apparent fondness for card games, what were they?'

'Oh, nothing really. There's not a man or woman on earth who doesn't have faults, and if you love someone you've got to accept that, haven't you? Samuel was a good man, but I just think he wasn't a natural businessman, and sometimes it all got too much for him. He was more of a dreamer, and you could say that's what all successful business people are – they have a vision of the future and they work to make it happen. Samuel had that kind of vision – he saw himself doing well, making money, having success. But the tragedy for him was that he'd never become what he wanted to be. I guess he was chasing a dream – but that's not a crime, is it?'

Jago knew that chasing a dream might not be a crime in itself, but it had led many a chaser into committing one. He also knew that Mrs Bellamy was not looking for an answer to her question, so he offered none. Instead he changed the subject. 'There's one more thing I'd like to ask you – it's not about debts or gambling, but it is connected with money.'

'Yes? What is it?'

'It's to do with your sister-in-law, Mrs Edison. She told us yesterday that you'd been kind to her and given her sums of money from time to time since her husband lost his job. I wondered how your husband might've reacted if he'd known you were giving money away while he was struggling with a major debt. Did he know?'

'No, I don't think he did. But it wasn't a question of large sums, so there was no reason why I should necessarily tell him. I'd like to think he'd have done the same, to help his sister, but he may not have known her situation as well as I did. She always confided in me more than in him – woman to woman, you know. She probably felt I was more likely to understand how her situation was.'

'And what was her situation? Apart from the financial pressures, I mean.'

'Well, things haven't been going too well for her for a long time. She probably wouldn't tell you herself, so I'm speaking in confidence when I say there are some strains in her marriage. Have you met her husband?'

'Yes, we have.'

'Well, as I said, my own marriage was short, but at

least I can be thankful that it was relatively happy. But when I look at Samuel's sister and that husband of hers, I wonder whether she knew what she was taking on when she married him. They've been together far longer than me, yet I don't envy her at all.'

'Why's that?'

'Well, he's not exactly Rudolph Valentino, is he? I can't imagine any woman mistaking him for a great romantic lover. I think a husband should be kind to his wife, and he's not – to be perfectly frank with you, he leaves a lot to be desired. Christine's a dear, but she's a timid creature – frightened of her own shadow. I think when she married John she thought she was getting a strong man who'd protect her, but it turned out he was strong in the wrong way. He can be . . . difficult, if you know what I mean.'

'I got the impression when we visited them that there was some sort of tension between them.'

'I think what you could probably sense was more likely fear on Christine's part, but she's learnt to cover it up.'

'I thought I noticed bruises on her wrist as we were leaving, too, but the lighting wasn't very good, so I wasn't sure.'

'I think you can safely assume those were bruises – as I said, he's a strong man. Was she wearing a lot of face powder?'

'Yes – now you mention it, I did notice that.'

'I've seen her like that many times. I think she does it to conceal marks on her face – marks that he's put there.

He's got a short temper, you see, and when he drinks . . . well, spite and alcohol aren't a good combination.'

'You mean he's violent towards her?'

'Yes – it's what people call knocking her about. I don't like that expression, because it makes the whole thing sound like some sort of game, but it's not. It's wicked, and he should be held to account for it.'

'Didn't your own husband intervene to protect his sister?'

'I don't know. He may have tried to, but Samuel wasn't a strong man in the physical sense, and I don't think he'd have made much impression if he'd tried to intimidate John or scare him off. He definitely would have come off worse if they'd come to blows. John's not the sort of person you can reason with – he'd just see that as a sign of weakness.' She paused. 'But you won't tell John what I've said, will you?'

'I won't be repeating what you've just told me to him, Mrs Bellamy, but thank you for sharing the information with us. I appreciate that.'

'It's the least I can do. Now, is there anything else I can help you with?'

'No, that's everything, thank you. We'll wish you a quiet night, if that's not too unrealistic these days.'

'Thank you – after what happened to Paternoster Row on Sunday night, all I pray is that I'll wake up alive in the morning.' She paused. 'But poor Samuel doesn't even have that hope any more, does he? I'll bid you good night, gentlemen, and I hope you catch whoever did it soon.'

* * *

Jago and Cradock went down the stairs and back into the street, Jago reflecting on what Marjorie Bellamy had said about her husband, a man who'd spent his life chasing a dream but never finding it, and what she'd revealed about her sister-in-law. Christine Edison's own marriage, whether it had started as a dream or not, had definitely turned into a nightmare. Not for the first time in his job as a police officer, today Jago had found himself on the outside of a marriage looking in, with no experience of being on the inside looking out. He'd always thought it must be nice to have someone to share your dreams with, but how could you tell whether they'd turn out to be good or bad? Perhaps someone like him would never know.

CHAPTER THIRTY-FOUR

It was Thursday. The day had barely started, and already Jago could feel the cold gnawing at his bones. When he got behind the wheel of his Riley Lynx, shivering, he wondered whether he should have invested in a new gadget he'd read about a year or so ago. It seemed some clever clogs had invented a device that took a small amount of hot water from the engine radiator to another small radiator, and then a tiny electric fan behind that blew heated air into the car. The report he'd read claimed that a garage could install one for about four pounds. It also claimed that with this heater, passengers wouldn't have to wrap themselves up in coats, gloves, rugs and foot-muffs any more to keep warm, but he assumed that only applied to saloon cars, not open-top tourers like his own, where even with the roof up the heat would surely leak away through the draughty gaps. As on the previous occasions when he'd considered getting one of these marvels, he reluctantly concluded it would be a waste of time and reconciled himself to being cold until the summer came. His quiet reflection ended when Cradock jumped in beside him, and they set off. 'I've been thinking, sir,' he said.

'Really?' said Jago. 'This early in the day? I'm impressed, Peter. What've you been thinking about?'

'Just trying to get it all straight in my head, sir. If I've got it right, Samuel Bellamy was afraid of Rossetti, and about what might happen if he couldn't pay off what he owed him, but then his wife steps in and has a quiet word with her old pal George Nicholson, and he lends Bellamy the money to clear his debt, but then that means Bellamy owes even more than he used to. If he told Ethel Rae he was over his ears in debt, borrowing even more would mean he was—well, he'd be over the top of his head, wouldn't he? Where's the sense in that?'

'You're right – on the face of it, Bellamy was jumping out of the frying pan and into the fire. But maybe he thought Nicholson might be a bit more understanding than Rossetti was, and that could buy him time.'

'Yes, right, or maybe he just thought if he got Rossetti off his back, something might turn up to get him out of the scrape he was in – some cash, I mean.'

'That's possible, but then again perhaps Nicholson wasn't in too much of a hurry to get his money back – maybe his plan was to get a hold over Bellamy and then offer to let him off the hook in return for services rendered, as they say. In which case the question would be, what services?'

'Yes – and that could be very interesting, couldn't it?'

'We'll have to find out – we'll call on Mr Nicholson this morning, I think. But first we need to see Christine Edison – I want to know what she's got to say about her husband knocking her about, as Marjorie Bellamy so elegantly put it.'

'So we're going to her flat?'

'Yes.'

'But what if Edison's there?'

'I don't care. I want to find out from her, and if he's there I'll have a word or two with him too.'

They drove to the Edisons' flat in Broadwick Street. This time it was the man of the house who opened the door to them: he was unshaven and had a black eye, with a conspicuous bruise developing on his left cheek. He looked and sounded surly.

'What do you want?' he growled.

'A word with you, Mr Edison,' said Jago. 'Can we come in?'

Edison said nothing, but stood aside to admit them.

'You look like you've been in the wars,' Jago continued. 'Been turning the other cheek, have you?'

'Very funny, I don't think.'

'What's happened to you, then?'

'I don't know. I was on my way home from the pub last night, minding my own business, when someone jumped me, started having a go at me. He pushed me back against the wall and then laid into me. It was as much as I could do to fight him off.'

'Who was this?'

'I don't know, do I? It was the blackout – I couldn't see a thing, let alone take down a description of some bloke who's knocking seven bells out of me.'

'You're sure it was a man?'

'Course I am – no woman's ever landed a punch on me like that. Besides, I could tell by his voice.'

'What did he say?'

'Not a lot. He asked if I was John Edison. I said, "Yeah, what's it to you?" Then he just said, "You're going to get what's coming to you, then, mate," and punched me in the face.'

'Did you recognise the voice?'

'No – it was just a bloke's voice, but nobody I know. I'm no pushover, though – I gave as good as I got, and I reckon if you find him he'll have cuts and bruises all over him. He'll regret picking a fight with me.'

'Be careful how you go, Mr Edison – I'm sure you know there are some dangerous people in Soho.'

'Don't you worry about me, Inspector – I can look after myself. If he crosses my path again I'll knock his block off – teach him a bit of respect.'

Edison's words were brave, but his general demeanour suggested to Jago that he was still shaken by whatever had happened to him. And if what Marjorie Bellamy had told them about his violent treatment of his wife was true, a black eye like that might almost seem like a case of poetic justice.

'Is your wife at home, Mr Edison?'

'No, she's out, and before you ask, I don't know

where she is. Looks like she's cleared off – she's been moody for weeks now, moping around all day, not saying anything. I don't know what's wrong with her – off her rocker, for all I know. She'll be back with her tail between her legs soon enough, though – I know what she's like. She likes to get attention, does our Christine.'

'Are you concerned about her?'

'No, she'll be all right. She's probably just gone to have a moan with one of her mates – maybe they'll be able to knock some sense into her.'

'Is that what you've tried to do – knock some sense into her?'

'What do you mean?'

'I mean knocking her about, Mr Edison.'

'No, of course not.'

'Well, you just watch your step. If you have, and she's gone because she's had enough of it, you could find yourself in trouble.'

'I don't know what you're taking about.'

'I'm talking about the magistrates' court – if they hit you it'll be in the pocket, and I imagine that might hurt you more than a punch in the face. Good day, Mr Edison, and think about what I've said.'

Jago and Cradock left Edison to nurse his wounds and returned to the car. 'Where do you reckon Christine Edison's gone, then, sir?' said Cradock.

'I don't know, but I think we should find her – I'd like to get to the bottom of this.'

'Do you think Mrs Bellamy might know?'

'She's the most likely to – she's the one who's helped out with a bit of cash from time to time, so she must care about her. I think we should pop back to Mrs Bellamy's place before Edison comes to the same conclusion and goes round there himself to cause some more trouble. I don't like men who hit women, Peter. There's enough trouble in the world already, without good-for-nothing bullies who can't cope with life taking it out on their wives. If you ever marry that Emily of yours, you make sure you treat her with respect, right?'

'Yes, sir.' Cradock looked alarmed that his boss might think there was even a possibility of him doing otherwise.

'Good. Let's go, then.'

They drove to Peter Street, where Marjorie Bellamy looked surprised to see them. 'Back so soon, Inspector?' she said. 'You were here only yesterday evening – has something happened?'

'We just need to check something with you, Mrs Bellamy,' said Jago. 'After what you told us about your sister-in-law last night, about her husband being violent to her, we wanted to see her so we could hear her story at first hand. But we've just been to her flat, and he's there but she's not. He seemed to think she'd "cleared off", as he put it, but said he didn't know where to, so I thought you might perhaps be able to tell us where she's gone.'

'I see. Well, you'd better come in, gentlemen.'

She took them up to the flat but stopped at the door. 'Before we go in,' she said, 'there's something I must tell you. Christine's actually here, in the living room, but she's very upset, and I don't want you to make her even more so. You will be gentle with her, won't you?'

'Don't you worry, Mrs Bellamy – we just want to hear what she has to say. She's not in any trouble.'

'Very good, but I'll go in first to tell her you're here.'

She went into the room, leaving them standing outside the door, then returned and took them in. 'Here they are, Christine,' she said, as an apprehensive-looking Mrs Edison rose from the sofa.

'Good morning,' said Christine. 'Marjorie tells me you want a word. Can you tell me what this is about?'

'Yes, of course,' said Jago. 'It's nothing to be worried about. Do sit down, Mrs Edison.'

She resumed her place on the sofa, and Marjorie Bellamy sat beside her, motioning Jago and Cradock to take the other two chairs in the room.

'We've just been to your flat,' Jago continued, 'because last night we were talking to Mrs Bellamy and she mentioned that your husband had been violent towards you.'

Christine Edison looked alarmed and glanced round at Marjorie, who gripped her hand reassuringly. 'I'm sorry, dear,' said Marjorie, 'but I felt I had to confide in the inspector. I'm just concerned about what John might do to you one day when he's in one of his rages – when a man gets drunk he doesn't always know what he's doing, and the person who's closest to him is the one who suffers the whole brunt of it. I don't want you to be hurt just because he can't control his temper. I do hope you understand – I only meant to help you.'

Christine nodded and spoke quietly. 'Yes, I understand. It's just that I don't want him to know I've told anyone about what he does.'

Marjorie shot an anxious look in Jago's direction. 'Inspector,' she said, 'you told me you wouldn't tell him what I'd said. You didn't tell him, did you?'

'No, I didn't. I did use the information you'd given me, but I didn't mention your name.'

She looked relieved and sat back. 'Thank you.'

'Now,' said Jago, 'Mrs Edison – as I said, we've just been to your flat, and that was because I wanted to hear what you had to say about your husband's inclination to violence. I'd noticed what I thought were bruises on your wrists the last time we saw you, and not to put too fine a point on it, when I mentioned them to Mrs Bellamy she said your husband's not averse to knocking you about a bit when he's drunk. Is that true?'

'Yes. He's been like that for years now, on and off, but since he lost his job it's got worse. I think sitting around idle all day with time on his hands makes him frustrated, and he just gets into a rage. But that's no excuse, is it?'

'No, it isn't, Mrs Edison. Do you know whether he ever gets into the same sort of rage with other people?'

'Who do you mean?'

'I mean anyone – friends, family, acquaintances. Strangers, perhaps. Or is it just you?'

'I don't know. If he does, I haven't seen it, but then again, he comes and goes as he pleases, and half the time I don't know where he is or what he's doing, so I suppose it's possible.'

'Now, when we called round to see you this morning, you weren't there, of course, but your husband was. He looked in a pretty bad way – he had a black eye, and bruises on his face, and he said he thought you'd walked out. His precise words were "cleared off". Can you tell us any more about that?'

'All right. It was a bad day yesterday. He'd been in one of his moods ever since he got up, and then when I made his tea he didn't like it for some reason, and he clipped me round the ear, then went off to the pub for the evening. As soon as I'd cleared up the tea things I came round here and Marjorie looked after me.'

'You weren't here when we called on Mrs Bellamy yesterday evening. What time did you get here?'

'It must've been about seven o'clock. I stayed for a bit, but I made sure I went home about half past eight in case John came home early for some reason – I didn't want him to know I'd been out.'

'And what time did your husband get home?'

'About ten, I think.'

'When we saw him this morning he looked like a man who'd been beaten up. Was he in a similar condition when he got home last night?'

'Yes, he was.'

'He told us he'd been attacked in the blackout when he came out of the pub. Did he say that to you?'

'No he didn't – I just assumed he must've picked a fight with someone, but I know better than to ask questions when he's in that sort of state.'

'Drunk, you mean?'

'Yes – I hate what that stuff does to people. I tried to help him, but he got angry again and hit me – that was the last straw for me. Marjorie's always said if ever I felt in danger I should go round to her place straight away, so I did – as soon as he fell asleep I came round and spent the night here. I didn't leave him a note to say where I'd gone, because I was scared he'd come looking for me here and cause a scene or worse. I thought if he's in a mess it'll be of his own making, so he can stew in it – I've had enough. That's about all I can tell you.'

'Did he say anything else about what had happened yesterday evening?'

'No, but he obviously wasn't in a mood to talk about anything like that, and I wasn't going to ask what he'd been up to. My husband's a violent man, Inspector, and when he's been drinking, the slightest thing can set him off. But like I said, I've had enough now – I'm not going back.'

Marjorie Bellamy leant forward and stared at Jago as though she'd suddenly realised something important. 'Inspector, do you think he could—no, it's impossible. Surely he wouldn't have . . .'

'Who wouldn't have done what, Mrs Bellamy?'

'John, of course. I'm just thinking – he's so violent, so unpredictable. And Samuel being killed right here in this flat on the morning after that terrible air raid. I know John didn't get on with Samuel, in fact I think he despised him. They might have had an argument, got into a fight. It's quite possible, isn't it? He was much bigger and stronger, and Samuel wouldn't have been a match for him if they'd come to blows.'

'Are you saying—'

Marjorie interrupted him. 'Yes, I am – I'm saying do you think it's possible he killed Samuel?'

Jago turned to Christine. 'What do you think, Mrs Edison? Was your husband capable of such a thing?'

'Yes, I'd say he would be, especially if he'd been drinking. When he gets into that terrible violent rage he loses control, and I don't think anyone could stop him. He's strong enough to hurt Samuel badly, and if they got into a fight he'd have been very dangerous.' She paused. 'But wait a minute – Samuel was shot, wasn't he? John doesn't have a gun, I'm sure of it.' She paused again, as if getting her thoughts into order. 'In any case, Samuel was killed on Monday morning – that's what you said, wasn't it?'

'Yes, that's right.'

'Well, part of me wouldn't care any more if I couldn't provide him with an alibi, because he's a brutal monster. But the fact is he was with me at home all day on Monday. He was getting under my feet and making a nuisance of himself, but he was there, and I can't deny it – so it couldn't have been him who killed Samuel.'

'I see. And you're prepared to swear to that?'

'Of course – I'd have to, wouldn't I? It's the truth. I don't suppose you'll be able to lock him up for all the black eyes and bruises he's given me, though, will you? The police don't get involved in things like that between husband and wife, do they? So do I just have to go back and put up with it?'

'No, you don't – have you heard of the Married Women's Act?'

She shook her head.

'Well, that's a law – its proper name's a bit longer than that, but that's what it's usually known as. It doesn't make what your husband's done to you a crime, but it does say you have the right to summon him to the magistrates' court on the grounds of his assault or persistent cruelty, and if the magistrates see fit they can grant you a separation order and require him to pay you a sum of weekly maintenance. That's the best I can suggest, I'm afraid.'

'Right. Well, I shall have to think about that – I can't see John having enough spare cash to pay me maintenance, but either way I'm not going to put up with it any more. Marjorie's made me realise I don't have to, and she's said I can stay on here if I want to.'

'I'm sure that must be a relief to you,' said Jago. He turned his attention to her sister-in-law. 'Now, Mrs Bellamy, there's one last thing I'd like to ask you. As you've heard, John Edison came home last night looking much the worse for wear, and when we saw him this morning he looked as though he'd been in a fight. It's also clear that you've been very kindly looking after his wife, but what I'd like to know is whether your care for her went as far as arranging for him to have some form of violent retribution visited upon him last night. What do you have to say to that?'

She smiled at him. 'Well, I can see what you mean – it's quite a coincidence that he should be the victim of an attack so soon after Christine had to seek refuge here from his own violence. But it would be absurd to imagine that I could beat up a man like John Edison.'

'I'm not suggesting that you beat him up, Mrs Bellamy. I'm just wondering whether you might've called on the services of someone else, like maybe a man who you knew was good in a fight and might do you a favour.'

'I can't think what you mean, Inspector. I'm a publisher of religious books – the people I mix with may sing hymns about fighting the good fight, but I don't think any of them are actually expert pugilists.'

'Very well, Mrs Bellamy, I shall be pursuing my own enquiries on that front, and in the meantime I'd advise you to resist any temptation to take the law into your own hands. And I'm sure you must know all about temptation.'

Marjorie Bellamy gave Jago only an inscrutable smile in reply as he made his way to the door.

CHAPTER THIRTY-FIVE

'Pardon my ignorance, sir,' said Cradock as they left the flat, 'but that thing she said at the end – there was a bit I didn't understand. It sounded like "expert pugilists", but what's a pugilist?'

'It's a synonym, Peter,' said Jago.

'Like the stuff you get in hot cross buns at Easter?'

'No – that's cinnamon. A synonym's a word that means the same thing as another word, like large and big. Don't worry about it, though – I don't think I'd ever heard it until I was sixteen. That was back before the King required me to serve in his army in the war, and I was still a trainee reporter on the *Stratford Express*. One day the editor sent me to cover a boxing competition the Essex Beagles Club were holding at the Cathall Road Baths in Leytonstone. When I came back and wrote it up he went through it with his red pen and tore it to pieces, trying to knock it into some sort of half-decent shape. One of the things he told me was never to use the same word twice, so if I said "boxer" I shouldn't say it again in the next sentence but use something like "fighter" instead – or even something like "the popular East End pugilist".'

'And you knew what it meant?'

'No, of course not – but I knew what a dictionary was, so I went and looked it up. It said a pugilist was a boxer or a fighter – simple, eh?'

'So what Mrs Bellamy meant was she doesn't know anyone who's handy with their fists.'

'That's right. But we do, don't we? In fact he told us so himself, didn't he?'

'You mean Ron Fisher?'

'Well done – you got it in one. So what I want to know is whether she knows him better than she's been letting on. Let's go and see if he's at home.'

They found Fisher busy in his flat, sorting through a pile of books on the table. 'I'm sorry to interrupt you, Mr Fisher,' said Jago, 'but something's puzzling me, and I'm hoping you might be able to help me get it straight.'

'Yes, of course – this lot can wait. What is it you want to know?'

'It's about you and Mrs Bellamy. When her husband was murdered, she gave me your name and asked me to tell you what had happened.'

'Yes, that's right – she sent you round here, didn't she? I suppose she couldn't bring herself to break the news to me, seeing as how she knew what good mates me and Sam were.'

'I dare say – she said you were his oldest friend.'

'I reckon I was, yes.'

'And she knows where you live?'

'Yes, of course she does.'

'Well, that's the thing that's been puzzling me – you see, when she asked me to tell you what had happened to Mr Bellamy she said she didn't have your address. What do you make of that?'

'It is a bit odd, yes – but I suppose it was the shock. I mean, she'd just found out her Sam had been murdered, hadn't she? Chances are anything could slip your mind when you've just had news like that out of the blue. So how did you track me down, then?'

'Actually it was Mrs Edison who gave us your address.'

'Ah, right – so all's well that ends well, eh?'

'Not exactly. There's been a few developments overnight involving Mr and Mrs Edison, and Mrs Bellamy too, including an incident that didn't end particularly well, especially for John Edison. Do you know what I'm talking about?'

'Can't say I do, no – sounds like mumbo-jumbo to me. Can I have it in plain English?'

'Yes – Mr Edison says he was attacked on his way home from the pub last night.'

'Oh, poor bloke. Mind you, I don't need to tell you what it's like round Soho – there's places here where you take your life in your hands just walking down the street after dark, and now we've got the blackout too it's like a crooks' paradise. Was it robbers?'

'No, it doesn't seem that theft was the motive for the attack.'

'What do you reckon it was, then?'

'I'm not sure, but I'm beginning to wonder whether the man who attacked him was you.'

Fisher looked shocked. 'Me? No – you're barking up the wrong tree there, mate. But hang on a minute – I get it. You're investigating Sam's murder, and he was my old pal, and you reckon I've found out John Edison did it, so I jumped on him in the dark and gave him a thick ear. That's a bit feeble, though, isn't it? I mean, it's not exactly an eye for an eye, is it? If I'd attacked the man who killed my oldest friend, I'd be more likely to stab him or strangle him or something, wouldn't I?'

'I didn't actually say what Mr Edison's injuries were.'

'Ah, no, you didn't, did you? That's me jumping to conclusions then – please excuse me. So what were they, these injuries?'

'He was beaten up.'

'Beaten up by me? What makes you imagine that?'

'As you said, Mr Fisher, Samuel Bellamy was your oldest friend, and when we spoke to Christine Edison she told us he used to say you were the kind of friend you'd want to have with you in a fight. And you yourself told us you were handy with your fists. I think you'd be more than capable of beating a man up, especially under cover of darkness.'

'But it still doesn't make sense that any man would get off with a beating if he'd murdered someone, does it?'

'I'm not assuming this attack necessarily had anything to do with Mr Bellamy's murder, in fact I think it might be connected with the way John Edison treats his wife. Yesterday evening he was violent towards her, and she had to go and seek refuge with Mrs Bellamy. So I'm just wondering whether Mrs Bellamy contacted you and asked you to teach him a lesson. I doubt whether she'd know many men willing and able to do that.'

'Well, I suppose that's quite an interesting theory, Inspector. She could've asked me, I suppose, and I could've gone and had a word with him to show him the error of his ways. I might even have reinforced the message with a bit of what you might call physical correction, but even if I had, I don't suppose there'd have been any witnesses, would there? I mean, who'd be able to tell it was me in the blackout? I don't know anything about all this stuff you're telling me, of course, but I can't help thinking it sounds like he got what he deserved, so maybe it's best to let sleeping dogs lie. You're the policeman, of course, so it's up to you what you do, but it seems to me we'll probably never know.'

'Where were you yesterday evening, Mr Fisher?'

'I was here, at home, enjoying one of those bottles of Bass I told you about. It's a nice ale, isn't it?'

'Can anyone confirm you were here?'

'Only that bottle of Bass, Inspector – such is the life of a bachelor boy. There's nothing more I can say, really, is there?'

'I think you've told me all I need to know.'

'Really? That's good, then. And looking on the bright side, if that Edison fellow's had a bit of a going-over like you say, perhaps he'll be a reformed character now.'

'Perhaps he will, Mr Fisher – perhaps he will.'

CHAPTER THIRTY-SIX

'So you reckon it was Ron Fisher who gave John Edison that thrashing, do you, sir?' said Cradock when they were back in the car.

'It makes sense, doesn't it?' said Jago. 'He didn't exactly go out of his way to deny it, and he was definitely giving us the run-around with all that hypothetical "I could've gone and had a word with him" nonsense.'

'No alibi, either.'

'Yes, but why wouldn't a single man living alone be at home on his own on a Wednesday evening? He can't prove he was there, but no one else can prove he was out beating up Edison. There's no witnesses, and we didn't see it, so he knows we won't be able to charge him with anything. As far as I'm concerned that's an end to it – Edison's had a good dose of his own medicine now, and I reckon justice is served.'

'Case closed, then, sir?'

'Yes. Now we can get back to what I was originally planning to do this morning, and that's find out what George Nicholson has to say about so generously bailing out Bellamy from his debts. We'll go round to the Blue Palm and see if he's out of his bed.'

The club in Dean Street was as dismal a place of entertainment as it had been on their last daytime visit two days previously. When they entered the premises from the street, the air that met them was stale with the residual odour of the night's cigarette smoke, beer and sweat. George Nicholson looked more tired than he had the last time they saw him.

'Ah, you again,' he said flatly, as if resigned to being interrupted. 'More questions, or have you come to tell me you've found out who killed Samuel Bellamy and you won't need to take up any more of my time?'

'More questions, but the straighter your answers the quicker we'll be.'

'All right, then, what do you want to know now?'

'It's about money, Mr Nicholson. I understand you lent a large amount of it to Mr Bellamy recently to clear his debts.'

'What? Who told you that?'

'It was Mrs Bellamy, actually.'

'Oh, I see.'

'The lady originally known to you as Miss Marjorie Hayle, who helped you when you first came to this country. That's right, isn't it?'

He hesitated. 'Yes.'

'Now, we've been told that in 1921 you were a young soldier in hospital in Greece, wounded in the war with Turkey, and you were nursed by Miss Hayle. Is that correct?'

His voice was sullen. 'Yes, it is.'

'I have to say I'm surprised you didn't mention that fact before, Mr Nicholson. After all, here we are with Mr Bellamy shot dead in his own home, and you're a pal of his, and you don't think to mention that you knew his wife twenty years ago, before she married him? A man like me with a suspicious mind might think you were trying to hide something – and might wonder why. So why didn't you mention it?'

'I don't know – it just didn't seem relevant. Besides, I thought if I did, you might jump to conclusions and make something out of nothing, just like you're doing now. Really, it was nothing.'

'Now that's strange, because we've been told that when you were being nursed by Miss Hayle there was what's been described as an "association" between you and her. So tell me, please, what was the precise nature of your relationship with Mrs Bellamy when she nursed you in Greece?'

'What do you mean?'

'I think you know what I mean – how close were you?'

'Oh, I see. Well, look, I don't know who told you that – they must've got hold of the wrong end of the stick.'

'This information came from a reliable source, Mr Nicholson.'

'I don't care if it came from the King of England, it was just one of those things they call hospital romances. It happens all the time. I was eighteen, just a kid, and she was a good-looking young nurse looking after me. I might've had a bit of a crush on her, or maybe she did on me, but it didn't come to anything. She was idealistic – she thought the idea of me fighting for Greece was romantic, but I was thinking of how I could get out of Greece and make a good living for myself somewhere else. When I got better and the hospital discharged me I saw her a few times. That's all.'

'I see. And I believe the help she gave you when you came to England included some financial assistance.'

'Yes, that's right – she helped out a bit.'

'So she must've still cared about you enough to do that. Did you lead her on?'

'Lead her on? Certainly not. She offered me money, and I gratefully accepted it. That's all there was to it.'

'Lucky young man. And despite the fact that this relationship was nothing, as you say, when you arrived in England you came to live here in Soho, where she happened to live too.'

'Yes, but I came here because it was where my uncle Ioannis was – the fact that she lived here too was just a coincidence.'

'So what was the nature of your relationship after she got married to Mr Bellamy?'

'Look here, I'm not sure what you're getting at, but if

it's what I'm thinking it is, all I'll say is I've got nothing to hide – we were just old friends.'

'Does your wife know about this?'

'Well, no, I don't think she does – and I'd rather you didn't tell her, if you don't mind.'

'Why's that?'

'It's because I care about her. When you were here on New Year's Eve and she was talking about her previous convictions and all that she probably came across as a bit aggressive, but that's not what she's really like. Life hasn't been a bed of roses for her, by any account, but she's a strong woman, and I admire her for that. She grew up in an orphanage, so there was no silver spoon in her mouth – everything she is today is what she's made herself. That's the kind of man I am too, and that's why she's the wife for me and always will be. I don't want anything to come between us, and I don't want you putting the idea that I've been unfaithful into her head. Me and Marjorie, that was all years ago, and there was nothing in it.'

'But enough in it still for you to lend her husband a large sum of money at her request?'

'Look – we were old friends, like I just said. She asked me to do him a favour, and I said yes, for old times' sake. But that loan was a straightforward business arrangement – no strings attached.'

'Had Mr Bellamy repaid any of it before he died?'

'Well, I don't see what that's got to do with it, but since you ask, no, he hadn't. But I'm sure he would've done before long. Now, is that all you want? I've got a lot on my plate today, and I'd be obliged if you'd let me get on with my work.'

'I don't have any more questions for you, but I would like to have a word with your wife. Is she here?'

'Yes, she's in the office. But what do you want to talk to her about?'

'Nothing that you need to worry about, Mr Nicholson – as you said, she's a strong woman. I'm sure she can speak for herself.'

'She can do that all right, but I'm not having you talking to her behind my back – I'm coming with you.'

'That's fine by me – but I must remind you that she has every right to speak to me in confidence if she wishes to.'

'All right, but I'm still coming with you.'

Nicholson led them across the room to the office door and opened it. His wife looked up as they entered. 'Oh, good morning, Inspector, Constable. You're here again, then.'

'They want a word with you,' said Nicholson.

'And your husband wanted to be present, Mrs Nicholson,' said Jago. 'I've got no objection to that, but if you'd rather talk to us in private, you can.'

'Oh, that's all right,' she replied. 'We don't have secrets from each other, do we, George?'

Jago couldn't tell from her tone of voice, nor from her husband's grunt in reply, whether there was any trace of irony or sarcasm in her response. 'Very well, then,' he said. 'It's just a quick question – it's to do with Mr Bellamy and Miss Rae, your singer.'

'OK – what do you want to know?'

'I'm trying to establish what exactly was the nature of their relationship. When we spoke to you before you said you thought he was obsessed with her. That's quite a strong term to use – do you have any evidence to support it?'

'Only the evidence of my own eyes – and of his, for that matter. You know how people talk about men making puppy-dog eyes? Well, that's what I caught him doing – it looked to me like he was taking more than just a polite interest. I didn't say anything to him, of course – none of my business. But young Ethel works here, so the way I see it, she is my business. I think sometimes she feels like she's in a fight and the whole world's against her, and I know how that feels. So I had a quiet word with her, asked her what was going on, whether he was making a nuisance of himself, if you know what I mean. She said he was a bit, and it was getting on her nerves, so I gave her my standard advice.'

'Which is?'

'It's simple. Make it crystal clear you're not interested, do nothing to give him the impression you might be, and if that doesn't work, kick him where it hurts – that usually gets the message across.'

'And how did she take that?'

'She said not to worry – she'd come across his type before, full of themselves, and she'd been able to take care of them quite adequately, so she wasn't going to take any cheek from Samuel Bellamy. I said, "Good for you, girl." I think she can look after herself, that one.'

'Thank you. There's one other thing I'd like to check with you before we go.'

'Go on, then.'

'It's just that your husband happened to mention a minute or two ago that you'd grown up in an orphanage. Is that correct?'

'Yes, it is, but so what? Thousands of kids do – it's nothing to be ashamed of.'

'I'm not suggesting it is. I just wondered, as a matter of interest, what the name of the orphanage was.'

'It was Dr Barnardo's – his home for girls, in Barkingside. It's quite a famous place, I believe, and I've no regrets. You could say it made me the woman I am today. But what's it to you?'

'Well, it's probably nothing, but we were speaking to Miss Langley, who worked for Mr Bellamy, and she happened to mention that she'd been brought up in the Barnardo's orphanage at Barkingside too. I gather it was a big place, but I wondered whether you knew her. Her full name is Judith Langley.'

Ivy looked thoughtful for a moment. 'Ah, yes, little Judith – I do remember her. She was younger than me – a bit of a shrinking violet, as I recall.'

'She told us she was bullied.'

'Yes, now I remember. She wasn't having a very happy time there – I did what I could to help her, but I think she'd brought it on herself, I'm afraid. She was her own worst enemy – wouldn't say boo to a goose, and you know what it's like when you're that age. Those other kids, they can see straight away that you're weak.

But I think she got through it OK – no harm done in the end. So do you know Judith too?'

'Yes, we've met her recently.'

'Really? Oh, I'd love to see her again and catch up on old times. Where's she living these days?'

'Here in Soho – she works in Mr Bellamy's bookshop in Old Compton Road.'

'Well I never – fancy ending up so close again after all these years. I must go and visit her – we'll have so much to talk about. Do say hello from me if you see her – I hope she remembers me.'

'I'll do that. What was your name back then?'

'My name? Oh, yes, of course – my maiden name was Johnson, Ivy Johnson.'

'Thank you – that's all I need to know for now. We'll see ourselves out.'

Jago left the office, followed by Cradock, and closed the door on the Nicholsons. He wondered whether they'd be comparing notes on their respective conversations with him during the last few minutes. And if they did, how would George Nicholson handle his admission that his wife didn't know about his old friendship with Marjorie Bellamy in the light of Ivy's assertion that there were no secrets between them? Sometimes, he thought, it would be nice to be a fly on the wall.

CHAPTER THIRTY-SEVEN

They wove their way through the tables and chairs dotted round the floor of the now-deserted club and found the exit, where Jago grasped the door handle and pulled it towards him. As the door swung open, a familiar figure came into view: it was Ethel Rae, hurrying in their direction with one hand in her pocket and the other holding a woollen scarf tightly round her neck to keep out the cold.

'Hello, Inspector,' she said when she reached him. 'Looking for me, were you?'

He stood back to let her in and shut the door behind her. 'No – we've just been talking to Mr and Mrs Nicholson. But there is something I'd like to ask you, actually, if you've got a moment.'

'Yes, of course. What would you like to know?'

'Well, it's just something that Mrs Nicholson

mentioned a couple of minutes ago – she said she thought you feel as though you're in a fight and the whole world's against you. Is that true?'

'I suppose it is, yes – I've felt like that since I was a kid.'

'I don't want to intrude, but can you tell me why that is?'

'Yes, I can. I was moaning about something one day, like you do, and I think my dad was trying to help me get my life in perspective. Anyway, whatever the reason, he told me something that brought me up short. I told you he's from Trinidad, didn't I? So were his parents and grandparents before him, and you can probably guess for yourself they weren't sugar plantation owners. He said his grandparents were slaves. That stopped me in my tracks – I was shocked. They'd both died before I was born, but it brought it all so close to me. I think that made me a fighter – I won't let anyone do me down.'

'So is that what you meant when you said you love jazz because it lets you sing your pain?'

'It's part of it, yes. But it's because I can sing my freedom too, in a world that's not free. That's why Hitler hates jazz, because it's free – he banned it, didn't he? The Nazis say it's degenerate, so I suppose they'd say I'm degenerate too, but all I want is to live free.'

'In a world that's against you?'

'I don't mean every single person in the world's against me – that'd be silly. But the way the world works is definitely against people like me – it's full of people like him who want to push us around and bully us and make us their slaves. And they don't all live in Germany – there's plenty of them right here in Soho. The sooner this war's over the better, as far as I'm concerned, but I'm not a fool – there'll still be bad people around, and I'll still have to fight to be who I want to be.'

'Does it make you angry?'

'I guess it does, yes. But I sing that too – if there's passion in my singing, that's where it comes from. I hope that answers your question.'

'It does, yes – thank you.'

'So, you said you'd just been talking to George and Ivy – how were they?'

'How do you mean?'

'Oh, I was just wondering if they were still at loggerheads – I think they've got their own anger. When I was here the night before last I heard them having what sounded like a row.'

'Is that something they often do?'

'Not to my knowledge – not in the club, anyway. Maybe they wait till everyone's gone home, but I wouldn't know.'

'What were they arguing about?'

'I don't know – they were on the other side of a closed door, so it was muffled, but it sounded serious, raised voices and all that. I hung around for a moment, but then the door opened and George came out. When he saw me he looked angry and asked me what I was doing there, so I said I was just on my way to the ladies', which I was, and made off quickly like it was an urgent call of nature.'

'Do you think he knew you'd heard them?'

'I don't think so, but one thing I can tell you. Since then he's not been as friendly as he used to be – and he looks at me as though he's not sure about me.'

'Do you think he might suspect you of eavesdropping?'

'It wouldn't surprise me – he's got a suspicious mind. But I've no reason to listen at keyholes where he's concerned, and in any case, I couldn't make sense of anything I heard coming through that door. I imagine he's got his fair share of secrets in that mind of his – not to mention a few on his conscience, I dare say. Anyway, is there anything else I can help you with while you're here?'

'There is one thing, actually. You remember mentioning the day before yesterday those odd things you'd seen going on in the building next door – people coming and going in the night, and vehicles parked there?'

'Yes.'

'I just wondered whether you've seen anything similar since then.'

'No, not as I recall – but I only happened to see them when I was on my way home from work, and I don't hang around when I'm doing that, not at four o'clock in the morning in the blackout.'

'Have you mentioned it to Mr or Mrs Nicholson?'

'No – I thought best not to, not with it being right next door. They might know something about it, and I wouldn't want them to think I was snooping. You think it's something interesting, then, do you?'

'I'm not sure. Let's just say I've got a passing interest – call it a copper's curiosity.'

'Right, well, no one's ever mentioned it to me, so maybe I'm the only one who's ever seen anything a bit odd going on there. Let me see . . .' She thought for a moment. 'Just trying to rack my brains. What about that bloke who's always hanging around in the street outside? He might've noticed something.'

'Which particular person are you thinking of?'

'The one who sells matches – have you seen him?'

'Yes, I have actually. I've seen him, but I think there's just one problem – he can't see me. The poor man's blind, so he won't have noticed anything. Or do you mean he might've heard something?'

'No, I mean seen. Remember, Inspector, this is Soho – you have to take everything with a pinch of salt. Just because a man's got a white stick it doesn't necessarily mean he's blind. There are people round here who'll do anything to turn a penny, honest or dishonest, and there's rogues on every street corner.'

'There are plenty of honest men who were maimed in the Great War too, Miss Rae – you can't just lump them all together as rogues, even if it is Soho. They fought for us and paid dearly.'

'I'm sorry, Inspector. I don't mean any disrespect – that could've been my own dad you're talking about. But it's just that . . . well, sometimes you see something that makes you think things aren't quite what they seem.'

'What do you mean?'

'Well, I saw him in the street out there yesterday. He tapped his way to the kerb with that white stick of his, then stopped to cross the road. I think his mind must've been wandering or something, because next thing I knew, he was having a quick look both ways to check for traffic before he crossed. And when he got to the other side he pulled a watch out of his pocket to see what time it was. He may be an old soldier and earnt those medals of his, and if he is I say good luck to him. But I reckon that man's no more blind than I am.'

CHAPTER THIRTY-EIGHT

Ethel Rae took her leave of them and continued on her way into the Blue Palm, while Jago and Cradock stepped outside onto the pavement. Jago looked up and down Dean Street. 'Can you see him, Peter?' he said.

'See who, guv'nor?'

'That match seller of course – who do you think I'm talking about?'

'Sorry, sir.' Cradock glanced down the road. 'No – no sign of him.'

'Well, I want a word with him. I want to see that Judith Langley, too – if she and Ivy Nicholson go back a long way together, and they both knew Bellamy, I'm wondering whether there might've been more to that little triangle than they're saying. But as soon as we've done that we're coming back here to find out whether our blind war hero's been taking us for mugs.'

* * *

When they arrived in Old Compton Street there were no customers to be seen in Bellamy's Books. Judith Langley was running a feather duster along the bookshelves near the front of the shop and looked round when she heard them entering. 'Ah, good morning,' she said. 'What brings you back here?'

'Good morning, Miss Langley,' said Jago. 'I thought we'd drop in and bring you up to date on a recent development in our enquiries. But before we do that, I wonder whether I could make a quick call on your telephone.'

'I'm sure that'll be all right, yes. It's in the office – that little room down there at the back of the shop, as I think I mentioned when you were here before.'

'Thank you. Peter, wait here for a moment with Miss Langley – I shan't be long.'

Jago headed off down the length of the shop, made his call and returned. To Cradock's quizzical look he replied only with a terse 'I'll tell you later.'

'Success?' said Judith.

'Yes, thank you very much,' Jago replied.

'Good. So what was this development you wanted to tell me about?'

'Only a small matter, Miss Langley, but I thought it might be of personal interest to you.'

'That sounds intriguing – tell me more.'

'Well, it's just that we've discovered that someone we've been talking to as part of our investigation was at Barnardo's orphanage with you.'

'Oh, really? Who was that?'

'She's married now, but she said her maiden name was Ivy Johnson – she said she hoped you remembered her and she asked us to pass on her greetings.'

'Right, thanks.'

'So I take it she must be the bigger girl you mentioned who stepped in to protect you when you were being bullied. She said she was older than you and did what she could to help you.'

Judith gave a brief, bitter laugh. 'No, Inspector – you must've misunderstood. She was a bit older than me, but she wasn't the one who protected me. Ivy was horrible – she was strong and knew how to fight, and everyone knew not to get on the wrong side of her. She used to pick on people she thought wouldn't stand up to her, and I was one of them. Ivy Johnson was the girl who bullied me.'

'Ah, I see – that puts a different complexion on things. She said she'd love to see you again and catch up on old times.'

'Well, that shows she's a liar too – she's already been here, back before Christmas.'

'So she already knew you were here in Soho?'

'Yes – she must've found out somehow, because I certainly didn't know she lived round here. Is she something to do with Mr or Mrs Bellamy? You said you'd been talking to her as part of your investigation.'

'I believe she was acquainted with Mr Bellamy, yes.'

'Maybe he told her, then, but I don't know. And by the way, you said she was married – so what's her name now, then?'

'She's Mrs Nicholson now.'

'Right. She didn't tell me that when she came calling here.'

'I see. And when she came here before Christmas, was it for a catch-up on old times?'

'You could say that, I suppose. She didn't say anything about the way she'd treated me – just went on about those days at Barnardo's as if none of that had ever happened. She acted like she was concerned about me – asked me what it was like working here, how much I got paid and all that, and when I said it wasn't easy she said she'd like to give me a little gift to help out. She got her purse out of her handbag, and before I knew it she'd taken a couple of pounds out and put them in my hand. Two of those new blue pound notes. I thought maybe now she'd grown up she felt guilty about making my life hell and was trying to make up for it.'

'Did you accept the money?'

'Yes. At first I thought I should throw it back in her face and tell her to go to blazes, but then I thought that's two quid she's offering me, and with the state my finances are in I'd be a fool to turn it down. So I took it. But then she said something funny. She said would I like to make a bit of money on the side, so I said, "Maybe, how's that then?" I thought she was going to say would I come and do her cleaning for her or something, but she said she could sell me pound notes like that for five bob each, so every time I spent one I'd be making fifteen bob for myself for nothing.'

'And what did you understand that to mean?'

'Well, it was obvious, wasn't it? I said to her, "You mean these are fakes, then? What do you think I am?" She said, "I think you're an intelligent woman who's not getting paid what she deserves, and bright enough to know an opportunity when she sees it." She said, "Look at those notes and tell me whether they're fakes or not," so I had a look and to be honest I couldn't tell. "They're good, aren't they," she said. I had to agree, so I said, "Yes, all right, it's a deal."'

'How many notes did you buy?'

'I haven't bought any yet. I had the two she'd given me, and I thought I'd better work out how many I could use before I bought any more.'

'What did you do with those two notes?'

She looked down, then raised her eyes to meet his. 'I reckoned Mr Bellamy owed me, so I decided I'd put them in the till and take out two of the old green ones. That way I'd have two pounds of real money straight away.'

'And you gave the blue ones out in change?'

'No – I couldn't bring myself to cheat one of my own customers. I thought I'd leave them in the till, and then if he banked them or spent them it'd be his problem.'

'Did you give out any other blue pound notes in change to your customers before this visit of hers?'

'Well, yes, of course – they've been out for months now, haven't they? But I had no idea there were fakes going round too. I couldn't even tell those ones that Ivy gave me weren't the real McCoy until she told me. I'm very sorry if I did, though.'

Jago acknowledged her apology with a brief pause

but made no comment on it. 'Does anyone else know about this "deal" of yours with Mrs Nicholson?'

'No. When I said I'd do it, she made me swear not to tell anyone she'd been here or that I'd had any contact with her – said it had to be our little secret. Then she got hold of my chin and tweaked it from side to side as if I was some little kid. I hated that. It was like she was trying to humiliate me, but I'm grown up now, and it doesn't work like it used to when I was a child. I just ignored her. But I did keep it secret – I only made one exception.'

'Who was that?'

'Mr Bellamy. It was on my conscience, and in the end I told him what'd happened and what I'd done with the two notes she gave me.'

'And what did he say?'

'Well, that's the funny thing – he didn't seem too bothered. It was as if he already knew all about it – what Ivy was up to, I mean. I still can't puzzle that out, and now he's dead I suppose I'll never know.' She paused, then looked at Jago with anxious eyes. 'But tell me, Inspector – am I in trouble?'

'That depends, Miss Langley,' he replied. 'It depends on whether you're telling me the truth. I'll be back, but in the meantime if you think of anything else you should've told me but didn't, I'd like to hear from you. Goodbye.'

She opened the door for Jago and Cradock and stood back for them to pass. The anxiety was still in her eyes as they left.

CHAPTER THIRTY-NINE

'That was interesting, sir,' said Cradock as he and Jago got back into the car. 'The way that conversation was going with Judith Langley back there, I thought we'd be taking her down to the nick. But I was a bit surprised we didn't arrest her – did you believe her?'

'Not necessarily, Peter, but at the moment I'm inclined to give her the benefit of the doubt – she might just be caught up in the middle of something bigger. The main reason why I didn't arrest her, though, is simply that we're a bit thin on evidence.'

'What about those blue pound notes Mrs Quincy brought in for us? She said Judith Langley gave them to her as change at the bookshop, and when we took them to that bloke at the Bank of England he said they were both fakes.'

'Yes, but she also said that was a few weeks ago, so

it was before Ivy turned up in the shop and offered to sell Judith counterfeit notes on the cheap. I'm sure you know what the Forgery Act 1913 says on the subject, don't you?'

'Er, not word for word, sir.'

'It says it's an offence to utter any forged document – which in this case includes something like a banknote – knowingly and with intent. And before you ask, I don't know why it says "utter" either – I think it's just an old word for passing off a forgery as legal tender. The point is, if Judith Langley's telling the truth, when she gave Daphne Quincy those two notes in her change, she didn't know they were counterfeits, so she didn't do it knowingly and with intent. And we haven't got any evidence that she did, so until we do, she's off the hook. Even the Quincy woman said she assumed Miss Langley must've accepted the notes in good faith from an earlier customer, so she obviously wasn't accusing her.'

'But Miss Langley did know the ones Ivy Nicholson gave her were counterfeits, because she told her they were – and she put those in the till and took two real ones out.'

'Yes, you're right. If she'd gone out with those fake notes and spent them somewhere else, that would've been knowingly and with intent, and she'd have committed an offence. And if Samuel Bellamy didn't know anything about these counterfeits, we might've been able to argue that she'd deliberately uttered them to him, to deceive him. But she says her conscience got the better of her and she told him, so she wasn't deceiving him. So all in all, if she's telling the truth, I don't think we've got enough evidence to charge her.'

'And Samuel Bellamy's not in a position to tell us she's lying.'

'Exactly. Now, while we're discussing this little visit of ours to the bookshop, I expect you're also wondering why I had to make a phone call from in there.'

'Me, sir? No – I just thought you, er, wanted to make a phone call.' He thought it would be unwise to confess what he'd actually been wondering: whether his boss had perhaps needed the phone for some private communication with the American journalist lady. 'I thought it might be none of my business, sir.'

'I appreciate your fine sense of discretion, Peter, but there was something I wanted to know. Like I said to Ethel Rae, I've been getting a bit curious about what's going on in that supposedly empty property next door to the Blue Palm, so I rang the Land Registry to find out who it belongs to.'

'Good idea, sir,' Cradock replied. 'What did they say?'

'They said it's registered in the name of a Mr George Nicholson. That's not an unusual name, of course, but the address they've got for him is the same as the Blue Palm Club's, so I reckon it must be our Mr Nicholson. Interesting, eh?'

'Yes – so do you think he's setting up some new dive in the basement, like she said?'

'I've no idea what he's up to, but I want to find out. Let's go and see whether that match seller's back on his pitch yet.'

* * *

They returned to Dean Street, and this time they were in luck: they found the man in question perched on the stone window ledge of a boarded-up building.

'Good morning,' said Jago. 'I don't know whether you remember my voice, but I was here the day before yesterday and bought a box of matches from you.'

The man looked up and turned his head towards Jago. 'Yes, I think I do,' he said, getting to his feet. 'By the sound of it, you're the kind gentleman who gave me half a crown for a penny-ha'penny box of matches that by rights should never've been more than a penny in the first place. I don't forget a kindness like that. Good morning to you, sir. I was just sitting here for a moment to rest my legs – feeling my age, I think. But we're none of us getting any younger, are we? Still, mustn't grumble – I get by for food, I've got somewhere to lay my head at night, and I haven't been bombed yet. And there's one consolation for not being able to see – unlike most people these days I don't have any trouble with the blackout. It's no challenge for me – I've been walking around in my own personal blackout for years now.'

'Yes, so I gather. But while we're on the subject of challenges, that's something I'm going to have to challenge you on.'

'What are you getting at?'

'It's a simple matter – a witness told me they'd seen you looking both ways before you crossed the road.'

'A witness? Are you a copper?'

'Yes, I am – Detective Inspector Jago.'

'Oh, blimey – that's done it. But you're still an old soldier too, right?'

'Yes, I am.'

'All right, then. Yes, I admit it – I pretend a bit. But I don't mean any harm by it. Thing is, you see, this little act helps me sell a few matches, and without that I don't know where I'd be. I had a touch of shell shock in the war and I still have troubles – you know what I mean? I can't hold down a proper job, because every so often I sort of go to pieces a bit, I get upset and all that. Do you understand what I'm talking about?'

'I do, Mr . . . ?'

'The name's Willis. I'm very sorry – are you going to nick me?'

'No, I'm not. Look, Mr Willis, I haven't come here to make trouble for you. I know shell shock's just as much a wound as losing your sight, whatever the army said at the time. I'm here for another reason.'

Willis took his dark blue glasses off. 'Well, that's a relief – thanks. But that's exactly the point, isn't it? If I hang a sign round my neck saying "shell shock casualty" no one's going to take a blind bit of notice— oh, I'm sorry, that wasn't quite the right thing to say, was it? But they wouldn't, would they, because they wouldn't understand. But a man with a white stick and his medals on his coat, well, they can see straight away he must've been wounded in the war and lost his sight. I'm wounded all right, so I reckon I'm justified.'

'I can understand that.'

'You're a real gentleman, sir. I could tell you were

when you gave me that half-crown. I mean, what does that work out at?' He screwed up his face in concentration. 'Two and six, that's twenty-four plus six – that's thirty pence, so at a penny-ha'penny a box that means you gave me, what, enough to buy twenty boxes of matches. Thirty boxes if we're talking before the budget. You know, you wouldn't credit it, but there's some miserable skinflints out there who slip me a useless coin like an Irish penny, not worth anything, just because they think I'm blind – and I can't say a word about it because then they'll know I can see it. It makes you wonder what we fought for, doesn't it? But look, you're an old soldier. I've got a pedlar's certificate, so I'm not breaking the law – do you think you could turn a blind eye to this little lark of mine?' He stopped. 'Oh, lumme, I've done it again, haven't I? What I mean is, could you see your way to doing a good turn to an old comrade and let me off? I can't afford to get arrested – I'll lose my certificate.'

'Don't worry, Mr Willis – I don't have any wish or intention to get you in trouble. I'm not going to arrest you, report you or charge you. But there is a small favour you can do for me.'

'Of course – what is it?'

'I'd just like to know if you've noticed anything going on in that building over there next to the Blue Palm Club. It's empty, but I understand people have been seen coming and going there in the night.'

'I don't know about the night – if I went round selling matches in the blackout, it'd be just my luck if some idiot struck one to check his change. Then one of your lads would be hauling him up before the magistrates to be fined, and I'd probably be arrested for assisting the enemy, wouldn't I? But in the daytime, yes, that's different – I have seen at least one bloke coming and going there quite recently, as it happens.'

'Did you recognise him?'

'No, sorry – it was no one I know.'

'Can you describe him?'

'Yes – average height, bit of a stoop, getting on a bit I'd say.'

'Anything else?'

'Yes – he had a stick, like me, but not white like mine, just the ordinary type old blokes use for walking. His hair, though, that's another matter – white as snow, that was, and a bit long, over his collar.'

'That's very helpful, Mr Willis – thank you for your assistance.' An image of Detective Superintendent Hardacre came unbidden into his mind. 'But a word of advice – you might be wise to review this little act of yours, as you call it. Some of my colleagues might take a stricter view about how and when to exercise their discretion. Do you understand what I'm saying?'

'Yes, Inspector – I can, er . . . see what you mean.'

CHAPTER FORTY

There was only one man Jago knew of who had white hair over his collar and a connection with the Blue Palm Club, and that was a man who more than likely favoured that style as a personal tribute to William Blake. It could, of course, be anyone, but until he was proved wrong his money was on Mr Ioannis Dimitriou. He and Cradock left the hapless match seller and went straight to Dimitriou's home in Greek Street.

'Hello, gentlemen,' said Dimitriou when he opened his door to them. 'How nice to see you again. Won't you come in?'

They crossed the threshold, and Jago pushed the door shut behind them. Dimitriou showed them into the living room. 'How can I help you?'

'Just a question, if you don't mind,' said Jago. 'I'd like to ask you something about Samuel Bellamy.'

'Of course. Do sit down. What do you want to know?'

'It's to do with something we were told yesterday. We were talking to someone who knew Mr Bellamy and who wasn't very complimentary about him – he said he was a "my country right or wrong" kind of person, with an unshakable sense of Britain's superiority over other nations. Was that your impression of him?'

'I think so, yes. He was what I think of as a typical British imperialist, who thinks it's a good thing that Britain rules over a quarter of the world and who likes boasting that its writ runs to every city in India and to African villages from Cape Town to Cairo. I suppose that was just his way of being patriotic – I remember him saying just before the war that the British Empire would make twenty-nine Germanies and that we shouldn't have an inferiority complex, so perhaps the logical response in his mind was to have a superiority complex. I think he was the kind of man who prefers to look back rather than forward – Britain's glorious past and all that. Maybe that's why he liked all those old books, because he wanted to live in the past. But that's not unusual – there are Greeks who think that way too, and certainly Italians.'

'Yes – it was actually an Italian gentleman that we were speaking to, and he certainly seemed to have strong views about the glories of ancient Rome. I believe you know him – Mr Rossetti. He runs a cafe in Frith Street. He said you'd been in there with Mr Bellamy, but he hadn't seen you for a few months.'

'Ah, yes, Mr Rossetti,' said Dimitriou grimly. 'I don't suppose he said why.'

'No, he didn't.'

'Well, when he says a few months, he means since last October. We had an argument, and I haven't set foot in there since.'

'An argument about what?'

'About what happened in October. It may not be as deeply impressed on your memory as on mine, but that was when Italy invaded my country. They said Greece had been giving too much support to Britain in the war and demanded that we let them occupy some of our territory. They even had the nerve to say their troops would not be arriving as enemies of the Greek people, and at the same time said that if we offered any resistance they would put it down by force of arms. Well, they tried, and we fought back. We pushed them back to the border with Albania, where they'd come from, and we're still fighting, with your help. Your king sent a message to my king, saying, "Your cause is our cause." Our army may be small, but it's brave, and it's fighting fiercely because it's defending our home.'

'I assume the argument was because Mr Rossetti took the Italian side?'

'Oh, yes. He was adamant that Italy was in the right and that the Greeks had brought it on themselves. I didn't want to discuss it any further with him then, and I haven't spoken to him since.'

'Do you know whether he ever discussed this with Mr Bellamy?'

'Yes, he did – Samuel told me they'd had a big row about it, almost came to blows.'

'Hmm . . . interesting. Thank you for that. Now, there's something else I've just been told that I want to ask you about, and it's a matter that concerns you.'

'I see – have I done something wrong?'

'That depends. A man answering your description has been seen entering the premises next door to your nephew's nightclub. What were you doing in there?'

'Ah . . . well, I shan't lie to you. My nephew needed a little help, and so I was, er . . . helping him.'

'And what form did this help take?'

'I'd rather not say.' Dimitriou paused, then continued hesitantly. 'I'm not a well man, Inspector. I'm old and I don't have long to live. You know what it says in the Bible – "The days of our years are threescore years and ten . . . and then we fly away." And then it says, "So teach us to number our days, that we may apply our hearts unto wisdom." Well, I've been numbering my days recently, and there are not many left. I don't just mean I'm well past those threescore years and ten that we're supposed to have – I mean I'm ill, seriously ill. I've done some good things in my life, and some bad things, and now I don't know whether I'm a good man or a bad man. Does anyone know?'

Jago said nothing.

Dimitriou sighed. 'You probably think I'm just an old man with too much time on his hands, and maybe I am, but I've been thinking a lot. You know, sometimes when there are no bombs falling I go outside and stare at the sky

– not watching for aeroplanes but just looking at the stars. That's perhaps the only good thing about the blackout – it means on a clear night you can see so much more of what's out there, stretching on for ever. I think about this world of ours, just a tiny dot in a vast universe, and London just a tiny dot on this planet, and me just a tiny dot in London. And that makes me think why do I worry about my petty concerns and grievances, why do we fight over scraps of land, why do we kill each other – all the terrible things that we do in this world. Maybe it's because I'm Greek – we love our philosophers, don't we? But maybe it's just because I'm human. I'm not a good man, Inspector, and I live in a world of violence, greed and lies. But when I make one of my icons I feel that I'm painting truth itself – that little Christ-child, the one who said, "I am the truth." And when I look at that night sky and all those stars, I know that truth exists. All through that universe, whatever it's made of and no matter how big it is, it's true – there's truth in every atom of it. Yes, I live in a world of lies, but when I paint I'm being true, and that comforts me. I'm tired of this world and its lies. I'm old now and I know I don't have long to live. I don't have to fear any Bow Street magistrate, but soon I shall face my Creator and be judged by truth itself.'

'But you've told us the icons you paint are fakes. Isn't that a form of lying?'

'You tell me, Inspector. I've told you the truth, haven't I? Is it still a lie if I've told you? I admit what I've done, but I only made those icons so I could pay my way and help my nephew – he's the only family I have. I love my nephew, and I admire him as someone who came to this country with nothing and made a success of himself against all the odds. I admire his wife too, because she's made of the same stuff. Did you know she's an orphan?'

'Yes, I do, but I don't know anything more, except that she was brought up in a Barnardo's home.'

'Well, let me tell you. She had nothing too, just like George – her father was a poverty-stricken German waiter working in a grubby little hotel in King's Cross. He could barely survive on the pittance he was paid and got tuberculosis, and she ended up in an orphanage. But she's worked hard and made a success of herself too, and I commend her for that.'

'That's interesting – I didn't know she had a German background.'

'Don't think badly of her for that – it's only an accident of birth, as they say. She still has relatives there, even a cousin of some kind who's a highly placed Nazi, I believe, but that doesn't make her a Nazi. If you asked her, I don't think she'd deny it – she doesn't tell lies about herself. She's had a colourful life, and I'm sure she'd be the first to tell you she's been in trouble with the law over the years. At least she's honest about it, and I admire that. I don't want to tell you any lies either. But there's a question I can't find an answer to – is it wrong to use a gift to create beauty if that very beauty itself can become an instrument of wrongdoing?'

The fact that Ivy Nicholson had German connections, if true, was news to Jago, and he made a mental note to pursue it with her as a matter of urgency, but first he wanted to cut through the Greek man's philosophising and find out what was really happening in the building next to the Blue Palm Club. 'Is this a theoretical question,' he replied, 'or does it concern something real in your own life?'

'It's real, Inspector. I think I've used my craft to do things that are wrong – or rather I should say to help someone else to do things that are wrong.'

'Are you talking about your nephew?'

He whispered. 'Yes, I am.'

Jago held his gaze. 'I know you've done good things for him. Are you saying you've done bad things for him too?'

Dimitriou bit his lip and looked down. 'Yes,' he said.

'Tell me.'

There was a silence while the Greek man seemed to be struggling with how best to reply, but eventually he spoke. 'When George came to this country he wanted to be a success. He'd had enough of living in poverty, but when he came here he found it cost even more to live than it did in Greece. That's why I helped him – I've never been a rich man, but I gave him what I could to help him start a business. As far as I know, that club of his has been a success, but there are always bills to pay, and I think he still struggles with money. He came to me recently and said he and Ivy were having some financial difficulties.'

'That's curious – I understand your nephew lent a large sum of money to Samuel Bellamy, so where did that come from if they were in difficulties? Do you know anything about that?'

'No, I'm afraid I don't. But that would be none of my business – all I know is what George told me. I think he said it was to do with some changes they'd had to make to the way the club operates – he said their turnover and profits had gone down as a result. I didn't need to know the details. As I told you before, family is very important where I come from – my nephew needed help, so I said yes.'

'Right, so let me ask you again – what form did this help to your nephew take?'

'He tried to make a joke of it, I think – he said he needed to make some money, but then he said he meant it literally, and I could see he was deadly serious. He wanted to print banknotes, and he asked me if I could engrave the plates for him. It's not something I would have chosen to do to make money for myself, but in my mind it seemed like making those icons – I was doing it for nothing, as a gift to my nephew out of my love and concern for him, and it was up to him what he did with them.'

'Even though you must know that making counterfeit banknotes is a criminal offence?'

Dimitriou smiled. 'Yes, Inspector, I do know, and I know my reasoning may sound very flawed to you. But as I mentioned earlier, I have a serious illness and I'm not long for this earth, and I also know that the wheels of justice move slowly in this country. I've had a good life, and I really don't mind if you arrest me – I've done my duty to my family, and that's all that matters to me. It's for you to decide whether I've committed a crime. I don't know whether I can persuade you that I'm not a criminal, and I won't try to argue my way out of my responsibility, but I will say only this. I haven't killed anyone, I haven't stolen anything, and I haven't tried to harm anyone – I'm an artist, and my only desire and duty is to produce the best art that I possibly can. As William Blake himself said, "I will not reason and compare: my business is to create."'

'I'm sorry to hear that, Mr Dimitriou,' said Jago. 'But unfortunately I have a duty that I must fulfil too. I'm arresting you on suspicion of engraving words and devices resembling those on Bank of England notes, without lawful authority or excuse. I must ask you now to come along with me.'

'Yes, Inspector,' Dimitriou replied, his voice sounding old and tired. 'I understand. I had my job to do, and now you have yours.'

CHAPTER FORTY-ONE

Dimitriou went meekly to the car with the two detectives and made no further comment on the way to West End Central police station, where they handed him over for charging. Once he was off their hands, it was clear to Jago that Cradock was bursting to say something. 'What's on your mind, Peter?' he said, his eyebrows raised sympathetically.

'I was just wondering – are you thinking what I'm thinking, guv'nor?'

'I don't know – I'm often uncertain about what exactly you're thinking.'

'Well, it's obvious, isn't it? Ivy Nicholson.' He paused for effect, but Jago only waited patiently for him to continue. 'Judith Langley said she was the one who was trying to talk her into giving out those fake banknotes, didn't she, and now it turns out our Ivy had a German dad and she's got a cousin who's a Nazi. And that stuff Mr Ford said about a Nazi plot to flood the country with forged notes – maybe what they're mixed up in is all part of that.'

'It's possible, on the face of it,' said Jago, 'although I don't think passing two or three dud pound notes is quite the same thing as flooding the country. I had made the same connection myself when Dimitriou mentioned the German side of the family, but as he might say himself, that doesn't necessarily mean it's a true connection. After all, what Mr Ford described was a very big operation. But still, on the other hand small things are often part of something bigger, so it's a fair point and we must keep it in mind. For the time being, I think we should simply report it to Mr Ford – if it's part of a German plot to undermine the British economy, it's definitely more up his street than ours. The days when we might've rung up the police in Berlin to ask for a bit of helpful cooperation are long gone.'

'Yes, I see, sir. But I've just thought – what about that thing Bellamy told Ron Fisher he'd come across, the thing he called a little gem that he thought was going to make him a packet of money. Supposing that wasn't anything to do with rare books or whatever – I mean, he'd found out Ivy Nicholson's secret, hadn't he? Judith Langley said she'd been sworn to secrecy about those fake banknotes and she hadn't told anyone – except him. Suppose this forgery business really is linked up with the Nazis and Bellamy knew she was involved? He must've thought his ship had come in – he could blackmail the Nicholsons and threaten to expose them unless they coughed up

335

some cash. Maybe he reckoned that little gem was going to be his meal ticket – he could bleed them dry.'

'Well,' said Jago, 'that is an idea – good thinking, Peter. It might explain why Nicholson was so ready to lend a lot of cash to Bellamy. We'll have to ask him, won't we? Let's pop back to the Blue Palm and see if he's still there.'

They left immediately, drove to Dean Street and parked outside the club. The front door was locked, but they rang the bell, then stood waiting in the cold for a couple of minutes until it opened. Ivy Nicholson looked surprised and a little irritated to see them.

'What do you want now?' she said. 'You've only been gone five minutes. We do have a business to run, you know.'

'We want a quick word with you and your husband, Mrs Nicholson,' said Jago. 'It won't take long if you give us some straight answers.'

'Charming,' she replied. 'In you come, then. George is in the office.'

She took them to him, and the four of them sat facing each other in the small room they'd left only hours previously.

'What is it you want to know, then?' said Nicholson.

'A simple question to start with. Do you own the building next door?'

'Maybe.'

'You don't sound very sure about that. I must say I'm surprised – the people at the Land Registry seem to be in no doubt. They say it's a freehold property and it's registered in the name of a Mr George Nicholson of this address, and to me that sounds very much like you. Do you have any comment to make on that?'

'Well, all right, then, yes, I do own it, but so what?'

'I understand there's been some activity occurring there of late, particularly in the night. What's going on in there?'

'Nothing – it's been empty since before the war started. Whoever told you that must've been mistaken. We don't use it.'

'Well, we can soon find out whether that's correct or not. I'd like to have a look inside that building – shall we go?'

'No – it's not convenient right now. Can you come back next week?'

'So you can do a little tidying up first? Very considerate of you, but that won't be convenient for me. In fact right now is exactly when it would suit me best.'

'No,' said Nicholson, with a new note of anxiety in his voice. 'You can't go in there without a search warrant.'

'And you imagine a justice of the peace would have any reluctance about granting me one? You sound worried, and that makes me think there's something in there you don't want me to see.'

'Well, that's where you're wrong – there's nothing to see. I've got nothing to hide.'

'In that case you won't mind me having a look.'

Nicholson gave a sigh and a resigned nod of the head. 'All right, then – but there's nothing to see in there except a load of old junk.'

He pulled out a bunch of keys from the desk drawer, then he and his wife took Jago and Cradock to the next-door property and let them in. The first room they entered on the ground floor was consistent with what Nicholson had predicted. The daylight outside struggled through the grimy window to reveal a few wooden desks and filing cabinets that suggested it had once been some kind of office, and the thick dust and cobwebs that covered every surface in sight gave the impression that it hadn't been used for months, if not years.

'There you are,' said Nicholson. 'Like I said, nothing to see. Do you want to see the rest upstairs now?'

'No, I don't think so.'

'Shall we go back, then?'

'No. Does this place have a basement?'

There was a brief silence, then Ivy Nicholson spoke, tight-lipped. 'Yes.'

'I think we'll go down there, then.'

The Nicholsons looked reluctant but took them to a door towards the rear of the property and opened it to reveal a narrow staircase going down. Ivy flicked a switch at the top, and an electric light came on at the foot of the stairs. At Jago's bidding they led the way down into the basement and switched on a second light to illuminate the space.

'Well,' said Jago, 'this is nice and clean – someone's been busy dusting down here.' He waved a finger round the room. 'So what's all this stuff?'

Nicholson's voice was sullen. 'It's just old junk we're storing for my uncle.'

'Mr Dimitriou?'

'That's right. He had a load of stuff left over when he retired from his business and he didn't want to get rid of it – he thought he might be able to sell it to someone younger setting up in the same line, but the war knocked that idea on the head. He asked us if we could store it for him, and we said yes.'

'Very good of you, I'm sure. You've certainly looked after it well – he told me he'd retired some years ago. I think he said his business was printing – is that correct?'

'Yes.'

'So that would explain what looks like a printing press over there – I am right, aren't I? It is a printing press?'

'Yes.'

'And it looks clean enough to be used today. Let's have a little look round.' Jago examined the area around the press. 'Here's paper, I see, and inks – it certainly looks as though there's everything here to run a small printing business. Are you sure your uncle hasn't come out of retirement?'

Nicholson was silent, and his wife looked the other way. Jago moved on to a workbench and scanned the shelf on the wall behind it. 'Now that's interesting,' he said. He picked up a cloth from the workbench and used it to take a glass-stoppered bottle from the shelf. He held it up so they could see the label on it. 'It says "nitric acid". Dangerous stuff to have around, but a man who knows a lot more about printing than I do told me yesterday this is what engravers use when they etch their plates. This man works at the Bank of England, actually.' He replaced the bottle carefully on the shelf. 'I believe your uncle was trained as an engraver, wasn't he? Just like William Blake,' he said. 'I wonder whether—' He broke off as he noticed a flat wooden box a little farther along the shelf.

He heard a snatched breath coming from Ivy Nicholson as he took the box down from the shelf and placed it on the workbench. He removed the lid and breathed his own sigh of satisfaction. In the box lay a copper plate engraved with what was, to his untrained eye, a perfect mirror-image representation of a Bank of England pound note.

'Well, well,' he said, showing the open box to the Nicholsons. 'What have we here?'

'I don't know,' said Ivy. 'Looks like a bit of metal.'

'And you, Mr Nicholson?'

'Never seen it before.'

'I'll tell you what I think it looks like,' said Jago. 'I think it's the kind of thing someone might've made if they wanted to print some counterfeit banknotes, and I'd like to know more about it. So I must caution you that you are not obliged to say anything, but anything you say may be given in evidence. I'd also advise you not to try wasting my time.' Their faces betrayed no clue to what they might be thinking. 'There's a couple of things I'd particularly like to ask you. Firstly, Mr Nicholson, is that why your uncle, Mr Dimitriou, has recently been seen entering this building?'

'What? Of course he hasn't – what makes you think that?'

'Simple – we have a witness. Has your uncle been creating plates so you can forge banknotes?'

'No. Look, this is nothing to do with him – leave him out of it. He's just a harmless old man.'

'I'm afraid I don't believe you. The fact is Mr Dimitriou is currently under arrest, and he's already told us that that's exactly what he was doing.'

Nicholson's shoulders dropped. 'Silly old fool,' he muttered. 'He never did know when to keep his mouth—'

'George!' Ivy interrupted him, spitting out her rebuke. 'You keep your own mouth shut. You heard what the man said – you don't have to say anything.'

'Actually, Mr Nicholson,' said Jago, 'I think it's pretty clear the game's up, and I think you can see that now, can't you?'

Nicholson pursed his lips in resignation and nodded his head.

'My husband's a fool,' said Ivy bitterly to Jago, and for the first time since he'd met her he thought she might be on the brink of tears. 'But this has got nothing to do with me – whatever was going on in here, it was just him and his uncle, not me.'

'I beg to differ, Mrs Nicholson. Judith Langley's told us you offered to sell her counterfeit banknotes. Do you know what I'm talking about now?'

'It's not true – she's lying. She's got a grudge against me and always has done, ever since we were kids in that blasted orphanage. She tried to make trouble for me then and she's doing the same thing now.'

'The way she tells the story, the boot was on the other foot. You were the one causing trouble – she says you bullied her.'

'Nonsense.'

'Is that why you reckoned you could bully her again now? You thought she'd do whatever you told her to with those banknotes, didn't you?'

'I don't know what you're talking about.'

'I think you know exactly what I'm talking about. And while we're on the subject of your childhood in that orphanage, there's another small matter that I'm interested in. I understand your family background's German, and that you still have relatives in Germany. Nothing wrong with that, of course, but I've also been told that one of them happens to be high up in the Nazi Party, and that I do find interesting. Is this counterfeiting you've been involved in connected with them in any way?'

'Look, this is mad – I told you it's nothing to do with me. Are you trying to persecute me just because my poor old dad was German? It's ridiculous.'

'Ridiculous or not, I have some colleagues who I think will be interested in exploring that with you in more detail, so you may find yourself having to explain it to them.'

She shrugged her shoulders and turned away from him.

'And now, Mr Nicholson,' said Jago, 'I've got a question for you.'

'Yeah?' He sounded despondent.

'It appears that Mr Bellamy knew about your little counterfeit currency business here that you were trying to keep so secret. So was he blackmailing you? Is that why you were so ready to provide him with a large sum of money?'

'Of course he wasn't – you're just trying to pin his death on me.'

'So it was just out of the kindness of your heart, right?'

Nicholson gave him a scornful glance and said nothing.

'All right,' Jago continued. 'Let's assume it was a genuine loan, then. It wasn't a gift – you'd be expecting to get it back. When I asked you about that money, you said you were sure Mr Bellamy would've repaid you before long. So what was the basis of your confidence? His wife told us that you'd lent him the money to help him pay off debts he owed to other people. I don't imagine many potential lenders would regard a man in that position as credit-worthy. They'd call it throwing good money after bad.'

'Maybe. Like I said, it was a favour, for old times' sake.'

'Did you actually intend that he should repay you in kind, as it were, with some form of service rather than cash?'

'What do you mean?'

'Listen, Mr Nicholson, it's time you stopped playing dumb. We're talking about a man who's been murdered, and it's in your interests not to lie to me. You need to give me some straight answers. What I mean is was there something he agreed to do for you – something connected with this little enterprise of yours here?'

'Well, you could say that, I suppose. I'd just say he was being helpful.'

'How, precisely?'

Nicholson eyed him warily. 'I'm a businessman and

I've got my fingers in a lot of pies, and some of them have what you might call a distribution aspect. Samuel said he'd help me out on that side of things.'

'You mean he took counterfeit banknotes from you and passed them off to anyone gullible enough to accept them?'

'I think you're trying to put words into my mouth, Inspector, but I've got nothing more to say. And listen – this was nothing to do with Marjorie. She wasn't involved in what he was doing, and she knew nothing about it, I swear.'

'How much did Mr Bellamy pay you for them?'

'Like I said, I've got nothing more to say. Look, the man's dead, isn't he? Why try to blacken his name now? You can't arrest him or take him to court, can you?'

'You're right, I can't, Mr Nicholson, but I can arrest you and your wife. You're both under arrest on suspicion of forging and uttering Bank of England notes with intent to defraud, and also of having in your possession without lawful authority or excuse material engraved with words and devices resembling those on banknotes. We're going to take a little ride together to West End Central police station.'

CHAPTER FORTY-TWO

With George and Ivy Nicholson both safely locked up, Jago put on his coat and hat and beckoned Cradock to the door. 'Right, Peter, we'll leave those two in the tender care of our uniform colleagues while they reflect on what they might say to the magistrate. And I think we'd better call in on Ethel Rae and tell her she won't be singing tonight – I rather think the Blue Palm's going to be closed until further notice.'

They drove back from the police station and parked the car near Newport Court, then walked to the house where Ethel Rae had her flat.

Jago was about to ring the bell when the street door opened and an elderly woman appeared.

'Oh,' she said, with a twitch of surprise. 'Are you on your way in?'

'Yes – we're police officers. We're here to see Miss Rae, on the top floor.'

'You'd better go up, then – sounds like a big row going on up there.'

They stood aside to let the woman leave, then hurried up the stairs. Jago could hear raised voices coming from the attic flat, one of them a woman's but higher pitched than Ethel's more mellow tone. When he knocked the noise stopped, and moments later the door was opened by the young singer, dressed in dark slacks and a red jumper.

'Ah, hello,' she said. 'You're just in time to join the party. Come in.'

She waved them in and closed the door behind them. 'Let me introduce you to my guests. I believe you know Mr and Mrs Abingdon.'

Jago gave a curt nod of his head to the couple, who had their coats on. Edith Abingdon's flushed face suggested to him that she'd been the one shouting, but he made no comment.

'To what do we owe the pleasure of this visit?' said Ethel, as if nothing out of the ordinary had just taken place.

'I just wanted to update you on our enquiries, Miss Rae,' Jago replied. 'But first I'd like to know what was going on here when we arrived. It sounded like an argument.'

He cast a glance in Edith Abingdon's direction: she gave a haughty scowl and looked away.

'We were having a business discussion,' said Ethel, 'but Mrs Abingdon seemed to take exception to what I had in mind and lost her temper. I expect it's something she ate – or drank.'

'Now look here, you little hussy—' Edith Abingdon began, but Jago interrupted her.

'What was this business discussion about, Miss Rae?' he said firmly.

'It was supposed to be private,' said Ethel.

'Well, it's not private now. Answer my question please.'

'All right, then. It was about my future career, Inspector. I don't see myself singing in the Blue Palm Club for ever – I told you before I want to make hit records, but that means I need a contract with one of the big companies. There's a recording business in Lisle Street where someone like me can hire a studio with a piano for my accompanist and an engineer to make a professional recording of me singing. They'll make copies that I can send to the companies. All that costs money, of course, and I invited Mr and Mrs Abingdon here in order to make them a business proposition.'

'Which was?'

'I was thinking lately that they might like to lend me the money I need for this project. I'd met Mr Abingdon at the club, you see, and I knew he was a big fan of jazz music. I'm not so sure about his wife, of course – she doesn't seem quite so keen.'

Jago's eyes went to Edith Abingdon: her face was set like stone.

'But Mr Abingdon seemed to think I had good prospects,' Ethel continued, 'so I thought he might be willing to support me.'

'So what caused the argument I could hear?'

'I think it was something I said – just an innocent

347

question. When I raised the subject of finance, Mrs Abingdon said the fact that they had a certain amount of wealth didn't make them a charity – people were always trying to get money out of them. She was quite rude about it, but I assumed she'd just got out of bed on the wrong side this morning and I ignored it. But it reminded me of something Samuel Bellamy said to me shortly before he died that puzzled me, so I told Mr Abingdon, and that's when they both got angry.'

'There's no need for this,' said Abingdon. 'Really, Inspector, this is a waste of your time.'

'No,' said Jago. 'I'd like to hear this – carry on, Miss Rae. What did Mr Bellamy tell you?'

'Well,' said Ethel, 'he said he'd got hold of something that was going to make him a lot of money. He was quite excited about it. He said he'd have enough to go away and make a new start – somewhere away from all this war and bombing – and he wanted me to go with him. He seemed to have gone quite mad at the prospect. He was virtually begging me to go, but I said, "No, don't be ridiculous, you're old enough to be my father." He wouldn't take no for an answer, though. He said his life was about to change for ever – he knew a man who had more money than sense, and he was going to make him hand a lot of it over. I asked him who this man was, but he wouldn't tell me. All he said was he knew how to force him to pay up. Then he said, "He thinks he's a big shot, but I'm going to knock him for six – yes, I'll knock him for six." Now, that's a cricketing expression, isn't it, and there's only one man I know and that Samuel

Bellamy knew too who's rich and loves cricket.' She inclined her head in the direction of Abingdon. 'Him. So I asked him whether he was the man Samuel was talking about, and whether Samuel had been blackmailing him or something.'

'And what was Mr Abingdon's reply?'

'Nothing. His face was like thunder, but he didn't say anything. But Mrs Abingdon – that was a different matter. Quite an eye-opener, you might say – she screamed at me and called me a lying little bitch, and said if I knew what was good for me I'd keep my mouth shut, or she'd shut it for me. And that's when you turned up.'

Jago turned to Abingdon. 'Well, Mr Abingdon, what do you say to that? Was Mr Bellamy trying to blackmail you?'

'Don't listen to her,' his wife shouted before he could reply. 'It's all nonsense, a pack of lies – she doesn't know what she's talking about.'

'Mr Abingdon?' Jago repeated.

'Of course not. This is all just a simple misunderstanding.'

'But if what Miss Rae says is true, and Mr Bellamy was planning to extort a large amount of money out of you, you'd have had good reason to want to be rid of him, wouldn't you? The man you'd trusted was about to try and cheat you. I think it's time you explained yourself – and I need to caution you that you are not obliged to say anything, but anything you say may be used in evidence.'

Abingdon's face registered outrage. 'I don't believe this – you're taking this woman's word against mine?'

He didn't wait for Jago to reply. Without a word he flung himself towards the door on the far side of the room. Cradock jumped forward and grappled with him, but Abingdon felled him with a blow from his elbow. He lunged again towards the door, but this time Cradock grabbed him by the ankle and brought him down beside him.

Jago was about to step in and restrain Abingdon when he glimpsed Edith Abingdon out of the corner of his eye. She stepped forward, her handbag gripped against her chest and a fire in her eyes that he hadn't seen before. She fumbled with the catch on the bag, opened it and reached into it. Before Jago could move she pulled out a small gun and aimed it in his direction. 'You stay exactly where you are, Inspector, and tell your man to let go of my husband.'

Jago complied, and Cradock released his grip on Abingdon. Both men got to their feet. Edith Abingdon shifted the gun towards Cradock, her hand trembling. 'You stay where you are, too. Do you understand?'

Cradock nodded.

She pointed the gun at Ethel. 'Look at her, Inspector – what is she? A vulgar little singer who can only get work in a miserable dive like the Blue Palm. She's the one who's behind all this trouble – I know what was going on between her and Bellamy.' Her voice shook with rage. 'She was taking anything she could from him, and now she's trying to drag my husband's name through the mud. It's intolerable.'

She waved the gun between Jago, Cradock and Ethel, panic in her eyes. Jago decided to seize his moment and took two rapid steps towards her. She shrieked, stumbling back towards the wall. Her husband broke away from Cradock and shouted, 'To me, Edith! Throw it to me – now!'

The one-time wicketkeeper crouched with feet slightly apart and hands cupped in front of him ready to catch the weapon. Edith threw the gun across the room towards him, but in a flash of red Ethel Rae leapt to her side and caught the weapon in mid-flight. She landed on the floor with her hand wrapped safely round it, sprang to her feet and handed it to Jago.

He took a quick look at the weapon. It was a snub-nosed revolver, its barrel little more than two inches long, and on its frame above the cylinder were engraved the words *British Bulldog*.

Well, well, he thought: Mr Cornwell knew his stuff.

He trained it on a now deflated-looking Abingdon. 'Right,' he said, 'I think we'd better sit down and have a little chat.'

The Abingdons and Ethel duly sat down. Jago remained standing, and Cradock stood in front of the door to discourage any more attempts to escape. Jago opened the back of the gun's cylinder and examined its five chambers.

'One shot fired, I see,' he said to the Abingdons. 'I'd be interested to know when that was.'

The couple remained silent.

'Whose gun is this?' said Jago.

'It's my wife's,' said Abingdon, his voice sullen.

'So nothing to do with you?'

Abingdon was silent.

Edith stared at him. 'Charles?'

Her husband looked down at the floor and gave no reply.

'Not such a gentleman when you're away from the cricket pitch, then?' said Jago. 'I suspect that when we subject this gun to testing we'll find it's the one that killed Mr Bellamy. That'll put your wife in a very difficult position, won't it? On trial for her life. I think it's time you started talking.'

'All right,' Abingdon snapped back. 'I gave her the gun.'

'Tell me more.'

'It was after that terrible business at Dunkirk. Edith was very nervous when all the talk about an invasion started – in fact she was downright terrified. She was convinced the Germans would invade at any moment, maybe even drop from the sky like they did in Holland, and she couldn't sleep for fear. I said I'd get her something to protect herself with.'

'And this was it?'

'Yes. Since then she's always carried it in her handbag.'

'How did you get it?'

'I bought it.'

'Who did you buy it from?'

'I asked Bellamy if he knew anyone, and he mentioned George Nicholson, the Greek fellow who runs the Blue

Palm. He said Nicholson had connections with people who'd probably be able to help.'

'So Mr Nicholson sold you this gun?'

'Yes.'

'Do you have a firearm certificate for it?'

'No.'

'You're aware that it's an offence to be in possession of a firearm without one?'

'Yes, all right, if you say so – but you've got nothing else on me.'

'We'll see. I think you'd better tell me exactly what happened when you went to see Mr Bellamy on Monday morning. You did go to his flat, didn't you?'

Abingdon mumbled something that sounded like 'Yes.'

'I beg your pardon?'

'Yes,' said Abingdon, his voice louder and resentful. 'Yes, all right, I did go there – and my wife came too. Bellamy had found something for me – he said he'd come by a very good copy of Linschoten's *Discours of Voyages*, published in 1598, and he'd like to offer it to me. I was sceptical, because fine copies with all the correct plates and maps are very rare, and I've been trying to get hold of one for years. But then he opened a drawer and took it out – not only was it in exceptionally good condition, but it had beautiful sixteenth-century hand colouring. I was immediately excited. But then he named his price. It was astronomical – he demanded fifteen hundred pounds. You can buy a house for that!'

Jago would have said three or more in the East End,

but the book collector clearly moved in different circles.

'I was shocked,' Abingdon continued, 'and offered him five hundred, but he said he wasn't in a mood to haggle.'

'And I suppose you weren't in a mood to agree.'

'Of course not – he was out of his mind. We argued over what it was worth, and in the end I said I wouldn't pay a penny more than six hundred, and then—' Abingdon's voice choked with anger. 'Then he said he'd had a good idea. He said there's quite a fashion for these old maps – people like to frame them and hang them in their house. They fetch good prices, he said, especially when they're copperplate engravings and hand-coloured, like the ones in this book. And then he opened the drawer and produced a single-edge razor blade. He said, "So I'm going to cut this up and sell the maps off one by one. What do you think of that, Mr Abingdon?"'

'I couldn't bear it – I grabbed his arm and smashed it down on the desk to force the blade out of his hand, and then I punched him. He leapt at me and began to hit me back. He was in a blind rage, and so was I – it was an act of sacrilege, you see, what he was going to do to that book. I could hardly see what I was doing. In the end I forced him back, but then I heard Edith scream. She pointed at his hand. I looked, and he'd got hold of the razor blade again – I thought he was going to use it on me. I shouted to her for the gun, and she threw it across the room to me. I caught it and . . . pulled the trigger. I wasn't in my right mind, you see – I didn't know what

I was doing. He was right in front of me, and the bullet hit him in the chest. He went down and . . . and died.' His lip trembled as he looked pleadingly at Jago. 'I didn't mean to kill him, Inspector – I did it to save the book.'

'You're under arrest,' said Jago, 'on suspicion of murder – and you too, Mrs Abingdon.'

'Me? I didn't shoot him.'

'Yes, but you brought the gun and gave it to your husband so that he could use it, so you're both liable.'

Edith Abingdon turned to her husband in distress, as if willing him to say something to secure her release, but he wasn't looking at her: his eyes were fixed on Jago. 'But what will happen to the book?' he said. 'It's mine – I must have it.'

'No it's not, Mr Abingdon,' Jago replied. 'You refused to buy it, didn't you? Even killing Mr Bellamy doesn't make it yours. I'd like to know what you've done with it – I don't believe you just left it there and went home without it.'

Abingdon glared defiantly at Jago without a word.

'Very well,' said Jago. 'I'll be taking a look round your home, and I expect I'll find it there – and whether I do or not, you won't be putting your feet up and enjoying it. You're both coming to the station with me.'

He and Cradock led them from the flat and down to the street. Charles and Edith Abingdon offered no resistance: they both looked drained and defeated. Ethel Rae followed them as far as the car, and as Cradock was putting the couple into the back seat she drew Jago to one side.

'Excuse me, Inspector,' she said, 'but what about me? Do I have to come too?'

'We'll need a statement from you, Miss Rae, but it doesn't have to be right now. Would sometime later this afternoon at West End Central police station be convenient for you?'

'West End Central – where's that?'

'It's in Savile Row, about five or six minutes' walk from Piccadilly Circus if you're coming on the Tube.'

'OK, that'll be fine.'

'Good. We'll see you later, then. And by the way, I'd just like to say I'm indebted to you. That was a neat piece of work you did with that gun. Thank you, and well done.'

She gave him a shy smile. 'My pleasure,' she replied. 'I told you I could catch for England, didn't I?'

CHAPTER FORTY-THREE

At West End Central police station, Charles Abingdon and his wife were charged jointly with murder, then consigned to the cells to await their appearance before the magistrate at Marlborough Street police court.

'All done and dusted, then, eh, sir?' said Cradock cheerily as he took his coat off the hat stand and prepared to leave the station.

'Almost,' said Jago. He glanced at the clock. 'It's getting on a bit now, and I expect we'll be hearing those blasted sirens soon, but I think we should try to see Mrs Bellamy before we pack it in for the day – we need to let her know we've charged someone with her husband's murder. Give her a call and see if she's in – if she is, we'll go straight over.'

Cradock went off to use the desk sergeant's telephone and returned to say Mrs Bellamy was at the flat in Peter Street and would be expecting them.

'So what do you think he'll get, sir?' said Cradock as they set off in the car. 'Do you think we'll be able to make that charge stick? Murder, I mean.'

'What do you think yourself?'

'Well, I don't know – he's admitted shooting him, hasn't he? But he was trying to make out he didn't know what he was doing and didn't mean to kill him, as if it was some sort of accident. There's got to be malice aforethought for it to be murder, hasn't there?'

'Yes, but he had a gun in his hand pointed at Bellamy and pulled the trigger, so the law says we regard it as murder until the contrary's proved – and it's for Abingdon to prove what he did wasn't murder. If he can satisfy the court that there was no malice in it, it might be reduced to manslaughter, but I'll be surprised if that happens. He might try to argue that all that business with the book and the razor blade was provocation and hold out for manslaughter, but it's got to be a big enough provocation to make him lose his self-control, so that'll depend on what the court thinks.'

'The way he told the story, he reckoned it was self-defence too, didn't he?'

'Yes, he said he thought Bellamy was going to use the razor blade on him, but who knows? It'll all depend on who the jury believe and what they make of it. But let's leave that for now – we've done our job, and now it's time for other people to do theirs.'

'Thank you, Mrs Bellamy,' said Jago when they joined her at her home in Peter Street. 'I won't be long – I don't want to delay you if you need to get ready to take shelter if the air raids come this way tonight. I just wanted to let you know that we made two arrests this evening in connection with your husband's death.'

'You mean you've got whoever killed him?'

'We believe so, although of course it's the judge and jury's job to decide whether they're guilty, not ours. But I can say that two people have been charged with your husband's murder. They'll be up before the bench as soon as possible, and the magistrate will decide whether there are grounds enough to send them for trial at the Old Bailey.'

'Who have you arrested?'

'Your husband's business associate Mr Abingdon, and his wife.'

'Oh,' she said, registering a look of surprise. 'But why them?'

'It appears your husband had got hold of a rare book that he knew Mr Abingdon would want to buy, but there was a dispute over the price. Mr Bellamy demanded fifteen hundred pounds for it, which Mr Abingdon thought was extortionate, and your husband threatened to destroy the book if he didn't pay up. There was an altercation and some sort of fight, and it appears that that resulted in your husband being shot. This'll all be picked over in detail in court if the magistrate commits the Abingdons for trial, no doubt, so it may turn out to be less straightforward than that, but that's all we know at the moment.'

'What was this book that they thought worth killing for?'

'I understand it was a very old book with maps in it, by someone called Linschoten.'

'And where is it now?'

'We don't know. Mr and Mrs Abingdon were the last people to see it, and they've chosen not to say anything, but given how much Mr Abingdon wanted to have it, the most likely explanation is that they took it with them. Is there anything else you'd like to know?'

'I don't think so – thank you for telling me. Not that it makes any difference really – no matter how much I know about what happened, it won't bring poor Samuel back, will it?'

'I'm sorry, Mrs Bellamy.'

'Thank you. I know there's nothing you can do about that, but it's all just so . . . I don't know – so final. But they say life goes on, don't they, and in present circumstances I know I won't be able to sit around feeling sorry for myself. There's a lot to do. But that reminds me – before you go, there's something I must show you.'

She moved to a bureau against the wall in the far corner of the room and picked up an envelope. 'This came in yesterday evening's post,' she said. 'It's addressed to Samuel, but of course I'm opening all his post now. I'll read it to you, and you can make of it what you will.'

She opened the envelope and took out two sheets of paper. 'It's a letter. I don't know the person it's from, but the address at the top is The Manor House, Apton Brazeley, Sussex. I've never heard of the place, but it sounds like one of those little villages in the middle of nowhere. It's dated the twenty-ninth of December, which shows what a state the postal deliveries have got into with all this bombing, and it's signed at the end by Mrs Evadne Littleton-Gore. This is what she says. "Dear Mr Bellamy, I hope I have used the correct address for this letter and that it reaches you. You didn't leave a card, but I remember you mentioning that you had to get home to London, and the girl at the village post office was kind enough to consult the London telephone directory for me. She said there were several entries for the name Bellamy, but only one of them had the initial S, so she gave me the address for that person and I'm trusting that it's you. If it's not, then please disregard this letter. If, however, you are the Mr Samuel Bellamy who called at my house just before Christmas, please read on. When you said you were having trouble with your car and asked if you could come in and use my telephone, I was of course pleased to be of assistance in your hour of need, and while we were waiting for a man to come out from the village I was quite touched by the interest you showed in my late husband's library. It was all inherited from his father and grandfather, but he liked to sit in there and read, especially in the last year or two before he died. To me it was just a huge dust trap full of fusty old books. I was disappointed when you were unable to find a copy of that book by your Huguenot ancestor that you mentioned, but I gather from what you said that it was very old and no doubt very rare by now. I hope you manage to find a copy one day."'

Marjorie turned the sheet over. 'She goes on – "But when you said you'd noticed a couple of books that you'd love to be able to buy from me as a gift for your wife, I was very pleased to accept your offer. The book of sermons didn't look terribly interesting to me, but the other one with the maps was rather pretty. I do hope your poor wife finds some appropriate treatment for that terrible disease she's afflicted with (I'm afraid I can't remember the name, but it does sound very challenging). For me, to be honest, your visit seemed nothing short of a godsend, because the roof's been leaking at the eastern end of the house, and the local builder said it would cost thirty pounds to repair it. Like many people these days, I may have a big house but I live in straitened circumstances, and ever since the Crash, the income I derive from my remaining investments is paltry. So when you offered me forty pounds for the books I was delighted."'

She paused to get her breath. 'On to page three. "However" – she says – "and this is why I'm writing to you, my daughter came to visit me at Christmas, and when I told her the story she chided me. She said the books were probably worth more than that. I'm sorry to have to say this, but she actually went so far as to say I'd been cheated. I apologise for repeating that, but she was adamant and quite cross about it. I'm sure it must have been an honest mistake on your part, but since my financial state is even worse than my daughter suspects, I'm wondering whether you might reconsider the situation. I don't wish to upset your poor wife by asking you to return the books if you've already given them to her, but I feel I should appeal to you as the gentleman you are to consider augmenting the sum you paid me for them. My daughter suggested that we might find an independent valuer to examine them and offer a professional opinion on their worth. Again, I hope this won't distress your wife – a crippling disease like that must be an intolerable cross to bear – but I very much hope you can see your way to giving this matter your attention. I look forward to hearing from you at your earliest convenience. Yours sincerely, Evadne Littleton-Gore (Mrs)."'

She was about to put it down, but then snatched it back up again. 'Oh, and there's a PS at the bottom. She says, "By the way, when I took the money you'd paid me for the books to the bank to pay it into my account, they rejected three of the pound notes on the grounds that they were counterfeits. I thought I should let you know – and if, as I'm sure, you are as shocked as I was to hear this, I would respectfully request that you reimburse me with a cheque for three pounds by return of post to the above address to make up my loss."'

She handed the letter to Jago, who examined it briefly.

'So that's how he did it,' he said.

'Yes – you mean that pretty book with the maps she mentions was the one he tried to sell to Abingdon and got shot for?'

'I think it was, yes.'

'So he swindled her, didn't he? After all that hand-on-heart stuff he gave me about never cheating anyone, he went and cheated some poor little old lady.'

'On the face of it, yes. But on the other hand, this letter suggests the lady in question was pleased to accept the forty pounds for it, and if your husband were here he might argue that if he hadn't bought it – at a price she agreed – she would've had nothing.'

'I think you're being too generous, Inspector – you don't need to spare my feelings. I'm suddenly seeing my husband in a new light. I suppose him buying a book of old sermons and saying it was a present for me was some kind of private joke for his own amusement, but telling that woman that I'm afflicted with a terrible disease – "crippling", she says, doesn't she? – that's outrageous. What on earth was he up to? Trying to make her feel sorry for him so she'd trust him? I can't believe he did that.'

'I suspect he felt trapped. He owed George Nicholson a lot of money, didn't he? You said so yourself.'

'Yes. I suppose when he saw that book he must've thought if he could buy it, it would solve all his financial problems.' She slumped forward in the chair, her head in her hands. 'It's my fault, isn't it? I asked George to help Samuel with the money he owed to that Italian, and I thought he helped him because there was a time when we were close and he loved me. But it must have been just another cold business transaction for George, and he wasn't going to let Samuel off repaying him. I put Samuel into a trap, and now he's had to pay a far greater price than anything he owed George.'

'Don't blame yourself, Mrs Bellamy. You're not responsible for your husband's actions any more than you are for Mr Nicholson's.'

She lifted her head. 'I know, but I was married to him,

and I feel as though his shame will hang over me for ever. He was a cheat, and now that's what he'll be known as, isn't it?' Jago did not reply, and she continued. 'But that book, the one he bought from that lady in Sussex – if you find it, what will happen to it?'

'I imagine that if it's true that your husband bought it from her, regardless of what he paid, it became his property, and it'll come to you.'

She nodded slowly. 'If it does, I shall give it to her – it's the least she deserves. And I shall tell her that a collector was willing to pay six hundred pounds for it.'

'Very good. We'll be searching the Abingdons' flat and I'm very much hoping we'll find it there. If we do, I'll get in touch.'

'Thank you, Inspector. You know, I said just now that life goes on, and I suppose it does, but a death like that leaves its mark on everyone, doesn't it? Samuel was my husband – I don't think I'll ever be the same again, no matter how long I live. And the strange thing is I know he treated that old lady abominably, but somehow I still can't help feeling sorry for him. Even though he found a very valuable book in her library, even there he didn't find the one he really wanted above all others, that Pierre de Bellême book, his Holy Grail, and he never made the fortune he'd always dreamt of either. Sometimes I wonder whether it's better not to wish for too much in life – at least then you're not disappointed.'

'Maybe,' said Jago. 'Perhaps you're right – but who can be sure?'

CHAPTER FORTY-FOUR

Ethel Rae arrived at West End Central police station at five o'clock, as arranged, and gave a statement. Once she, Cradock and Jago had signed it, Jago invited her to join them for a cup of tea in the police canteen.

'That would be very nice,' she said. 'I could do with something to drink, and I've never had police tea before, I'm glad to say. I hasten to add that I've never seen the inside of a police station before, either, in case you were wondering.'

'I wasn't, Miss Rae, you can rest assured.'

'Oh, do call me Ethel, please – I mean, it's all over now, isn't it? You've finished your case – you can relax.'

Jago smiled. 'There's still a lot of work for us to do, but I must say I'm glad to see Mr and Mrs Abingdon behind bars – and I must thank you again for your assistance.'

They adjourned to the canteen and got their drinks.

'First of all,' said Jago once they were seated, 'I should let you know that earlier this afternoon we also arrested Mr and Mrs Nicholson on suspicion of forging banknotes.'

'Wow – is that what was going on in that empty property next door?'

'We believe so – it wasn't as empty as it seemed. But I feel I should apologise to you – it probably means the Blue Palm will be closing, and I've put you out of a job. I'm very sorry.'

Ethel laughed. 'That's very sweet of you, but don't worry – I'll be OK. In fact, I've had a very interesting morning. Shall I tell you the story?'

'Please do.'

'Well, the thing is, I had an unexpected visitor. I'd barely finished eating my breakfast when he turned up, and I had no idea who he was until he introduced himself. He was a young man, very confident and energetic, and as soon as he opened his mouth I knew he must be American or Canadian. It turned out he was American and he'd been working over here for a couple of years – one of those who decided to stay when the war started rather than run off back home. He's called Clark Hayworth and he seems to be, well, a pretty special kind of man. But this is the exciting bit—' She paused as if to calm herself. 'When he told me what he was, I couldn't believe it. He said he ran a small record company here in London – it's one I've heard of, because they do quite a lot of jazz records. But anyway, the really amazing thing is that he said he'd heard me sing at the Blue Palm yesterday and wanted to sign me up – so as of this morning I've got a recording contract, and he says my first record will be out in March. Can you believe it? I don't know whether to laugh or cry.'

'Congratulations – no wonder you're excited. So that means you don't need to pay for your own recordings and do all that hard work to get noticed by the music industry?'

'Exactly – it's noticed me. It's all going to happen – everything I've dreamt of.'

'That's what they call a lucky break, isn't it. Did he say why he happened to go to the Blue Palm?'

'Yes, he said an American acquaintance of his here in London had tipped him off, so he'd gone along to see for himself, and he loved what he heard.'

'That sounds wonderful. Did he say who this acquaintance of his was?'

'No – he didn't mention a name. All he said was she's a journalist.'

'Really? Maybe you'll get into the papers as well – I'm very happy for you. And this record man – can you trust him?'

'Oh, yes – he seems honest and genuine, and he's young and full of life. Good-looking too – in fact, all things considered, he's rather lovely.'

Jago couldn't help noticing the dreamy look in her eyes. 'Well, Ethel,' he said, 'it looks like you may've just made the catch of your life.'

* * *

After further excited details from Ethel about the events of the morning, she bade them farewell and left.

'So this mysterious American journalist, sir,' said Cradock with a smirk. 'Is that another lead to follow up?'

'Never you mind,' said Jago. 'If any further enquiries are required, I'll do it myself.'

Cradock was about to attempt another witty question, but the expression on Jago's face clearly indicated that this was his last word on the subject.

CHAPTER FORTY-FIVE

It was eight o'clock that evening when Jago called for Dorothy at The Savoy. The sirens had not yet unleashed their nightly wail, and there was just enough moonlight reflecting off the Thames for them to take a stroll down the Victoria Embankment, gazing at the anonymous broken silhouettes of bomb-damaged wharves and warehouses on the opposite side. But the cold soon drove them to take refuge in a pub near Charing Cross station. It was a rough and ready place, but the fireplace in the saloon bar had a roaring fire by which they could warm themselves.

'So tell me what you've been doing today,' said Dorothy when he'd fetched their drinks.

'Haring round Soho, basically,' said Jago. 'But bringing our case to a successful conclusion, I'm pleased to say – although whether there can be any pleasure in it when a man's lost his life I'm not so sure.'

'This was the man you mentioned last time I saw you – he'd been shot dead, you said.'

'That's right. He worked in the book trade – a world I knew nothing about. We met one man who seemed to make a good living out of selling old books to some of your wealthy collectors in America.'

Dorothy laughed. 'Oh, yes, we've got plenty of them. There's a man called William Randolph Hearst, one of our big newspaper owners. He collects just about everything – he once bought a complete monastery in Spain and shipped it back to the States in pieces to make it into a home in California but then ran out of money, so it never got built. Some of these people will spend anything it takes to get something they want. Was your man selling books to people like that?'

'To wealthy collectors, yes, but not Americans, as far as I know. I never met him, of course, but it seems like he had a hard life. He grew up in a poor family living from hand to mouth and wanted something better for himself, but ended up in debt. People said he was always searching for something – his Holy Grail, they called it, but no one ever knew quite what it was. I reckon he thought he'd finally found it – some priceless book that was going to make him rich. He must've thought his ship had come in at last, but in the end it cost him his life.'

'How sad. What was his name?'

'Samuel Bellamy.'

'Really? We had one of those in Massachusetts, you

know, only our Samuel Bellamy lived two hundred years ago and had a very different profession. He was pretty successful in it too – they called him the prince of pirates. He came from England originally, but he lived in Cape Cod – it's only about seventy miles from Boston, and I've spent a lot of time there, especially in the summer. They say he had a kind of Holy Grail too – there was a fleet of Spanish galleons loaded with silver that sank in a storm off the coast of Florida, and he sailed off to try and find it. I don't think he ever did, though, and in the end he drowned. Was your Mr Bellamy some kind of modern-day pirate?'

'No, I think he was just a man who couldn't make life give him everything he wanted. But look, let's not talk about him right now – or who killed him, for that matter. It feels too much like more shoptalk.'

'Quite right. I agree – let's change the subject.'

'OK. But there is one thing I need to ask you first – something serious – and it's to do with this case of mine.'

'Is this a formal interview, Inspector?'

He laughed. 'No, it's just a small matter I'd like to clear up.'

'OK, you may proceed.'

'You remember I told you about that girl we met in a nightclub – the jazz singer who wanted to be a star?'

'I do, yes.'

'Well, I saw her this afternoon and she was so excited she could hardly contain herself. She said a man who runs a record business came to see her this morning because he'd had a tip-off about her from a journalist – an American journalist who happened to be female. I'd just be interested to know who that journalist was.'

'And you think I can help?'

'I'm hoping you can.'

'I see. If I know but decline to reveal my source, will you have to arrest me?'

'I hope that won't be necessary.'

'Well, I suppose I'll have to confess – it was me. I went to check for myself – you were right about that voice.'

'Do you mean you've been to the Blue Palm? On your own?'

Dorothy smiled. 'I have, and I believe she's landed herself a recording contract as a result. There's no need to worry about me, though – I've been to plenty of worse places in my time. And besides, I didn't actually go alone – I took a man with me. After what you said about her and that club, I mentioned it to someone I know in the record business called Clark Hayworth, and he said, "Let's go see her, then" – and we did, last night. I'd say he was more than impressed – he said he'd fallen in love with her voice. So, all in all I think Ethel Rae could be a name to watch – she's a very determined young lady.'

'She is. But that same determination meant she found herself up against a man with a gun today. It could all have ended very differently.'

'Oh, my word. But she's OK?'

'Yes, she's fine.'

'Thank the Lord for that. It's no bad thing for a girl to have a bit of determination – you don't get far in this world without it, especially if you're a woman, if my experience is anything to go by. I got the impression she likes to make things happen, and so do I. Sometimes you can't just sit around and hope they will – you have to take life by the scruff of the neck and make it happen, don't you?'

Jago wanted to say yes, but his life had taught him otherwise. At the mention of Ethel Rae's name, a picture of her leaping into the air to catch Abingdon's gun had flashed into his mind: a picture of grace, energy and freedom. It was a scene he'd imagined himself in when he was a boy, catching the last man out in a Test match drama and saving the day for England. He smiled at the thought of it, but now he knew better. It was a boyish fantasy – the kind that life's knocks gradually beat out of you.

'I know what you mean,' he said, 'but there are limits, aren't there? Sometimes you can't just make things happen, no matter how much you'd like them to. I spent two years of my life fighting in that terrible war in France, and there wasn't a day when I didn't want it to stop. But I couldn't even take my commanding officer by the scruff of the neck, never mind Field Marshal Haig, or the Prime Minister – or Kaiser Bill himself for that matter. I couldn't stop death having its way, not even to save just one of my men. So I think . . . well, maybe it's just because I'm probably a good twenty years older than her, but I think those days have left me feeling I'm not very good at taking life by the scruff of the neck. I know you didn't mean it that way, and I'm really pleased to see what you've done for her. I hope she'll get everything she wants, but it doesn't always happen.'

'I know what you mean, John,' said Dorothy, 'and you're right. Ethel Rae's just a kid, and she's got her dream come true. I guess when we're her age, we've got a lot more future than past, and there's plenty of time ahead of us for that to happen, but the more past we have, the more unlikely it seems it could. But that's not a reason to let our dreams die, is it?'

'No, of course not. But sometimes there are things that you see—' His voice broke off as he struggled to know what to say next. 'This is probably just me, but there's this thing I haven't been able to get out of my mind since Monday morning. It's the picture of that woman in Paternoster Row sitting on the ruins of her family business. Her grandfather and then her dad had spent their lives building it up, and now there it was, all gone – completely destroyed in one night. And now I'd come to tell her someone had killed her husband. She was all alone, with no future, no hope – nothing. It reminded me—'

He halted again, but Dorothy waited silently for him to continue.

'It reminded me of something I saw in France,' he said quietly. 'It was 1918, October I think, and we were tired and filthy, marching through a place called Amiens. I'd never been there, but one of the men had, before the war, and he said it used to be a beautiful city. I could only take his word for it – all I could see was ruins, the whole place shelled to pieces. We went past what looked like it must've been a big church once, but now it was just a few stone walls with holes blasted through them. Those old stonemasons hundreds of years ago spent their whole lives building churches and cathedrals, and their sons and grandsons followed them – generations working on those beautiful buildings without seeing them finished. Then we came along and smashed them to pieces. And here we are now, doing the same thing all over again, destroying places and destroying lives. I can't get the pictures out of my head – not just the ruins, but all those men I saw killed and maimed, all the friends I lost. I just can't help thinking – what's the point?'

Jago felt the hot sting of tears coming to his eyes and steeled himself to hold them back. 'I'm sorry,' he said. 'This wasn't how I wanted this evening to be. It just all came back to me when I wasn't expecting it.'

'It's OK, John,' Dorothy murmured. 'It's good for you to talk about it.'

'But that's just it. When I came back from the war, no one wanted to know about it. They all wanted to move on and put it behind them, try to be happy again. I didn't want to talk about it either – I don't think any of us who'd been in the real fighting did. Why would we tell horrible stories to people who wouldn't understand? So I just kept it all inside me. I didn't deal with it – I just tried to push it all down deeper where it couldn't hurt me.'

'Do you think people were worried about reopening old wounds in you? Maybe they didn't want to hurt you.'

'Maybe. Perhaps they meant well – I don't know. All I know is it felt like there was an empty space between me and them that no one ever tried to cross. They didn't want to ask and I didn't want to tell. No one ever got close enough to understand what was going on inside me.'

'But maybe it doesn't have to be like that.'

'What do you mean?'

'I mean do you think someone could get close enough to understand?'

Jago hesitated. 'I suppose so – it's just that it's never happened.'

'Well,' said Dorothy. 'If it is possible, I think I'd like to be that person.'

Jago was silent: he was afraid of what might happen if he tried to speak. All he could do was nod his head wordlessly, his eyes closed.

Dorothy said nothing more, but waited as he struggled with his thoughts. Then, slowly, she edged her chair a little closer to his, reached out and gently but firmly gripped his hand.

ACKNOWLEDGEMENTS

This book began with a happy three-way coincidence. My publisher, Susie Dunlop, suggested the Blitz Detective might delve into London's Soho district, and my agent, Broo Doherty, thought the world of bookselling could prove fertile ground for a murder case. The triangle was completed by Susan Wilcox of the Police History Society, who out of the blue passed on to me her copy of *Death of a Bookseller*, a charming 1956 novel by Bernard J. Farmer, a keen book collector and former Metropolitan Police officer. These three elements combined to spark *The Soho Murder*, the ninth outing for Detective Inspector John Jago in the Blitz Detective series.

As Jago gets to grips with his latest challenging case, I'd particularly like to thank Susie and Broo for their commitment to these books and for all the energy, wisdom and skill they've put into making them a success: I hope they've enjoyed the journey as much as I have!

Soho has for generations been one of London's best-known districts, and not always for the most flattering of reasons. At the time my story is set, this square mile of London's West End, bounded by Regent Street, Oxford Street, Charing Cross Road and Shaftesbury Avenue, was regularly portrayed in the racier sections of the press as a seedy hotbed of crime, corruption and clip joints, where racketeers thrived on separating mugs from their money, and 'dens of iniquity' of all varieties kept the Vice Squad at West End Central police station busy by day and by night. And it wasn't just the press that saw Soho this way: a retired Metropolitan Police detective inspector writing in 1937 said, 'Regarding criminal haunts in London, there are districts which are known as haunts of vice and depravity, full of bolt-holes for hunted men. Soho is one such region.'

It was also a magnet for crime writers, not least the prolific John G. Brandon, who in the 1930s and 1940s set several of his books in Soho, including the entertaining *A Scream in Soho* and *Murder in Soho*, both of which sit on my shelf as I write this. The same was true of the film industry: as Stanley Jackson noted in his fascinating post-war memoir *An Indiscreet Guide to Soho*, the movie gangsters typically had their headquarters in Frith Street, 'and everyone packs a gun or razor, usually both'. He was perhaps fairer in his own assessment, however, observing that while Soho was 'a slum district teeming with good hide-outs' for crooks, it was still a place where thousands of people led 'dull, honest lives' and struggled to make ends meet 'without the aid of knuckledusters, razors and dope'.

Fakery, forgery and deception of various kinds were part of the stock-in-trade of the criminal world depicted in DI Jago's latest case, and they didn't stop when the war started: forgers were still being jailed for counterfeiting coins and banknotes in 1939 and 1940. On this subject I'm particularly grateful to the late Ronald Allport of the Bank of England for his meticulously detailed history, completed in 1950, of the bank's operations from 1939 to 1945, and to the bank for making this unpublished work available to the public.

Counterfeiting offences prosecuted at the time were small-scale operations: international conspiracies were another matter. While my story is fiction, it may be worth noting that there really was a secret Nazi plot to undermine the British wartime economy with counterfeit Bank of England notes, and it was known to the British security services and government and the Bank of England from late 1939. The scale of the threat it posed was so great, however, that it wasn't made public until after the war was won. History has also left us a curious link with the world of crime fiction. In 1941, while all knowledge of this operation was still classified, crime writer Margery Allingham's novel *Traitor's Purse* was published, in which her detective hero Albert Campion uncovers an enemy plot to wreck the British economy by flooding the country with counterfeit banknotes. Whether this was simply a coincidence or whether the author had gained knowledge of the Nazis' top-secret operation and used it to inspire her plot, and if so how, remains a literary mystery to this day.

My research for my own plot for this book took me

down a number of fascinating byways. One of these was into a world previously unknown to me – that of the antiquarian book trade – but fortunately I did not have to travel alone. I'd like to say a special thank you to James Tindley, Tim Bryars and Laurence Worms for inducting me into that world and for so generously sharing with me their time, expertise and reading matter. Sitting in Tim's London shop with pen in one hand and a hospitable glass of wine in the other as he and Laurence poured forth information, anecdotes and ideas is a fond memory – and my thanks go to Laurence for lending me some precious volumes from his own collection.

Soho in 1940 was famous not just for its underworld but for its links to the creative industries, particularly film and music. It was still, despite Blitz and blackout, home to many nightclubs of varying reputations, and the place to go to hear hot jazz. One of my characters is a singer in that world, and I'd like to express my appreciation to modern-day jazz instrumentalist Laura Jurd and singer Polly Gibbons for helping me to understand what makes a jazz artist tick.

As always, I thank David Love for his advice on the medical aspects of the case, and Rudy Mitchell for his on American English. And as always again, I must note that any errors in this book are mine, not those of the kind people who've shared their expertise with me.

Finally, thank you to my dear family, without whose constant love, encouragement and support I would not be here once again, writing this, the concluding sentence of a new Blitz Detective book!

down a number of fascinating byways. One of these was into a world previously unknown to me – that of the antiquarian book trade – but fortunately I did not have to travel alone. I'd like to say a special thank you to James Tindley, Tim Bryars and Laurence Worms for inducting me into that world and for so generously sharing with me their time, expertise and reading matter. Sitting in Tim's London shop with pen in one hand and a hospitable glass of wine in the other as he and Laurence poured forth information, anecdotes and ideas is a fond memory – and my thanks go to Laurence for lending me some precious volumes from his own collection.

Soho in 1940 was famous not just for its underworld but for its links to the creative industries, particularly film and music. It was still, despite Blitz and blackout, home to many nightclubs of varying reputations, and the place to go to hear hot jazz. One of my characters is a singer in that world, and I'd like to express my appreciation to modern-day jazz instrumentalist Laura Jurd and singer Polly Gibbons for helping me to understand what makes a jazz artist tick.

As always, I thank David Love for his advice on the medical aspects of the case, and Rudy Mitchell for his on American English. And as always again, I must note that any errors in this book are mine, not those of the kind people who've shared their expertise with me.

Finally, thank you to my dear family, without whose constant love, encouragement and support I would not be here once again, writing this, the concluding sentence of a new Blitz Detective book!

MIKE HOLLOW was born in West Ham and grew up in Romford, Essex. He studied Russian and French at the University of Cambridge and then worked for the BBC. In 2002 he went freelance as a copywriter, journalist and editor. Mike also works as a poet and translator.

blitzdetective.com   *@MikeHollowBlitz*